T0162069

There's No Story There

Also published by Handheld Press

There's No Story There

Wartime Writing,

1944–1945

by Inez Holden

Handheld Press

Handheld Classic 19

This edition published in 2021 by Handheld Press
72 Warminster Road, Bath BA2 6RU, United Kingdom.
www.handheldpress.co.uk

ISBN 978-1-912766-36-9

1 2 3 4 5 6 7 8 9 0

Series design by Nadja Guggi and typeset in Adobe Caslon Pro
and Open Sans.

Printed and bound in Great Britain by Short Run Press, Exeter.

Contents

Lucy Scholes writes about books, film and art for *NYR Daily*, *Granta*, *Literary Hub* and *The New York Times Book Review* among other places. She writes 'Re-Covered', a monthly column for *The Paris Review* about out-of-print and forgotten books that shouldn't be, and is the Managing Editor of the literary magazine *The Second Shelf: Rare Books and Words by Women*. A version of this introduction originally appeared in *The Paris Review Daily* (2019).

Introduction

BY LUCY SCHOLES

'London's Bright Young People have broken out again,' announced the *Daily Express* in July 1927, reporting on the latest antics of the city's infamous juvenile society set. 'The treasure hunt being *passé* and the uninvited guest already *démodé*, there has been much hard thinking to find the next sensation. It was achieved last night at a dance given by Captain Neil McEachran at his Brook Street House' (Taylor 2008, 68). Now the stuff of legend, this was the 'Impersonation Party', whose guests were asked to come dressed as well-known personalities. There is a famous photograph from the evening, that serves, according to D J Taylor, as 'a kind of Bright Young Person's symposium' (Taylor 2008, 145). The line-up in what he describes as this 'dazzlingly arrayed' tableaux includes 'the scene's long-term ornaments and conductors', the 'brightest' of them all, the socialite Stephen Tennant, his hedonistic partner in crime, Elizabeth Ponsonby, and the photographer Cecil Beaton; their 'proud attendants', the writer and aesthete Harold Acton and Georgia Sitwell; as well as 'exotic passage migrants,' here in the form of the American actress Tallulah Bankhead. Despite the obvious visual draws of the scene – Ponsonby's wig, Sitwell's false nose, Tennant elaborately dressed as Queen Marie of Roumania – one can't help but be intrigued by the beautiful, fresh-faced young woman wearing a simple Breton top in the very middle of the mob, her clear-eyed gaze looking straight into the camera. Her name is Inez Holden.

'In those days she was very pretty,' recalled Holden's friend, the writer Anthony Powell, in his memoirs, 'with the fashionable type of beauty Lambert used to call "consumptive charm" (he thought her attractive but too *difficile* for involvement), a fragility of feature well suggested in two drawings by Augustus John' (Powell 1978, 23–4).

It is by means of cameo appearances like this one that we're able to piece together a portrait of the woman whom Taylor goes as far as to describe as 'a wholly mysterious figure' (Taylor 2008, 145). Indeed, readers are perhaps more likely to be familiar with one of the fictional characters Holden supposedly inspired – Roberta Payne, the female lead of Powell's fifth novel, *What's Become of Waring?* (1939), for example, or Topaz in Stevie Smith's *A Novel on Yellow Paper* (1936) and later Lopez in *The Holiday* (1949) – than the real woman behind these literary guises. This is regrettable though, not least because the story of Holden's life is just as fascinating as anything dreamt up by her more famous literary friends.

Holden was a journalist and writer. Her first novel, *Sweet Charlatan*, an entertaining if rather absurd comic ghost story, was published in 1929, two years after the Impersonation Party. She went on to publish six further works of fiction, a wartime diary titled *It Was Different at the Time*, two collections of short stories, the first of which, 'Death in High Society' (1933), was published in linguist Charles Kay Ogden's experimental Basic English – limited to a vocabulary of only 850 words and envisioned to accelerate communication between different classes and nations. Anyone with a phonograph was supposed to be able to teach it to themselves in only thirty hours, and it later came to be associated with Orwell's 'Newspeak' in *Nineteen Eighty-Four* (1949). Holden also published a notable body of journalism.

Although her early work had a certain '*succès d'estime*', as Celia Goodman, Holden's cousin, friend and original literary executrix, described it in the 1994 memoir she wrote about the writer for *The London Magazine* (Goodman 1994, 30), it's in the work she produced during the war, a series of social documentary-inspired projects set amongst the working classes, that Holden really came into her own as an writer. Handheld Press's publication of *Blitz Writing* (2019) introduced readers to Holden's acclaimed novella *Night Shift* (1941), which follows workers in a London factory making camera parts for reconnaissance planes over a period of six nights during the Blitz, alongside *It Was Different at the Time*. This was writing that covered the period 1938–1941, detailing Holden's war-work in hospitals, at a government training centre, as a fire watcher, as an occasional broadcaster for the BBC, and as a resident at a BBC Centre in Worcestershire. Now, with this re-issue of Holden's wartime novel, *There's No Story There* (1944), as well as three pieces written during the same period – 'Exiles in Conversation', 'Musical Chairman' and 'Soldiers' Chorus', all of which were originally published in *To the Boating and Other Stories* (1945) – readers are able to appreciate the full and impressive breadth of Holden's social documentary project during the war years.

A particularly notable and immersive work – richer and more fully realised than the deft but admittedly slight snapshot of urban factory life Holden portrayed in *Night Shift* – *There's No Story There* details the lives of conscripted workers at Statevale, an enormous rural munitions factory somewhere deep in the English countryside. In it, Holden paints a vivid and moving portrait of working-class life. She attentively describes the workers' daily routines, while also exploring their individual pleasures and pains, not to mention the risks they habitually face in what is an exceptionally dangerous work environment. Unlike in *Night Shift*, where the regular bombing raids are endured by Londoners as they go about their work, here the explosives being manufactured in the factories present a more immediate hazard. Much like life itself, there are moments of farce, and there are moments of tragedy, and Holden's considerable skill in constructing stories enables her to situate these side by side with devastating effect. *There's No Story There* is a detailed and compassionate portrait of life during wartime.

Crossing Boundaries

Wartime factory life might seem like a surprising subject for a Bright Young Thing, but the story of Holden's life is anything but predictable. In the 1920s and 30s she was at the heart of the most famous, feckless party-going set around, and fittingly, her writing during this period tended towards satirical depictions of the giddy antics of the moneyed, frivolous upper classes. Her first three novels – *Sweet Charlatan*, *Born Old, Died Young* (1932), and *Friend of the Family* (1933) – for example, should be considered alongside novels like Michael Arlen's *The Green Hat* (1924) and Evelyn Waugh's *Vile Bodies* (1930). Yet, by the end of the Second World War, Holden had transformed herself into a writer of documentary realism with a serious socialist agenda, empathetically depicting the lives of the working classes. J B Priestley, for example, described *Night Shift* as 'the most truthful and most exciting account of war-time industrial Britain' (Priestley 1941), and when H G Wells first read it he wrote to Holden, 'Your book is first-rate... I'll admit you *can* write.'[1]

So how did a Bright Young Thing become a socialist champion of the working class, not to mention a writer who was able to render the lives of others with such verisimilitude and understanding? Born Beatrice Inez Lisette Holden, the family of her father, Wilfred Millington Holden, is listed in *Burke's Landed Gentry* (1952), while her mother, Beatrice Holden (née Paget), was an Edwardian beauty and 'the second best woman rider in England' (Goodman 1994, 29). Yet despite these rather grand beginnings, Holden was what Kristin Bluemel describes as 'working poor' for most of her life (Bluemel 2019, xv), in large part due to an early schism between her and her immediate family. To describe Holden's parents as neglectful is something of an understatement. As Goodman dramatically elaborates, 'Her mother and father quarreled incessantly and both drank a good deal: the sound of voices raised in anger and swish of the soda-water syphon were familiar background noises throughout her early years' (Goodman 1994, 29). Holden didn't even know whether she'd been born in 1903 or 1904, because they hadn't bothered to register her birth. They favoured her older brother, Bill, and sent their daughter to a school for poor tradespeople. Not that Holden let this disregard hold her back, even if it did have lasting implications on her adult character.

She severed ties with her family when she left home at fifteen, going first to Paris and then to London. As such, suggests her current literary executrix, Ariane Bankes, Goodman's daughter, the 'crossing of boundaries' that seemed so extraordinary in her later life was actually 'entirely explicable in terms of her early rejection by her family and her subsequent rejection of all that her family stood for—class values and all' (Bluemel 2919, x). Powell too parsed a similar judgment, believing that Holden's political opinions were a 'a sharp reaction [...] against the hardness and selfishness of Edwardian smart life' (Powell 1974, 90).

All the same, as Taylor points out, 'Holden's ability to move seamlessly from high bohemia to a political position that may have included membership of the Communist Party was comparatively rare' (Taylor 2008, 234).[2] However justifiable, the fact that she was a woman between worlds and classes – what Bluemel describes as Holden's 'radical border crossings, from adventuress to socialist, party girl to novelist, writer to worker and back' (Bluemel 2004, 105) – as familiar with privilege and plenty as she was with privation and hard scramble, makes her a fascinating anomaly for the period.

In his book, *Lost Girls: Love, War and Literature, 1939–1951*, Taylor draws a direct line between the Bright Young Things of the 1920s and a particular group of young women at large in Blitz-era London, all of whom orbited Cyril Connolly, the charismatic editor of *Horizon*, the most celebrated literary magazine of the 1940s. Taylor's book focuses on a neat quartet: Lys Lubbock, Sonia Brownell (eventually Orwell), Barbara Skelton and Janetta Woolley. 'From one angle they are a way into a certain kind of war-era bohemian life in which glamour and sophistication and something very close to poverty are inextricably combined,' he explains. 'From another, they exemplify a unique moment in twentieth-century British social history in which a tiny group of upper-middle-class young women broke free from the restrictions of their upbringing and achieved a degree of personal freedom that would have been unknown a generation before them' (Taylor 2019, 9–10). That Holden isn't even mentioned once in *Lost Girls* shouldn't, perhaps, come as a surprise – she was not quite of the previous generation, but she was older than these girls by slightly more than a decade. She had been given only the briefest of mentions in Taylor's earlier book, *Bright Young People: The Rise and Fall of a Generation, 1918–1940*, and she was at the heart of the action described therein – but what is she if not a proto-Lost Girl? There is less evidence in what is known of Holden's life, admittedly, of the vulnerability, isolation, pain and loss that Taylor knits into his subjects' life stories. 'In spite of having had a childhood that would have made many people maladjusted and neurotic,' Goodman points out, 'Inez was a remarkably well-balanced person, free from any complex except a rooted objection to marriage, and with a love of life that adversity did little to diminish' (Goodman 1994, 38). But the courage and tenacity of Taylor's subjects, not to mention what he describes as 'the intensely precarious nature of their lives' (Taylor 2019, 10), are certainly elements that resonate with what we know about Holden's existence. What was outlier behaviour for a well brought-up young girl like Holden in the 1920s and the 1930s was clearly becoming more widely acceptable by the middle of the century.

That acknowledged, Holden's interest in and depiction of the working classes in her writing sets her apart from the crowd, from the women who followed her, as well as from her contemporaries. As Bluemel rightly observes, Holden's immersion in and her writing about the world of the working-class in the 1940s wasn't entirely without precedent, but she was something of a lone female figure on the scene. George Orwell, Christopher Isherwood, and Henry Green were all middle- and upper-class writers who 'wrote convincingly about the working class' during this period (Bluemel 2004, 107). But what was different about Holden's situation was that what she was doing was far from 'poverty tourism'. She was 'motivated as much by financial desperation as literary ambition or socialist commitment' (Bluemel 2004, 107). It's important to remember that she had no safety net to fall back on, her 'hold on the privileges that distinguish the typical writer's life – food, paper, books, a room (or desk) of one's own, and time to write – was unstable' (Bluemel 2004, 107). Bankes, Powell and Goodman all note just how often Holden was desperately short of money, living hand to mouth from her writing.

When tracing Holden's developing political consciousness throughout the 1930s, towards her ultimate self-identification as an anti-Communist socialist, Bluemel cites her 'increasing intimacy' with Orwell as one of the key factors (Bluemel 2019, xv). What began as a brief affair – Orwell having 'pounced' on Holden one afternoon in May 1941 after they'd been for lunch at the zoo in Regent's Park: 'I was surprised by this, by the intensity and urgency', she wrote in her diary at the time (Bluemel 2004, 13) – developed into one of the most significant friendships in Holden's life. Three years later, in June 1944, the relationship between them had progressed to the point that she generously offered both him and his wife, Eileen, the use of her London flat when they were bombed out of their own. Even more notably, *It Was Different at the Time* originally began life as joint project between the two writers, but their difference in styles – in her unpublished diary, Holden records that Orwell characterized her writing as 'feminine impressionistic' (Bluemel 2019, xxvi); or, as Goodman describes it, Orwell's diary was 'objective and confined to facts, while Inez's was full of personal observations, character sketches and dialogues' (Goodman 1994, 32) – combined with the demands on Orwell's time made by his journalism and BBC work ultimately saw him pull out of the undertaking. Nevertheless, the two writers remained close, both self-identifying as what Goodman recalls Holden describing as 'dyed-in-the-wool socialists,' strongly opposed to Communism (Goodman 1994, 32). Indeed, it was due to the closeness of this friendship that Holden found herself dropped by another friend, H G Wells. After her own flat had been bombed in October 1940, Wells suggested that Holden rent the mews flat of his London home in Hanover Terrace overlooking Regent's Park. She took him up on his offer, often having her meals with her landlord for the duration of her stay, but their friendship came to an abrupt end when Wells famously fell out with Orwell the following year, incensed by the latter's published attacks on his work. It's a story that's been recounted often, climaxing, as Powell recalls in his memoirs, 'in Wells's famous note to Orwell saying: "Read my early works, you shit"; a recommendation many authors must have been tempted to prescribe at one time or another, in just those terms for suspected carpers' (Powell 1978, 25). Although what happened between the two men was technically nothing to do with Holden, unfortunately for her, her connection to Wells's nemesis was all it took for him to unceremoniously evict her from his flat and his life.

Wartime Camaraderie

As Holden became increasingly dedicated to socialism, the focus of her writing shifted accordingly. A different reality to the world of giddy socialites had caught her eye, and one that would resonate with a different class of reader. Her friendship with Orwell was clearly instructive, but it certainly wasn't the only element at work on her broadening political consciousness. When she'd cut ties with her family, she had not swopped one class for another, but now regarded herself as classless, an 'outsider', someone who could just as easily write about the wealthy and the privileged as about the working classes. She'd also long sympathized with the latter – perhaps due to the uniqueness of her own liminal position – particularly in terms of the social inequalities that grew from discrepancies of wealth and poverty. This is a woman, remember, who had supported herself from the age of fifteen, a reality that many of the people closest to her couldn't have even countenanced. 'There was a period in my life,' Holden once told Powell, referring to the mid-late 1920s, 'when I knew only millionaires. That was when I was working on the [*Daily*] *Express*. They were always asking me to arrange for them to buy the paper for a halfpenny, instead of a penny' (Powell 1978, 24). But if there was a single event or experience that helped to radicalize Holden more than anything else, it was the Blitz.

In her introduction to *Blitz Writing*, Bluemel draws on *The People's War* (1969), Angus Calder's landmark social history of the Second World War, to show that Holden wasn't alone in her egalitarian outlook. This was, Calder theorises, the moment during which Britain came closest to social revolution than any time since the seventeenth century. After all, it was the working classes, particularly those who lived in the East End, in Stepney, Whitechapel and Shoreditch, and who worked in the factories, warehouses and gasworks of Poplar, or the docks of West Ham and Bermondsey, who suffered the most during the famously violent bombing raids inflicted on London between 7 September 1940 and 11 May 1941. The working classes lost their homes and their lives at the highest rates, yet they were also the city's poorest residents, least equipped to deal with the huge losses, both material and emotional, that they suffered.

This is the world Holden draws us into in *Night Shift*. Although set entirely in the factory, and focused on the comings and goings of the workers, their conversations set to a background noise of machinery, like the book's characters themselves, the reader is never quite allowed to forget the ever-present danger overhead and outside, apparent here in a cacophony of sounds: 'the air-raid orchestra of airplane hum, the anti-aircraft shell bursts, ambulance and fire bells' (Holden 1941, 4). An anonymous female worker who's new to the factory narrates the novel. She has 'no very definite personality,' as the book's original jacket copy put it, 'acting rather as the lens of a moving camera.' Hers are the eyes through which we see the monotonous shift work unfold; hers are the ears through which we hear the conversations of the other workers, the nuances of which Holden excels at picking up. We see something similar in both the short stories 'Exiles in Conversation' and 'Musical Chairman', the narrator of each assiduously reporting all she sees and hears:

'all these images ran through my head quick as machine-gun fire', explains the narrator of the former (220). Not, however, that the narrator of *Night Shift* should necessarily be identified as a stand-in for Holden herself: even though the novel was based on her first-hand experiences of working in an aircraft factory in North London, another character, Feather, described as 'the sort of girl who would have been 'ladying it' at a First Aid Post attached to some auxiliary service' (Holden 1941, 5), belongs to something closer to the milieu from which Holden herself hailed. Wells, for example, assumed the connection was obvious. 'Bravo Feather,' he wrote in the note quoted earlier that he had sent to Holden, praising the book as 'first rate.' Assuming 'something had happened to shake up her journey in the slow coach of security' (Holden 2019, 5), the other workers can't quite understand what the bourgeois Feather is doing here with them, but her inclusion is significant: she provides a way into the narrative for non working-class readers.

In assessing both Holden's descriptions of her factory work in *It Was Different at the Time* alongside a piece Holden published in *Horizon* in 1941 called 'Fellow Travellers in Factory', Bluemel details what she describes as Holden's initial 'struggle with the representation of relations between bourgeois author and working class subjects, overt political context and hollow documentary fact' (Bluemel 2004, 127). In her reportage, Holden maintains a degree of distance between herself and her subjects, to whom she refers as 'they' throughout. In her diary, this division is obliterated, Holden easily identifying herself as one of the women she's writing about. By the time Holden writes *There's No Story There*, this transition is complete and she is completely immersed in the working-class world. There's no middle-class character like *Night Shift*'s Feather to bridge the divide: Holden is wholly comfortable amongst her factory-worker characters, able to portray 'diverse working-class lives and accomplishments, dialects and characters' (Bluemel 2004, 127). Due to this ease she is in a position to see a story where many other writers wouldn't even have recognised one in the first place.

Seeing the Story That Others Didn't

In a move that echoes the opening of *Night Shift* – '"Follow me," one of the engineers tells the narrator' (Holden 1941, 1) – *There's No Story There* also begins with a command. '"Search, please,"' barks the police inspector in charge of Statevale's security (1). This immediately situates the reader amongst the workers arriving for the morning shift: 'people from the Potteries; volunteers of the first war years; new conscripts, old and young; housewives from the villages; women from the towns; from Scotland and Ireland; men just discharged from the Army and invalids of long-time unemployment; ex-miners, greengrocers, builders, bakers, men from the south, from the north, middle-aged men wounded in the last war, young me soon to be called up and casual labourers. The sons of preachers; the daughters of dockers; the children of crofters' (3). This exhaustive, inclusive list is the first example of Holden's ability to detail the sheer diversity of experience contained in the label 'the working classes'. Whereas the engineer's instruction in *Night Shift* is aimed at the narrator alone, here the inspector is speaking to every single one of the workers. Writer and reader too can be counted amongst the multitudes.

Statevale, which employs an astonishing 30,000 people, is described as 'seven miles of carefully-planned human paraphernalia: the 'contraband' huts where all the workers had to give up their cigarettes and matches, the shifting houses where they must change into asbestos suits, the workshops, the canteens, surgeries, cleanways, explosive storehouses, truck sidings, and the intricate internal railway lines' (8). In *Night Shift* the 'workshop sounds' are relayed in great detail:

> The thump-hum-drum of the machinery was only the foundation of noise. From time to time there was, also, the sudden violent hissing of the steam jets which were used for cleaning out the bits of work, and the clattering sound of someone dropping or tripping over some castings they

tried to count or pile up. This last noise was the worst of all; it ran along the workers' nerves like monkeys jumping on telephone wires; whenever it happened someone muttered 'Clumsy', or 'Why can't people look what they're doing?' (Holden 1941, 3–4).

Noise isn't just integral in terms of the important role it plays in rendering the reality of what life in the workshop was like; Holden also incorporates it into the structural fabric of the novella. The action of the week culminates in a tragic event 'sandwiched' between two small and innocuous sounds: that of a penny whistle and birdsong (Bluemel 2019, xvii). And it's the memory of these to which the narrator returns at the very end of the novella: 'Between these two sounds there showed a chink of light through which I could see the start of a more hopeful life, a future in which the courage of people could also be used for their greater happiness and well-being' (Holden 1941, 85). As Bluemel explains, 'this quiet vision of a more just, more egalitarian Britain emerging from the noise of total war was the motivation guiding many workers back to their dangerous posts day after day, night after night, as they fought their war in the factories of London' (Bluemel 2019, xviii).

It's strange then, to come to *There's No Story There* with the sounds of *Night Shift* still humming in one's head. Inside Statevale's workshops, all is quiet and still. It's a place devoid of both loud equipment – 'humans […] took the place of machines' (117) – and lighthearted chit-chat: the silence is described as having 'guillotined down' (3) on the workers as they enter the factory's well-guarded gates. It is heavy, forceful and absolute. This is a different kind of war work to that happening in cities. It's also at more of a removal from the actual war. Due to the factory's rural location, air raids aren't the ever-present danger they are in London, and many of Statevale's workers have been drafted in from elsewhere, living in the factory's nearby dormitory accommodation for the duration of their stay, away from their homes and their families. As such, the little details of ordinary life that couldn't help but slip into *Night Shift* are more broadly absent here. But this is probably useful; distractions are the last thing these workers need as the work here is much more dangerous than that depicted in *Night Shift*. The making of shells and bombs is an intricate, risky process that requires the utmost concentration.

The threat of an accident hangs heavy in the air throughout the text. Something, according to Kate O'Brien in her review of the novel in the *Spectator*, that 'gives the book a very special quality' (O'Brien 1944, 488). Once in the official 'Danger Area', even the most mundane and tedious of tasks have to be undertaken with the utmost care and attention. A worker named Julian (a man whom we learn has recently been discharged from the forces after he was injured when his ship was torpedoed) is tasked with wheeling trucks loaded with explosives between workshop – 'surface-sunk, mounded-up [and] blast-proof' (13) – and storage facility. 'Supposing one of them tipped over and fell to the ground?' he thinks, assessing the boxes awaiting his attention. 'What would happen – well, you know! A small speck of powder spilled, some sort of friction, what they call a 'blow,' and I should disappear instantly' (15). His fear is no idle exaggeration. Halfway through the book, a young female worker trips while carrying a papier-maché boat of 'Powder K' (the explosive compound that the detonators are filled with). There's a sudden flash, 'as if we were being photographed at the seaside, or something,' and her hands fly up to her face, blood pouring down between her fingers (70). In the time it takes to stretcher her to the Rest Room, she's already dead.

Although the factory life described in *Night Shift*, from the noise of the machinery to the Blitzed city setting, is more familiar from wartime writing, the world of *There's No Story Here* is no less real. As well as working in an aircraft factory in North London, Holden also spent some time at an ordnance factory in Wales, so she was writing with a degree of first-hand experience. And yet, what she is describing is also decidedly alien: 'the strange, hushed, unnatural life of those who work in shell-filling factories' (O'Brien 1944, 488). There's something especially eerie about the image of the workers, wearing rubber-soled 'sneaker' shoes and dressed in white flannel suits 'impregnated with asbestos' (13), their faces covered with the 'protective cream and powder' (9) they're obliged to apply before they enter a workshop. It's an image that seems to belong in a science fiction novel – 'scientific, robotic, serious and aseptic' (9) – a far cry from the turbaned, overalls-wearing factory girls with their red lipstick – commonly known as the 'red badge of courage', a defiance of war (Grant 2009, 33) – painted by Laura Knight, our go-to image when we think of Second World War female factory workers. One of the applicants to the Local Appeal Boards in 'Musical Chairman' is a fourteen-year-old girl who's bored stiff at her office job and longs to go and work in a factory. There is a lure in working with other young women, the hustle and bustle of factory life, a glamour is attached to this world. But these things don't quite apply at Statevale.

There's also something discombobulating in the way in which Holden, for all the authenticity of her documentary-style writing, doesn't use traditional exposition. It isn't until the very final chapter of the novel – written in the form of a letter from a newly arrived worker, nineteen-year-old Mary Smith, to her younger sister – that we are given the introduction we might expect to this world; that which echoes the sort of explanation Holden saw it important to provide in the opening of *It Was Different at the Time*, for example:

> I am working on an eight weeks' course in a government training centre. A certain amount of training in technical engineering is given by workshop practice, lectures, and so on. The works superintendent acts in an advisory capacity on behalf of workers leaving the training centre at the end of their course. He tries to tell them something of the factories asking for employees, and the conditions. Women who are finishing their training course often come

in and tell us about their interviews with employers and the ridiculously inadequate wages some of these people still dare to offer them. These stories are always received with laughter, because we feel it is the only thing to do. We often hear that even with overtime, war bonus, and so on, it is exceedingly difficult for a woman worker spending seventy hours a week in a factory to earn more than £2 a week, although the cost of living on the 1st of January this year stood at 96 points above the level of July 1914, and has risen one point above the figure of December last year, due again to increases in the prices of coal and clothing. The Purchase Tax also raises the cost of living figure. (Holden 1943, 168)

Instead, for the most part of *There's No Story There*, Holden forces the reader to slowly piece together the details of this strange world she's describing. We're like the workers themselves, people 'whose war-time job had jerked them out of their own surrounding and brought them down suddenly into a strange unfamiliar setting' (42).

'The cloud of humanity approached the first factory gates,' writes Holden in the opening scene – workers disembarking from the bus that brings them from the nearby purpose-built hostel, a 'big place, almost like a small town,' where most of them live – 'and broke up into individuals' (1). Of these 30,000 workers, Holden's novel follows only a handful, each of whom is both representative and personalized. Among them is the nameless Austrian chef whom everyone knows was in a concentration camp, though he himself never speaks of it. 'Must be sad for him living amongst a lot of strangers,' writes Mary in her letter (164), but by this point in the story, we've learnt that everyone at Statevale is an outsider.

Having said earlier that there is no Feather character in the novel, someone from a middle- or upper-class background that mimics Holden's own roots, there is a character who could loosely be described as the author's fictional alter-ego: Geoffrey Doran, a bespectacled, brown-suited intellectual and 'One-Man-Mass-Observation Centre' (39) who carries a notebook with him wherever he goes, in which he obsessively records the conversations and routines of those around him. In a similar way that the narrator of *Night Shift* was identified as a 'lens of a moving camera'. Doran's are the eyes and ears by which we most often perceive the lives and opinions of Statevale's workers. Mass-Observation was a social research organization founded in 1937 with the aim of recording everyday life in Britain. Workers on the project compiled their material by means of both unpaid, untrained volunteers – who kept diaries, which they then submitted to the project – and hired investigators, who recorded the conversations and behaviour of their neighbours or work colleagues, or that of people attending public events. Doran sits somewhere between the two; he spends as much time as possible observing what's going on around him, but he's not under any particular contract to produce work. 'Dressed in his reasonable brown suit, with collar and tie to match, and carrying a modest attaché case, Geoffrey Doran had the appearance not of one clerk but rather of a composite clerk, but he kept to himself the consolation of his own secret counterfeit career. His rather ambitious goal is to produce 'the greatest one-man volume of mass observation ever' (33). He likes to think that his endeavours are discreet, but his colleagues are well aware of what he's doing. 'I can tell these mass observers from a mile off,' one of the workers tells another when they're joking about Doran rushing off to write down the conversation he's just overheard. 'Don't know why it is. Must be the shine on their spectacles, or something of that' (55). Not that Holden takes poor Doran (or herself) too seriously. 'He found he had no opinions of his own,' she writes when, earlier on in the evening, he tries to initiate a conversation with the men he wants to observe, if only to start them talking, 'only the opinions of the masses docketed down in his notebook' (50). Then, later in the novel, Doran loses his precious notebook in a blizzard that sees the factory buried under large drifts of snow. He's completely bereft, and rushes to scrabble around in the snow trying to find it, to everyone's else's bemusement: 'There was a mass of workers observing him', writes Holden, tongue in cheek (172).

All the same, when *There's No Story There* was first published, what the critics praised most were Holden's observational skills. She's 'a very careful listener,' the *Times Literary Supplement* pointed out, 'these snatches of conversation in canteen or pub that she sets down so shrewdly carry cumulative force and illumination' (anon 1944). She's just as keen an observer of psychological states too, not to mention a sly critic of the governmental and institutionalized structures that keep the working masses in line.

In Mary's letter home she also tells her sister about the 'cinema girl' Nordie, who used to be a journalist but who now screens films in the canteen to entertain the workers. 'I asked her once why she didn't write about the factory,' Mary relates, 'but she said, "There's no story there." I don't suppose there is, neither. The way you know people at work is different to ordinary life. It is jagged and uneven, not just straightforward like in a storybook' (173). It's not lost on the reader that we are reading this supposedly un-writeable novel, the fragmented nature of which is precisely what makes it so compelling. Holden doesn't just neatly prove Nordie wrong. More broadly, *There's No Story There* challenged the prevailing notion that the lives of ordinary working-class people weren't a suitable topic for fiction, a sentiment held by many during this period. It's something we see again in 'Musical Chairman'. The narrator – a clerk at the Labour Exchange – spends all day at the Local Appeal Boards hearings, in the course of which she learns the stories of countless applicants' hardship cases. One of her colleagues – a girl obsessed with music hall celebrities – expresses how glad she is that she didn't have to waste her day at the hearings. 'I like something with a bit of life in it,' she tells the narrator (205). The irony, of course, is that the narrator has spent the whole day learning more about life – what makes it hard, what makes it valuable, of certain people's stupidity and cruelty, of the kindness and love of others – than her colleague could ever hope to understand. Holden's great gift, Bluemel explains, 'was to find plot where others saw random events, see heroes when others saw workers, create stories when others saw no story there' (Bluemel 2004, 134).

Notes

1   Holden transcribed Wells's words into her diary entry for 18 December 1942.

2   It is thought that Holden might have been a member of the Communist Party at an early point in her life. She definitely wasn't by the 30s, when she identified herself as an anti-Communist socialist. But, as Powell points out in his memoirs, 'Her later passionate hatred of the Communist Party suggested close knowledge of its methods' (Powell 1978, 24).

Works Cited

anon, Review of *There's No Story There* by Inez Holden, *Times Literary Supplement*, 25 November 1944, 569.

Bluemel, Kristen, *The Radical Eccentrics: Intermodernism in Literary London* (Palgrave Macmillan 2004).

Bluemel, Kristen, 'Introduction' to *Blitz Writing: Night Shift & It Was Different at the Time* by Inez Holden (Handheld Press 2019), vii–xxix.

Calder, Angus, *The People's War* (Ace Books 1969).

Goodman, Celia, 'Inez Holden: A Memoir', *London Magazine*, Dec/Jan 1994, 29–34.

Grant, Linda, *The Thoughtful Dresser* (Virago 2009).

Holden, Inez, *Night Shift* (1941), in *Blitz Writing. Night Shift & It Was Different At The Time* (Handheld Press 2019), 1–85.

Holden, Inez, *There's No Story There* (1943), in *Blitz Writing. Night Shift & It Was Different At The Time* (Handheld Press 2019), 87–181.

O'Brien, Kate, Review of *There's No Story There* by Inez Holden, *Spectator*, 24 November 1944, 488.

Powell, Anthony, 'Inez Holden: A Memoir', *London Magazine*, Oct/Nov 1974, 88–94.

Powell, Anthony, *Messengers of the Day*, Volume 2 of *To Keep the Ball Rolling: The Memoirs of Anthony Powell*. 3 Volumes (Heinemann 1978).

Priestley, J B, quotation from dustjacket of 1941 edition of *Night Shift*.

Taylor, D J, *Bright Young People: The Rise and Fall of a Generation, 1918-1940* (2007; Vintage 2008).

Taylor, D J, *Lost Girls: Love, War and Literature, 1939-1951* (Constable 2019).

Further Reading

Feigel, Lara, *The Love-Charm of Bombs: Restless Lives in the Second World War* (Bloomsbury 2013).

Gardiner, Juliet, *Wartime: Britain 1939–1945* (Headline 2005).

Gardiner, Juliet, *The Blitz: The British Under Attack* (HarperCollins 2011).

Hartley, Jenny (ed.), *Hearts Undefeated: Women's Writing of the Second World War* (Virago 1994).

Hartley, Jenny, *Millions Like Us: British Women's Fiction of the Second World War* (Virago 1997).

Madge, Charles, and Tom Harrison, *Britain by Mass Observation* (1939; Faber and Faber 2009).

Orwell, George, *The Collected Essays, Journalism and Letters* (David R Godine 2000).

Spalding, Frances, *Stevie Smith: A Biography* (Norton 1988).

Taylor, D J, *Orwell* (Chatto & Windus 2003).

Works by Inez Holden

Holden wrote dozens of pieces of journalism and short fiction for fashion and middlebrow magazines like *Harper's Bazaar*, *Punch*, *The Cornhill Magazine*, and *The Strand Magazine*, as well as short fiction published in the wartime magazine, *Horizon*. All of this work is uncollected, as are Holden's postwar film scripts written for J Arthur Rank.

Novels

Sweet Charlatan (Duckworth 1929)

Born Old, Died Young (Duckworth 1932)

Friend of the Family (Arthur Baker 1933)

Night Shift (John Lane 1941)

There's No Story There (John Lane 1944)

The Owner (Bodley Head 1952)

The Adults (Bodley Head 1956)

Story collections

Death in High Society (Kegan Paul 1934)

To the Boating and Other Stories (John Lane 1945)

Non-fiction

It Was Different at the Time (John Lane 1943)

There's No Story There

by Inez Holden

The text for this edition of *There's No Story There* was scanned from the first edition, and was silently corrected for typographical errors and punctuation consistency.

Chapter One

Inspection

'Search, please.'

A fleet of red buses loomed up through the morning mist, as purposeful as troop-carrying aircraft, fast following each other into the clearing-ground before pulling up. All the passengers descended and massed forward. Only the darkness of the clothes they wore separated them from the slow starting day. The cloud of humanity approached the first factory gates and broke up into individuals.

'Search, please.'

The morning shift was going through the first inspection. The men filed through on the left, the women on the right. They walked in single file. People from the Potteries; volunteers of the first war year; new conscripts, old and young; housewives from the villages; women from the towns; from Scotland and Ireland; men just discharged from the Army and invalids of long-time unemployment; ex-miners, greengrocers, builders, bakers, men from the south, from the north, middle-aged men wounded in the last war, young men soon to be called up and old casual labourers. The sons of preachers; the daughters of dockers; the children of crofters.

Old Charlie went into the inspection hut followed by Lofty, the foreman, wearing 'sneaker' shoes. Gluckstein, the overlooker of Group IV, Section I, moved more quickly than the others. He caught up with them and then passed them by.

Silence guillotined down on the workers as they went through these first inspection huts; but, getting safely out on the other side, let loose some of the stored-up talk in them.

'Morning, Bill.'

'Morning.'

'This new inspector Jameson's a bit of a bastard, isn't he?'

'That's right, regular bastard he is.'

A man with tattooed arms and a black beret set far on the back of his head said, 'Inspector Jameson, huh!' and spat to the ground. A sweat strand of hair fell forward over his face; looking out in hatred through the dark lock, he walked on towards the Danger Area.

Gluckstein was almost through the Danger Area gate now; the distance between them made him seem smaller to the others.

'Look at old Gluckstein off there on his own.'

'Yus, independent beggar he is.'

'Yus, always first at work, he is.'

'Gluckstein's a regular glutton for work and no mistake about it.'

'Where's Old Charlie?'

'He ain't come through the inspection yet. That's the fifth time they've frisked Old Charlie this week.'

'They're supposed to search one in thirty, but if it goes on like this they'll be searching thirty in one.'

Julian, discharged from the Army, had not been searched to-day. A tall, thin man whose face had been burnt in a pit explosion told him, 'It never was this way when Inspector Davies was here. He was all right, Inspector Davies was. You'd never have knowed he was a policeman at all unless you'd seen him in his uniform.'

Hate-lock pushed the black beret farther to the back of his head and answered at once: 'This here Jameson's got inspection on the brain, always acts like he knows you've done something wrong and he's only got to find it out. His life must be a regular misery to him, always bothering about other bastards' lives.'

'That's right.'

Julian listened to the talk around him. 'There was a man who followed *Les Misérables* through the sewers of Paris. I wonder if Inspector Jameson ever read that book? It might do him good to take a look at himself from the outside.' Julian did not think aloud, but he thought in words. He found it difficult to speak at all. The sound of his voice made him feel afraid. Between the thought and the speech there was a shadow. When he had been in hospital it had been the opposite. At that time he had been obliged to speak out everything that came into his head. The man in the next bed had complained that he could not sleep at night because of Julian's incessant talk. 'Just my luck to be put next to a delirious sod!' But now it was the opposite process with Julian. He talked in silence. 'I never used to think like this, not in words. I used to think visually in pictures, but now it's all words. Nothing but words; they keep coming into my head, and it seems that I can't get them out. It was soon after I arrived in hospital that it happened this way, after the treatment from the "Trick Cyclist". It's curious the way everything comes into my head in verbal form. I wonder why it is ... It seems as if I had no control over it.'

Now that Gluckstein had got through into the Danger Area, he felt much safer. He was farther away from the first inspection huts. Every morning the same fear swept over him. It made no difference whether he was searched or not; in the experience itself of going through inspection there was a hint of some horror to come—hidden, but already on the horizon, as if indistinct and difficult to read, but addressed to him personally. Gluckstein got the same fear on a moving stairway. Of course it was irrational, he knew that. Now that he was safe inside the Danger Area he might as well slow up his steps. No need to hurry, because he would still be at work a minute or two before the others. The voices of his workmates travelled over the few yards between them. He did not look back. Although he could not recognize the voice of every speaker, there were one or two he knew each time. Old Charlie's gentle monotone; Linnet's clear controlled treble; Julian's rather weary way of breathing; and the harsh sentences of Lofty, the anti-Semite, which Gluckstein hated to hear.

'Wot's the use of them searching Old Charlie? Wot do they expect to find?'

'A whole Karl Marx library.'

'I keep that in my head, see,' Old Charlie answered up, 'where no one can't look.'

'Fancy looking into Old Charlie's head! You wouldn't 'arf find some slogans.'

On impulse Gluckstein looked back towards the first factory gate. Inspector Jameson had come out from the police-office, and was standing there, very straight and thin in his loose brown suit, watching the workers file through the huts.

Linnet had just come through the inspection hut on the right. She worked on the detonator group, and at this moment was closely followed by Ysabette Jones, the schizophrenic, who stumbled along after her, talking as though tripping over her own ill-assembled sentences.

Inspector Jameson stared at the people passing by like a man watching a pageant. It was impossible to tell what he was thinking. Lofty saw him too. Lofty did not say anything about Inspector Jameson but his face instantly twisted itself into an expression of disciplined dislike.

The beret-topped man said, 'Look at little Mr Sunshine.'

'Wot a clean clothes per-lice man.'

'Ah reckon Jameson's the most unpopular man in our factory.'

'Yus, they don't 'arf luv 'im 'ere.'

The young assistant foreman asked Julian if he had seen Geoffrey Doran during the morning. 'He sleeps in your block up at the hostel, doesn't he, Julian?'

Julian nodded.

Lofty said, 'Doran works on Time and Motion, so he won't be in until about nine o'clock or thereabouts.'

'That's right,' the assistant foreman answered, 'Doran works gentleman's hours. But I seen you having a bit of a discussion up at the hostel supper-time last night. Of course I noticed it, see, because you don't often see Doran in a conversation. Writing's more in his line. Write, write, write, that's Geoffrey Doran all over. Seems to me as if he'd be as lonely without his notebook as a witch without her broomstick. Still, Geoffrey ought to be able to write; he's had a good education. What is it, BA, or MA, or something of that? You can't do nothing without education these days. You can get to being assistant foreman, same as me, but after that, stop, finish; an assistant foreman in a factory, but no education – then no further. I'm a practical man myself, always have been. I like to be doing something even in my spare time, making a rabbit-hutch or something of that. But there's old Doran, even on a fine day when everyone as can is out enjoying themselves, there's old Geoff, writing in his notebook. Seems as if he must get snowed under with his notes. All the same I wish I could write. I wouldn't 'arf put down some of the things I bin' noticing 'ere.'

Julian and the assistant foreman reached the second gate together. A policeman was standing there staring straight ahead of him. The blue bicycles which were kept especially for factory messengers were up-ended on an iron rack; through the criss-crossed bars various visitors could be seen going into the Office of Works, the Security Office or the Policemen's Office known as the Cop-shop. Labour officers, cinema projectionist messengers, bill-posters, and Captain Quantock, the Security Officer, Mr Lyons, the Public Officer, and Colonel Flore of the Home Guard went past, weighed down with portfolios.

Julian saw them as figures set there ready for a careful drawing, squared up by the bars of the bicycle rack. The two men walked on through the gate into the Danger Area. Before them lay the long avenues, tree-less and dead straight, and leading off each avenue the streets, each one marked with a shin-high signpost, Street I, Street II, Street III. The streets were empty of traffic, and free from people. Six years ago this had been unorganized country where cattle grazed at will, but now there were seven miles of carefully-planned human paraphernalia: the 'contraband' huts where all workers had to give up their cigarettes and matches, the shifting houses where they must change into asbestos suits, the workshops, the canteens, surgeries, cleanways, explosive storehouses, truck sidings, and the intricate internal railway lines.

The assistant foreman said, 'At this time of the morning it looks like a regular city of the dead, and yet there must be near on seven thousand of us on this early shift alone. I always like this shift better than the night shift, you know. On the night shift you don't have no private life at all. You like noons, do you? I can't abide that shift myself. When we're on noons, we don't have no day nor no night life, so where are we?'

One of the internal buses was going by on its way to Group 8.

'Here comes a budgie-cage,' the assistant foreman said. He stopped it and got in. 'So long, soldier.'

Julian walked on alone till he reached the contraband hut. The man next to him was handing over a paper-backed poetry anthology.

'Here, Joe, you look after this for me. I don't want those fellows in the shifting house to start reading it.'

Julian gave up a cigarette-case and a watch, then he moved on into the shifting house and changed into his magazine clothes.

At the same moment, Linnet, on Group IV, was going through the ritual of getting ready for work. She no longer noticed the centre and clock number printed on the back of her white flannel coat. 'You don't when you've seen it several hundred times.' Linnet put on her white flannel trousers and her rubber-soled shoes. After she had pushed some of her hair back under her cap she was almost ready. There remained only the ritual of walking to the 'ablutions', then putting protective cream and powder on her face. After this she would drink a cup of tea in the canteen, go up into the detonator workshop and begin the day's work.

She thought about Willie, but she could not get any clear idea. Already her image of him was becoming confused. His life in the Army was unknown to her. She could not imagine his camp. She did not know any of his companions. She thought of her marriage with Willie, and their life together before the war. It was only a little while ago, but now their two lives had diverged.

Linnet walked down the cleanway, a long black rubber composition path. It was a pity Willie couldn't see her now. It would seem strange to him, this sight of her, scientific, robotic, serious, and aseptic. Linnet supposed that Willie would think it 'a rare old joke'.

Ysabette Jones came out of the shifting house. She pattered pigeon-toed along the cleanway.

'I had two letters from my boy this morning,' Ysabette Jones said. 'He's a Group Captain.'

Linnet wondered if she would have any news of Willie when she got back to the hostel. Perhaps there would be some hope that he might get leave soon. There was no post in the morning before Linnet left because it did not arrive until nearly eight o'clock, and sometimes on the work of the morning shift she was unhappy wondering if there was a letter from Willie waiting for her. Ysabette Jones was still talking, but there was no sense in her words.

'Almost all my men friends are Group Captains,' she said. Enclosed in her own thoughts Linnet did not answer. It was four minutes to seven now; the Blue shift was starting work.

Chapter Two

Cleanway

At one minute after seven Julian was walking down the cleanway on his journey to the truck-store. He wore the white asbestos suit, he had the protective cream on his face and his time of arrival at work was already marked on the time-card. A sentence skidded through his mind.

'It's one minute after and I'm on the group. I've got into my magazines, clocked on, and made-up.'

Julian was still speaking in silence. His thoughts sifted slowly through his mind, put together in sentences. 'How easily one takes to jargon. It seems strange at first to hear the tough men of Statevale talking about "getting made-up". There is that heavy fellow from Cornwall working on 'smoke', name of Darling. It's funny to hear them say "Darling's making-up". The first time I heard it I wondered why no one else smiled. It often happens to me like that. Expressions that seem odd to me don't matter at all to the others because they are used to it. It was that way when I went to see my cousin Edward at the Training College. The moment I walked into that red brick suburban house and saw Edward, he said, "I've got leave to go ashore; we can just catch the liberty boat if we hurry." Then we ran like hell and caught up with a cumbersome green omnibus which jogged us down that damn ribbon development right into the local town. I felt irritated with Edward that day, and kept thinking that it was stupid of him to be dressed up as a sailor for the sake of drilling in the precincts of a small but well-appointed city gent's residence. All through our conversation I resented this meeting with Edward as if I had been somehow manoeuvred into acting in a musical comedy – and an indifferent one at that. I considered my cousin a cardboard character. Funny, though, the way he made a quick jump right into reality by going to sea three weeks later. He got torpedoed first trip out. I remember the way it impressed me at the time. I think he always was the lucky one. I don't remember feeling so insanely jealous of anybody since another boy at my school showed me a pair of buckskin cricket boots when I only had the regulation canvas kind myself. Funny idea, being jealous of a man getting killed. But I couldn't control it somehow. I hated hearing people talk about him.'

Julian walked on towards the truck-store. He walked slowly, steadily, bullied and tyrannized by his thoughts. 'It's odd about jargon, the way it slides about and shifts its meaning. The expression "make-up" is an example of that. When I hear it now I only see myself going through this routine of smearing on the protective cream before starting out to take my rubber-tyred truck up and down the cleanways and in and out of the workshops. But a year or so back the word "make-up" would have touched off a completely different group of associations. I'd think about my mother making-up at home, fussing over me at first, and then abruptly forgetting all about me in order to pin-point all her thoughts on the reshaping of her eyebrows with a curious kind of cosmetic pencil. That was the way it always happened. She did not take her eyes slowly away from me. She suddenly shifted the whole of her attention off me and on to the making-up of her face, leaving me each time isolated with a panicking sense of emotional insecurity. It's very odd the way one can go cantering about on the back of a contemporary slangism such as "make-up". It takes me over other ground far away from my home – the faces of chorus girls waiting to go on, young intellectuals at the Cambridge Festival Theatre, also waiting to go on. Long-legged and useless young ladies in peace-time restaurants, peering into little mirrors at meal-times, and cissies getting ready to go willowing down Piccadilly on moonlit nights.'

A stone-shouldered giant of a man wearing an asbestos suit came walking down the cleanway towards Julian. He had red hair, and his blue eyes were paler than his face. He went by muttering, 'Two minutes after seven, and I ain't got that blurry powder on my face yet.'

As soon as Julian reached the truck-store the foreman, Lofty, came in and gave him his instructions.

'Go to H Magazine and take Lot 6246 to B7.'

Julian set out on his first-errand with a light truck, light now because it was still empty; rubber tyres on his truck, rubber soles on his shoes, a round white cap on the back of his head, and wearing a white flannel suit impregnated with asbestos. He moved rapidly over the black rubber composition cleanway. He seemed to be skimming through the work-day. No effort anywhere, everything easy, but then the nagging sentences started coming back into his mind as if the words were the motor which made him move.

'What am I doing now? Wheeling my truck towards a magazine store. I've got to get it filled up there. Of course, Old Charlie will be in the magazine, and he'll help me; and then when we have got it loaded up I shall set out again and take the truck down to B7. But it will be rather heavy by then, so that I shall have to go very carefully. Still, I ought to be used to it. I've made the journey often enough. Thousands of times I must have travelled with this truck along these shiny black cleanways, and thousands of times, too, I have seen these straight lines before me subjecting me to the same symmetry and solitude. The solitude is the most subtle part of the whole set-up when you think there are seven thousand workers on the shift, but nearly all of them are out of sight now in their surface-sunk, mounded-up, blast-proof workshops. Sometimes the workshops make me think of those semi-basements—the kind that house agents used to advertise when they wanted to put over a hint of half-refinement, suggesting that the dwelling was not as beetle-like as a basement, and not as ordinary as the common or garden ground-level building which could be overlooked by passers-by.'

Julian walked lightly, aware of no weight but that of his own sense of guilt. 'I know I ought not to be scrim-shanking above ground like this. I ought by rights to be working in one of those semi-sunken combined explosive shops.'

As if the sun had the strength to bring them out, other truck men appeared now, making their white-coated way along the various avenues. None of them were near enough to seem life-size. Those not too far distant could have been children at play, and those farther away toys in action. Julian could see two dark-suited shop-managers escorting a brown-dressed visitor over one of the colossal steel bridges. They walked slowly, leisurely; a visitor who might be interfering, distinguished, technical, or perhaps even all three at the same time. Straining his eyes towards the suspending bridge, Julian thought 'You would expect folk to work their way up from the dark-suited stage of those three men, stepping on steel, to the white-suited stage of the fellows moving along the cleanways, but in this curious kind of other-ether world it all seems to scheme out the opposite way round. As you go on the up-grade from worker to foreman you change over from angel-white suit to black bowler hat.'

Julian reached his first objective, opened the doors of the magazine shop and backed his truck into it. Stacked on three sides from floor to ceiling were white wooden boxes with rope handles and yellow lettering—DLG/150. There were no windows in this room, the only light from outside was let in through the portholes as in a ship. The ceiling was high, there was a low white table in the centre of the room, a form and a bench. 'The room, the womb, the steamship, the school with form and bench, the unbroken crystal in which every individual lives.' Julian looked up at the top layer of boxes, and as he did so his death-wish overwhelmed him again.

'Supposing one of them tipped over and fell to the ground? What would happen—well, you know! A small speck of powder spilled, some sort of friction, what they call a "blow", and I should disappear instantly. Sudden violence is something which I can never be clear about in my own mind. Confusion comes creeping round it both before the impact and afterwards. I remember waiting in a queue on a beach after having lost most of my equipment, but I don't remember being torpedoed. I don't remember the clearing-station, all that is part of what they filled in for me afterwards. I do remember a hospital-train, though, and the surgeon who stuttered. He said: "You'll be all-all-all ..." and I waited for him to say "right" but he never did. He said, "You'll be all-all-all—set for home soon." That was what he told me and he told me true enough. I did get home after I left the Army and I got well enough to come and work here now. But I cannot get all the events in their right order. That is what seems to haunt me all the time as if I cannot do anything without arranging it all in words in my mind first. Now supposing there was a "blow" here; it would be the same sort of thing again. Another part of my consciousness would be taken clean away from me a second time. I don't suppose I should remember wheeling my truck along the cleanway before I came in here. I wouldn't remember the two shop managers and a visitor walking over the bridge, nor putting on my magazine clothes, nor the conversation of the assistant-foreman fellow after I got through the inspection gate. Maybe I wouldn't even remember leaving the hostel this morning and waiting for the bus at the cross-roads; all that would be forgotten, even the sight of the hills behind us in the misty morning air.

There would be a parting in my memory as if a zip fastener had been ripped back and then got stuck suddenly–probably stuck at that game of chess I had with Geoffrey Doran last night. Funny fellow, Geoffrey, he seems rather isolated from the others up at the hostel, works on time and motion, but of course the Time and Emotion men, as they call them, are bound to be a bit out of things. They wear their own clothes, and work "Gentlemen's" hours. But even Geoffrey's way of talking is strange: it's punctuated, and he ends his sentences on a sort of signalling note, something like a typewriter bell at the end of a line. Certainly Geoffrey Doran doesn't seem to take off his spiritual stays in company. Geoffrey Doran–is he human? Oh well–to hell with him; here I am into the magazine shop to load up the truck!'

Old Charlie got up from the bench where he sat, and stood ready to help with the loading-up.

'Old Charlie sits here all day as quiet-calm as a fellow in a wicker chair outside a country pub on a sunny evening. He doesn't trouble about anything. He likes to talk of old "Red Flag" singing days, though; if anyone comes in, he doesn't expect any answer. I'm glad of that, because although I don't mind talk going on around me, I can't speak out loud myself. I've got these sentences chasing each other through my mind all the time, but I think if I tried to translate them into sound I couldn't keep my complete consciousness. It's a funny business. I can't speak words out neither can I move without them.'

Old Charlie said, 'I hear as they've closed the cinemas on Sundays up in the town. People can make explosives for blowing each other up on a Sunday, but they mustn't go and sit quietly in a cinema. They tell me as the people marched through the town with placards, "Open the cinemas." You'd think that if anyone wanted to march they'd have plenty more to march about than that: something a bit more worthwhile.'

Old Charlie picked up a white wooden box, lifted it down by its rope handles, and put it gently on the truck.

'There was a time when they closed the pubs on a Sunday in London,' he said, 'and all the toffs went into the park wearing their top-hats, same as they did every Sunday. And what did they find there this time but the proletariat shouting at them, "Go to church!" The next Sunday the pubs were still shut, and ten times the number of proletariat told each dressed up dummy, "Go to church!" 'Course I wasn't there myself, mind you, but my dad told me about it; and Karl Marx was there, and he knocked off a topper hisself! My dad seed him do it, and heard him call out, "Go to church! Go to church!" with the rest of them. Well, when the next Sunday came round, every pub was open again.'

Old Charlie had put three white wooden boxes on the truck now. Julian had not moved or spoken. In the silence the words went through his mind, 'I must help Old Charlie. I feel ashamed that I've let him do all the work. I'm picking up this box now, carrying it very gently; better give all my mind to it. We're told everything's safe enough if you're reasonably careful and take the ordinary safety precautions provided; but the people who say this are not the same as the ones who work on eight or twelve-hour shifts six days a week themselves. This second box of combined explosives I'm lifting down now must be the same weight as the last, but somehow it seems much lighter. Between us we've managed to get a good few loaded up already. It's not so bad at this time of the day, but towards the end of the shift that awful mood of monotony comes creeping over me as certain sure as slow paralysis. Boredom isn't a negative thing as people say; it's an active kind of poison, a malady that drags you down with it and into a deep morass where treacled-up time ticks slowly over you. It's not carelessness, but monotony that's the enemy of safety in industry.'

By now the truck was three-quarters loaded. Old Charlie came back again to the same subject.

'But wot do they do in the town to-day? A few unorganized workers go carrying bits of papers on sticks, saying, "Open the cinemas." Now that won't get them anywhere – not even into the cinemas. The cinemas will be open every week-day and shut of a Sunday, same as ever. An ordinary worker don't know which way to act no more than a blooming kid does. They 'aven't got any leaders over the cinema trouble – that's what they want, leaders to tell them not to be content till all the cinemas are closed Sundays and week-days alike, because anyone that's watched events, same as I have, could see that all cinemas are capitalist propagander. Of course they are, the shareholders see to that!'

Charlie moved a box of combined explosive quickly from pile to truck. Julian thought: 'If he were to drop it now? But, of course, Old Charlie couldn't do that. His thoughts go gavotting to an old-time revolutionary march. They don't dance to any other tune, but his hands have a life of their own; strong, responsible hands. I heard that all the years Charlie was unemployed he used to make toys for children, and sometimes he sold them in the streets. It must have taken some skill, making those toys.'

'Mind you, there have been workers' films,' Old Charlie said. 'Good ones, too. *Battleship Potemkin*, and those.'

Charlie loaded the three last boxes on to the truck.

'I've been glad to have this talk with you,' he said 'I get proper despondent down here. In London it was different, we were always having a bit of a discussion, or something of that; and I often used to speak in Hyde Park of a Sunday.'

The truck was loaded up and ready to lead out of the store. Old Charlie did not seem to notice Julian's silence. He was pleased to be able to go on talking without being challenged.

Julian thought: 'Funny about Old Charlie. He keeps his

ideas in store, like those far-sighted women who keep all their clothes until the same fashion comes round again.'

Julian did not say 'Good-bye,' because somehow he could not get the sound out. He could not interrupt the talk that ran on through his mind; but he smiled at Old Charlie, wheeled his truck out on to the cleanway and walked slowly forward with the heavy load down Street III, Avenue B, and into filling shop B7.

B7 was a mixed shop. Most of the men were lifting and working on presses; the girls filled shells through a paper cone. Julian had once heard a foreman describing this operation to a visitor; the sentences worked their way through his mind again.

'With a plunger you pull the slide, adjusted to a certain tension, so that the spring sends it back at the proper moment to where it first came from. Yer see, yer gets paid yer money and yer don't take yer choice, but yer can't go wrong. It's as 'safe as 'ouses, or as safe as 'ouses were before they knocked 'em in the Old Kent Road.'

Blue-band Gluckstein was acting as senior overlooker in charge. He said to Julian, 'Just give me a hand, and we'll lift them on to the bench here.'

Gluckstein worked at such a speed that almost at once he was lifting two boxes to Julian's one; a little while after he was working on a load of three to one, and finally on four.

Julian thought: 'Gluck's a good fellow, but he works overtime all the time. The girls can't do that; they've got to work to an exact rhythm, all at the same speed. This shell-filling shop makes me think of that occupational therapy they ran at the hospital for anxiety neurosis cases.'

Gluckstein said, 'Will you take these empty boxes back to the box-shop? Look at the untidy way those bastards on the last shift have left them here! They should have cleared the shop before they went home.'

Someone said, 'It must be that fourth shift again.'

It was an answer that Julian knew well. There were only three shifts–his own, which was the White shift, the Blue, and the Red. There was no fourth shift, but it was an imaginary scapegoat, often brought into the conversation of the workers on every shift. Julian wheeled his truck out of the workshop down the cleanway towards the box store. The mist was clearing, it was going to be a fine day. There were four tough girls with chisels and hammers, waiting in the box shop. They cleaned the boxes and screwed down the tops ready for them to be sent back to the key factory from which they came. An old Welshman was wheeling a truck.

'Here comes Sid Walker,' said the tallest tough girl.

The Welshman unloaded the boxes very slowly. One of the tough girls set to work to help him. He was a short man, Spanish-dark, with deep-set eyes. 'You could see by the way he breathed that he had an industrial disease. Some of the ex-miners had silicosis. They get given light jobs here now. Same as they give me since I've been discharged from the Army.'

When the Welshman with the hesitant breathing had gone away, one of the girls said, 'Welshman, weren't he, that larst fellow?'

'That's right.'

'Welshmen is always singing bloody 'ymns. Ar like a bit of music in the right place, but bloody 'ymns is only for church.'

Julian began to unload the boxes. None of the girls gave him any help, because they knew he was stronger than the man who had just left.

For the next few hours Julian walked back and forth with these loads. The mist cleared slowly; the sun shone forth more strongly. It was not very long since Julian had made the decision to let the State take him over. That was the way he saw it later. The State took him over. He had been directed to work in an ordnance factory, and had come here fearing the strict static existence. But as a truck-man he moved about all day, spent most of his time in the open air, and had the sense of space he needed. The work did not cause him any great anxiety; he did not have to take difficult decisions.

The sun shone out now on to the avenues and cleanways, and at this moment he felt quite free, wanting nothing as he moved back and forth from magazine to filling-shop and to box-room. The rubber-tyred truck smoothed its way along until the time when he left it in the truck store from where he had fetched it at seven o'clock. He went to wash then, and afterwards went into the canteen. In the doorway he saw the Welshman.

'Half-past ten in the morning. What a time to have dinner, man.'

The clock-hands jerked on to half-past ten. The men and girls came into the canteen, rushing forward like players in a baseball game Julian had seen in a film. Most of the workers ran to the racks to fetch the dinners they had brought from their homes in tin cases and parcels. Then they ran for their places at the long tables. But Julian went up to the counter.

A man went by with soup in a bowl. 'Could wash my socks in it, I could,' he said.

Another explained to Julian: 'It's funny to think I had to come here to see that man. We knew him when we were kids, see. He was a great boxer—a local champion he was! We used to follow him round, sort of hero-worshipped him we did, and now he's turned up here. Funny, isn't it?'

Julian smiled and nodded his head. He watched the White shift come crowding into the canteen, most of them talking, some shouting. He stood awkwardly against the food counter, alone in his silence, feeling as isolated as a man walking by himself on a heath.

Chapter Three

Joint Production

At half-past eight in the morning, Henry Whistler, the superintendent of Statevale, came stride-stepping down the quarter-mile factory drive. His raincoat, a bulky Burberry, was slung over his left shoulder, his dispirited flop-eared spaniel followed on his heels. Whistler went past the inspection huts and on up to the Administration Building.

The tall, sad-seeming policeman came out of the cop-shop. It was time for him to come up to the gate on Group Six. He was ready to take over from the square-shouldered police officer with the splay hands, who stood waiting outside for him.

'They come in at all hours, don't they?'

Splay-hands was staring out over the valley. He could see a little boy rounding up sheep in the far distance.

'Who come in at all hours?'

'Whistler and his dog.'

'That's right.'

The tall police officer was glad to be out of doors and able to look round him. This morning he had been going through routine jobs, checking up on lost property, looking over identification cards, signing people in and out, and odd jobs of that sort. Nothing to complain about except the monotony of staying indoors seeing the same four walls.

'What do they call him?' Splay-hands asked.

'Who?'

'Super's dog?'

'Pitcher.'

'That's a funny name for a dog.'

'Ah, but there's a reason for it, see. Super told me hisself one evening, up at the gate it was, just when he was going out. "Little pitchers 'ave long ears," he said, and laughed fit to bust hisself.'

The superintendent was lost to sight behind the swing-doors of the Administration Building, but the two policemen could see the spaniel squeezing through after him on the second swing.

'So long,' said Splay-hands to the tall policeman, 'see you later.'

He went into the cop-shop, and almost at once two women talking came in after him. The leading talker was the film unit supervisor, Mrs Karslake. She wore a sailor-shaped beaver hat on the back of her head: she fussed forward with words.

'One of my girls has lost a flapjack. I've brought her along with me.'

The girl looked ill at ease, wishing herself elsewhere. She had tied a scarf peasant-wise under her chin, and her fair curls had been carefully crowded forward to the front of her forehead, giving her the look of a pretty hare.

Splay-hands sighed heavily. 'A flapjack, you say? That's one of them cases for face powder, isn't it? One of them things you women set such store by. Well, let's look in this book then and see if it's come in.'

He sat down at the table, opened a big book and ran the whole bunch of his fingers down the list of objects brought in.

'There ain't no flapjack here, nor anything like it either.'

'And we've lost some instructions sent to us from head office. It's the list of films we're to show next in the canteen.'

Mrs Karslake looked restlessly round the room. 'They told us it was sure to turn up here, so we comes straight round to see if you could help us.'

Another armed police-officer came in and moved heavily round the room, as if weighed down by his revolver.

'Nothing ain't come in yet,' Splay-hands said, in his stubborn way.

'Well, if anyone's taken those instructions, I'll see Mr Whistler himself gets to hear of it. My girls can't spend all their time being sent from pillar to post looking for things that someone else has laid their hands on.' Splay-hands started to yawn. The cinema supervisor stood her ground, as if frozen from frustration she was unable to move on.

'I sent two of my girls up to the Office of Works once already this morning to see if they'd been holding back some films that should have arrived, and that we were supposed to be showing in Canteen C8. Of course they couldn't tell us anything about it. And now C8 haven't had a cinema show this break-time at all. If it's that young labour officer in the Office of Works that's been keeping back the films addressed to us, I shall tell Mrs Teglar about her myself.'

Pretty hare shifted from one foot to the other and gave a tug to her scarf-knot.

'Well, it's not your fault. I know that,' said Mrs Karslake. 'Thank you for helping us. We'll come in again and see if those instructions have arrived.'

The film unit boss bustled her assistant out of the room before her. As she went, Splay-hands heard her say, 'We've done damn-all again to-day! When are we going to get really started? That's what I want to know. We've come here to show flaming films – and we're going to show flaming films instead of all this messing around.'

The second police-officer said to Splay-hands, 'It wor' funny when she wor' on about telling Whistler. Much he'd worry about a cinema lot losing their instructions. She ought to know that Super's got more to think about than that. She said she was going to tell Mrs Teglar too, as if the head labour officer in a place like this hadn't enough on her plate already. How many are there of them there in the film outfit?'

'Six so far.'

'Well they should know their jobs better than to go losing their instructions. Well, I suppose it's difficult for them. They're neither factory nor management; they don't work shift hours nor "gentlemen's" hours either, so where are they?'

'Here to-day and gone to-morrow,' said the splay-handed policeman.

The other police officer was staring at a notice on the wall: 'NO LIVESTOCK ALLOWED WITHIN THE FACTORY.'

'I must have seen that notice dozens of times since I've been here, but I often wonder if old Super's ever taken a look at it.'

'Oh, well, Super's different. His dog Pitcher don't do no harm so long as he stays up there in Admin. Dogs is all right in their proper place, but I don't reckon a dog is much of a companion to a grown man; more for kids' company dogs are.'

'Super's a grown man all right, ain't he? Fancy being in charge of some thirty thousand people like he is here. You've got to be grown-up for that. Of course he's only a figure-head, we know that, but I often wonder how people get them jobs.'

'He's a very clever chemist, Super is, you know; very clever chemist indeed he is.'

Whistler walked down the first floor of the Administration Building and into his office. It was the second office from the first staircase and had a glass door on which was written in big black block letters: 'SUPERINTENDENT. H D WHISTLER.' The next room on the right was not quite so large, but it also looked directly on to the bit of lawn centred with the Union Jack floating from the top of a flagmast. The glass of this door was black-blocked: 'MRS TEGLAR. CHIEF WOMAN LABOUR OFFICER.' The office on the left, occupied by the Public Relations Officer, was about a couple of feet in size and the lettering on the door was a quarter of an inch smaller: 'CHAS. LYON. PRO'.

All along this passage there were glass doors: the Registry room, the Chief Production Manager's office, the Second Production Manager's office, the First PAD man, and so on. In the basement of the building where the green-dressed girls moved about getting the tea, there were more PAD men, an office for the chief electrician, the chief telephone man, and many others. Whistler knew them all by sight and by name; he had got them carefully documented in his mind.

Whistler went into his room and sat down at the desk, staring gloomily at the letters and notes waiting for him there. This was the morning of the Joint Production Committee meeting, and already along the passages glass doors were opening and shutting, harassed men were hurrying in and out handing each other notes and saying, 'I shall bring it up at the meeting.'

Whistler walked along the passage to the glass-doored lavatory for 'Managerial Staff Only'. This hierarchy of lavatories was a curious clue to the new kind of snobbishness. Whistler was always thinking what a strange thing it was. He turned to the washbowl, and turned on some water. The tap gave out a startled sound and let loose a torrent of tepid water. Outside, a series of messengers kept coming in up the stairs carrying large yellow envelopes. They had been sent by the Shop Managers' Committee from the Group. Every now and then Whistler could hear one of the glass doors opening, and the voice of a manager. The glass doors opened and shut as they took them into the various Production Managers' offices. 'The SM told me to bring this to you, sir—he said you'd know what it was. He said you was to have it before the meeting started, sir—he said I wasn't to give it to no secretary, sir. He told me to go straight to the Production Manager's office and hand it to you personally, sir.'

Steam came out of the tap now, but no water anymore. Whistler turned the tap off and put the soap back in its tray. The words 'ROF, Statevale' stamped on the soap were getting very faint now. Whistler redrew them in with his green pencil. He could hear some of the young secretaries walking along the passage, their heels tapping on the lino-muffled stone.

'The old man's in a terrible temper to-day,' and 'Can't do anything with my boss this morning.' ... 'It's always the same with the Joint Production Committee.' ... 'I haven't washed yet; never wash before I come to work.' ... 'I always bring this sponge-bag to work with me; my aunt gave it to me last Christmas and sewed my initials on it herself.'

The swing-doors of the young lady-secretaries' wash-room and lavatory were continually opening and shutting. Whistler thought: 'The secretaries have all kinds of modern inventions in their wash-place. There's a central washbowl there, with no taps showing, that you can turn on from the walls. Wonderful thing, that! We ought to have one here.' He sighed, thinking, 'I suppose it's meant to be grand when things aren't properly poshed up, like Eton being uncomfortable because it's for the upper classes.'

He dried his hands on the towel marked 'Government Property.'

Geoffrey Doran came in. He carried his notebook with him; he was never separated from it. Captain Quantock, the Security Officer, followed. Whistler thought: 'They're like a couple of character actors.'

'Are you going to the JPC?' Quantock was saying.

'Yes,' Geoffrey answered. 'I've been co-opted to-day. That question of the ventilation on Group V is coming up again.' Geoffrey's spectacles had a rather frosted look. 'That comes from condensation,' Whistler thought.

Captain Quantock asked, 'You've got some Irishmen working for you down on Group V, haven't you? Do you find they grumble a great deal?'

Geoffrey blinked behind his frosted glasses and then answered in his heavy way, 'It's been found that those in the lower income group get through a greater percentage of grumbling than those in the slightly higher income groups. All those below a £5-a-week level grumble irrespective of nationality.'

Geoffrey saw that Whistler was just about to leave.

'Good morning, Super,' he said, 'we shall see you later at the JPC.'

'Good-oh, good-oh!' answered Whistler, and went out.

Five minutes later he came back, filled Pitcher's water-bowl from the cold tap, and then went out again. He went back to his office for twenty minutes. He read through letters; dictated answers; had a quick consultation with Twizden, the Chief Production Manager, on several problems which had already been decided in London; saw two semi-important visitors—one very confident and the other so ill at ease as to be almost silent; answered five insistent disembodied voices coming to him through the dictagraph; and had two conversations with shrill, persistent, long-distance talkers, scamping their sentences through the threatening black upright telephone which stood on his desk. Only two minutes before the Joint Production Committee was due to start.

He could see the outline of his own reflection in the glass door. There he was, Henry Whistler, Superintendent of Statevale, dealing with the business of the day at his desk, but it was difficult for him to match up his own identity with this glass-pane reflection. His Burberry coat was hanging on a hook at the end of the room; it bulged on one side because of the 'Oo-Done-It' detective story book he had left in the pocket. He had collected thirty of these paper-backed detective books now, and arranged them in a row on the white bookshelves by the fire in the sitting-room, part of the bungalow which the Government had given him near the factory gates. On the other side of the fireplace there was the wireless he had made himself from spare parts. He was very proud of it.

People were walking down the passage past his room. His dog, Pitcher, was lapping great gulps of water out of the bowl by the desk. The minute-hand of the electric clock set in the wall pointed to one minute before half-past ten. Whistler went to the Joint Production Committee.

The Board Room was centred by a long polished table and at each place one of the clerks had put a clean piece of blotting-paper and a typed copy of the agenda. There were no pens, no paper, no ink, and no pencils. The executives were asked to 'Bring your own'. The windows looked out on to the railway track. Trucks passed back and forth, marked Mansfield, Newport, Tredegar, Cory, and so on.

Superintendent Whistler sat at the top of the table on his swivel-chair, and on his right, the chairman of the workers' side. Down the table, two or three representatives, shop stewards, and also the women's shop steward. At the bottom of the table Mrs Teglar, the senior Labour Manager, as if she and Whistler were the father and mother of the factory. Mrs Teglar rested her elbows on the table and thought, 'It's a great strain having to sit opposite and look at the Super all the time.' On her right was Geoffrey Doran, the 'Time and Emotion' man. He was next to his own chief, and then there were two or three production officers, Twizden, the Chief Production Manager, and also the chief clerk. Just behind

Super's shoulder, in an upright chair, sat a young stenographer; she sat there as if she were Whistler's conscience, but all the time she was taking notes down on a pad on her knee.

Whistler opened the meeting. He asked the chief clerk to read the minutes. It was a preliminary, but it went on too long. Boredom came down over the Superintendent's mind. He swivelled round in his chair, looking nervously at the clock behind him. Some facts arising out of the minutes came up for discussion; then at last they got to the main business of the day.

The meeting began to warm up as soon as they started discussing the varying density of the powder used on Group VI. Should the temperature of the magazine be lessened? Should doors be opened or shut? The workers' representative said the inspectors continually came round stopping the incorporators, saying that the mixture was wrong. Well, what happened? Just what you would expect. The men did not get their target, the men were very upset about not getting their target.

The talk went on. The workers' representative was very young. He kept saying my men don't do this, or that. The Production Manager was old; he kept saying the boys don't take it like that. The Super smiled the first time this happened, but soon he could not smile any more. He swivelled round on his chair staring down at his brown boots. Finally, he said, 'The samples of powder there were tested by the Research Department, you know, so we'll have that on by next week.'

But this was only half the meeting, and only half the trouble. Soon the talk started up about the ventilation in the incorporators' shop on Group V. It was proposed that fans should be placed in the roof to circulate the air. The Super said that he thought the only way to approach this problem was with fans in the side walls opposite each other to ensure a through current. The workers' representative came in with, 'We don't get nothing we want done. It's always the same now. The management just sit in their offices; they don't seem to realize it's a very urgent problem for us down there. The hot air rises so it gets hottest near the roof. The men get very warm, then they catch cold when they walk down to the canteen. Why can't we have these ventilators?'

Whistler wondered why they did not see at once that fresh air must be continually drawn, it was no use stirring up used air.

'You could have the ventilators,' he said, 'but not in the ceiling,'

'Why can't we have them in the ceiling?' the workers' representative asked. 'I can't go back to my men saying we can't have these ventilators, and that we aren't going to have them. They sent me to this meeting to see that we get them. We ought to have ventilators.'

'Yes,' said Whistler, 'but not in the ceiling; in the side.'

It seemed that they did not hear or understand what Whistler was saying. The argument went back and forth, with the workers' representative worrying it. Probably there was some injustice which was troubling him all the time, but he did not speak about it, he only talked about the ventilators, and they would not be able to get to the real trouble until this talk of the ventilators was ended.

Whistler was getting tired. Whenever things went badly, he put in a bit of politeness. He looked now at the Senior Labour Officer facing him at the end of the table.

'Is it true that there's an increase of sickness on Group VII?' he asked.

Mrs Teglar answered up, 'Well, Mrs Davis, the shop steward here, is the representative for that group. She has taken a great interest in this question and has supplied me with a lot of data.'

Mrs Davis thought, 'For once Mrs Teglar hasn't taken all the credit to herself after getting all that dope for nothing.'

But she was pleased that some of her work had been brought up at the meeting.

The workers' representative was returning to worry the old subject. 'Ventilators in the roof; why can't we have them? We did ought to have them!'

'Not, in the ceiling,' said the Super. He was going to add, 'You can have them in the side wall'—but the workers' representative was down on the subject again, 'We did ought to have them; they've got them at Kindale, and that's not even a State factory. All private enterprise it is at Kindale and we know what we think about that; but all the same they have got ventilators.'

One of the other shop stewards near Geoffrey said to him, 'Yes, sometimes I think they look after their people better at Kindale. I've got a brother that works up there.'

Mr Twizden's quiet voice dropped down on the meeting. 'Please address all your remarks to the chair.'

Mrs Davis smirked, hugging her thoughts to herself. 'How could you talk to a chair?'

The shop steward said in an undertone, 'Might just as well be talking to a chair for all the sense you get out of it.'

Whistler wished the meeting was over. The swivel of the chair had worked loose, so that the nervous movement of his shoulder set it turning on its axis. This was the sort of thing that made him laugh. He was afraid now he might get giggling and not be able to stop. He wished it were possible for him to swivel away in his chair altogether and get back to his own office work. He thought, 'I'm not the owner of Statevale, why do they all act as if they thought I wanted to be here? All I want is to get the war over as quickly as possible, the same as they do.'

Whistler, watching the meeting of the Joint Production Committee, was overcome by a feeling of melancholy.

Twizden was still explaining that the men must speak directly to the chairman in the meeting. They did not seem to understand what the chairman of the meeting was for, he said.

Whistler started thinking about the new C E explosive. With the point of his green pencil he began elaborately to draw trench mortars on the blotting pad before him, marking in signs for the various components and chemicals. 'Put a funny hat on it,' he thought, in his childish way, as he drew the top of the trench mortar.

Twizden was still talking, explaining that the ventilators would be no good in the roof, because the hot air rising would only get stirred round and round. But ventilators in the wall on either side—now that was another story altogether; that would really be getting somewhere. The ventilators on the side walls would draw the new good air, and expel the old air; and what was more, and even better, it could go on doing this indefinitely.

Geoffrey Doran was waiting and wondering if he would be asked any questions. Would they ask him why the men hadn't got the target the Time and Motion boys had fixed for them?

Geoffrey had dotted down most of his answers already. Most of his ground had already been covered by the meeting. He was glad the workers' representative hadn't said that the target was too high. It was becoming clear that there was no grudge against his department at the moment. He was glad of this. Geoffrey looked at his notebook and wished he could write in it. It was going to be the greatest one-man volume of mass observation ever made, even in the last five minutes he had thought of a lot of new stuff which he wanted to get down. He thought, 'You can't regard Super Whistler as a worker, of course. He isn't exactly one thing or the other.

But he's never been in any private enterprise, always kept his hands clean of that. Whistler's always been a State worker, so in that sense at least he's a practical worker.'

Geoffrey began to divide the people round the table into income groups.

First Income Group–Whistler, £1200 a year.

Second Income Group–Twizden, £1000 a year.

Third Income Group–Mrs Teglar, Head Woman, Labour Office, £800 a year.

Mrs Teglar and Geoffrey's own chief Time and Emotion man came into the same income group. This seemed very funny to Geoffrey as he thought it over, because after all they were working at opposite poles. 'One is treating people as if they were machines, the other is treating machines as if they were people.' And so it went on, the two executives putting the same amount of energy into the work and getting the same wage out of it.

Fourth Income Group–the Divisional Production Managers, all at £750 a year.

Fifth Income Group–Geoffrey himself, and one of the male Labour Officers at £450 a year.

Geoffrey, thinking along his notebook lines, observed that all these executives were on the same side of the table and all of them got salaries–and salary is paid once a month. On the other side of the table they were all wage-earners–wage is usually paid once a week.

Geoffrey began thinking out his wage-earners' list. First wage-earners–the workers' representative, who was a senior overlooker and a skilled man. Geoffrey began working out the basic 63s plus War Bonus (danger money in the old language), plus Production Bonus if any, plus his senior overlooker's rate of another 10s. That made it up to £8 a week if all went well. But, thought calculating Geoffrey, they didn't reach their target this week owing to all this incorporator-inspector trouble, so last week the workers' representative would only have earned £6 10s. Then there was always the income tax to come off, and some of the fluctuations of the wages depended on how many children the worker had. But all the same, the workers' representative was a skilled man, so taking it all in all he ought to average out a clear £7 a week.

The second wage-earners' group included some of the shop stewards.

Geoffrey went through his calculations carefully, totting up the various amounts in his mind. He decided these two groups were interchangeable, because one of the shop stewards in the second group worked on detonators where he would probably earn a higher rate of production bonus, and on some weeks this might put him in a slightly higher wage-group than the workers' representative.

Third wage-earners' group – the woman shop steward, Mrs Davis. She was an overlooker in her workshop, so she would probably clear about £4 10s a week.

Fourth wage-earners' group – the efficient young secretary sitting behind Super's swivel chair. She was getting £3 10s a week.

Geoffrey felt frustrated because he couldn't write all this down in his notebook. But he tried to memorize it so that once having got it clear he could sit down in his leisure hour documenting notes for his grand mass observation enterprise.

'About this target question?'

Geoffrey was turning his mind now towards the age groups, so that he did not hear this question until it was repeated again.

'Mr Doran, about this target question, your chief tells me …'

Geoffrey realized suddenly that the Super was talking to him. He shifted his thoughts back to the subject in hand as quickly as he could.

'... your chief tells me that you worked out the target for Group VII. Do you consider now that they were set too high?'

Geoffrey remembered the weeks of wrestling with figures before finally submitting the targets to the head of his department; he had done this several times; each time he had arrived at a conclusion they had suddenly changed the process, so that it all had to be gone through again.

'In my opinion,' he said, 'I think they are not. Of course, sir, in this specific case, the adverse conditions now under discussion are responsible for the target not having been reached by the men last week.'

Mrs Davis, the woman shop steward, thought, 'Wot does all that rot he's been saying mean? It's always the same with these intellectuals. They never do a day's work; they couldn't. Otherwise they wouldn't talk such a lot of fizzle. Of course, he's one of the Time and Emotion men, as they call them. He must be clever though, because he wears spectacles, and they say that's a sign. I wonder if he eats fish as well to give himself brains. You can't get it now, though. Not fish, you can't get, unless you stand in a queue a couple of hours.'

The Chief Production Manager, Twizden, handed Whistler a piece of paper on which was written the words: 'It's a quarter to twelve.'

Whistler looked at his watch and nodded. The meeting was on its last legs.

'Is there any other business to discuss?' Whistler only paused for a few seconds after he said this. Then he went on again very quickly, 'Oh well, if there's no other business ...'

Geoffrey Doran was now going over the age-groups in his mind. This was quite another sequence. The oldest age-group would have one of the shop stewards alone in it. The second age-group, Mrs Teglar, the chief Woman Labour Manager, and two of the Production Managers with her. Third age-group – Superintendent Whistler, Geoffrey himself, Mrs Davis, Mr Twizden, and two or three of the others.

Geoffrey did not realize the meeting was over until he heard Mrs Teglar say, 'Are you coming along with us now, Mr Doran?'

He blushed, got up and moved towards the door, and then was overcome by a sense of panic. He had left his notebook on the table. He hurried back to get it.

Whistler returned to his office. Captain Quantock, the Security Officer, was peering through the glass door of his room as he came out. Two PAD men were standing in the passage. Geoffrey Doran heard one say to the other, 'Did you see Whistler and Twizden coming out of the JPC?'

'Yes, they looked as if they'd been through a rough house.'

'Yes, that's right; course Whistler's tie's always is crooked, isn't it. He's always thinking of something else.'

'He's a very clever chemist, Super is.'

'Yes, he is; but Twizden's tie was crooked too, and it takes a lot to upset him. It must have been a stormy meeting.'

Chapter Four

War Hostel

Geoffrey Doran finished work in the early evening. Through the thick lenses of his horn-rimmed spectacles he blinked upwards towards the sky, saw no signs of rain there, and started to walk up the hill homewards. There was no shift going out at this time. Only one bus stood in the clearing ground. This great grey bus was filling up slowly. A few of the clerical staff were waiting for it to start. They sat inside and goldfished their gaze out through the glass windows. Geoffrey decided there was nothing to be gained by travelling with them; he found it difficult to hear what people said inside a locomotive lumbering up and down hills. Besides this, he had heard so much of their talk before, it was all written down in his notebook now; perhaps he would prune it later, because although it was observation it was material that did not really represent the masses.

'Are clerks folks?' Of course they are, but to record any more clerks' conversation might be a deviation from the central theme. Where would he go this evening? Hostel, pub, or local town hotel? He decided to start his tour from the hostel. In his right hand he held a small brown attaché case; he held it loosely; he had filled it with the statistics he had been working out for the Government. In his left hand he held his notebook; he held it tightly; it was three-quarters full of recorded observation on the workers; inside the book itself two patent clasps gripped two pencils with red and blue lead, both at the alert.

Dressed in his reasonable brown suit, with collar and tie to match, and carrying a modest attaché case, Geoffrey Doran had the appearance not of one clerk but rather of a composite clerk, but he kept close to himself the consolation of his own secret counterfeit career. He never ceased to think of himself as a One-Man-Mass-Observation-Centre. Observing the masses was only the first stage; then there was the work of getting the notes down and afterwards going through them, compiling, collating, listing, subdividing, valuing, and sifting; he turned the work over in his mind and rearranged it in his notebook.

Doran took twenty-five minutes to reach the cross-roads. Then he turned up to the left and came upon the long low grey hostel buildings.

Ysabette Jones was walking ahead with six or seven girls of her shift. But she walked a little distance away from them, near the roadside, hitting savagely at the blades of grass with a straight bit of stick she had broken off from an overhanging branch. 'You'll hear a lot about me one day,' she was saying. Although the other girls did not take any notice, Ysabette talked on as emphatically as if there was an enemy arguing against her. Her companions continued to behave, in every way, as if Ysabette Jones was not there. They were twitter-talking together about their friends.

'I like Mabs, don't you?'

'Oh, do you? I'm not so keen on Mabs. Doll's a sport though.'

'I'll tell you who I like, I like Curly.'

Inspector Jameson's bungalow had been built down outside the entrance to the hospital grounds. Geoffrey could see him now, staring out through a corner of the net curtains of his parlour, white-cheeked, questing, querulous. As Chief Inspector of Factory Police, Jameson had no jurisdiction over the hostel. He resented it.

Geoffrey Doran had been wrong about the day. An anaemic shower of fine rain started its dismal down-drizzle.

Workers were coming over from the sleeping-blocks, from the sick bay, the laundry, and allotments. They quickened their steps and came running into the main building. They ceased to smile, and got a guilty look as though hearing that the rain was some strange God's-punishment sent from the skies. Geoffrey thought he might start a new section in his notebook. It would be headed, 'Workers and the weather.' Geoffrey walked slowly forward thinking it over.

The reception hall was almost empty when he reached it. Most of the residents had already moved on down the passage into the dining-room. Old Charlie was still at the bookstall buying a Penguin Special. Linnet was reading Willie's letter which told her that he would be getting forty-eight hours' leave and coming down to the hostel to see her; she stood quite still making the effort of readjusting her mind to this new situation. All these months Linnet had been too toned down to routine to expect any sort of happiness, and now she was overwhelmed by Willie's letter as if at a too-quick return to consciousness. One of the shop stewards was in the passage pinning a notice up on the board. It was about the Residents' committee meeting. Two of the men from the Smoke Section were standing there watching him. When they saw Doran come in one said, 'Slow sort of blighter that Time and Emotion Man, isn't he?' and the other answered, 'That's right, hasn't got enough sense to come in out of the rain, has he?'

The dining-room, of concert hall proportions, was divided down the centre by the great kitcheners. Each half of the room had the same rows of wooden tables and chairs, but one side was quite empty of eaters. This was the space being kept free for the bread-cheese-and-tea late arrivals; they would wander in afterwards from an evening in the town or an extra shift. The other half of the room filled up fast at this hour.

The kitchen staff stood behind the long counter putting the hot plates down on it–'Austria' the refugee chef, Miss Lazenby, the head kitchen supervisor, the green-overalled canteen girls, and the young canteen supervisors with their white coats, film-starrish hair sets and continual inner conflicts as to whether they should stay here at all, or try to enlist in the Wrens, Waafs, or Ats–they all lined up now to wait on the workers while the workers queued up to get the food. The kitchen machinery, the steel cupboards, steam heaters, great stoves, ovens, and cauldrons used for the preparation of every meal were so large that they seemed to dwarf down eaters and servers to the size of marionettes.

The canteen girls, with their frivolous heads and hard high heels, gave the impression of a group of pretty centaurs handing out suppers in tune to hoof sounds on kitchen tiles.

The head manager of the hostel was away on sick leave, so that his only substitute was the young diabetic discharged from the Army who usually acted as Social Entertainments Manager. They called him the 'Acting Manager'. He wore a blue, high-necked jersey and grey flannel trousers. He was not interfering, had agreeable easy manners, and was well liked.

Geoffrey fetched the first part of his dinner, some soup and two slices of bread. He took the two plates to a table where several of the cinema projectionists were sitting together.

The Hostel Manager had been fond of saying, 'There are no rules in our dining-room as to geography, folks can just sit where they like,' but most of the hostel staff were preoccupied with the same problems and tended to sit together at the same end-table; the next table was nearly always occupied by the same research doctors, welfare officers, labour managers, and two or three shop managers, while the third table filled up with foremen and their wives. The cinema projectionists also grouped together. There were only six of them, and five were united by their lack of confidence in Mrs Karslake, their supervisor. They continually told each other that she did not know her job, had not been educated, was not used to dealing with staff, and that she had let a little authority go to her head. Instead of superintendent, they had nicknamed her 'pretendant'.

The tall, fair girl, the 'pretty hare', was picking at her food and telling the others about the shop manager who had asked her to dance. 'Last night when we were just coming out from supper, I was walking up towards the "Ladies" when he came up and said something to me. I couldn't hear what it was at first, so I leant forward to catch what he was saying. Before I knew where I was, he had whisked me off into a dance, right into the assembly room, and there we were, waltzing away in a giddy-go-round!'

One of the other projectionists, the wife of an officer in charge of a motor transport boat, came into the conversation: 'Where's our perfect "pretendant" this evening?' she asked in her acid way.

A tall, blonde woman, who had been a peace-time nurse for backward boys, answered, 'She's gone back to the factory.'

'Mrs Karslake does love her work, doesn't she, Nordie?'

Geoffrey decided that here was material for more notes. The use of nicknames among people whose war-time job had jerked them out of their own surroundings and brought them down suddenly into a strange unfamiliar setting. It was very interesting about these nicknames. It was the tension of the time that caused them to crop up everywhere. 'Acting Manager,' 'Pretendant' for superintendent, 'Austria' for the refugee chef; and then even nick-names for nicknames, such as 'Nordie' for Nordic, a nickname for the big blonde Juno who had been jurisdicting over retarded kids way back in peace days.

'What's the Pretendant doing up at the factory, Nordie?'

'Oh, I don't know, there was no need for her to go up there really. She says she had got some reports to write out for the head office, all about the film showings in the canteens.'

'Can she really read and write?' asked the 'pretty hare'.

'Makes out she can.'

'Did I tell you about the way she acted in the town the other night. You see, we went up there after we had shown the last picture in Canteen B8 and put away all the equipment, and when we got to the Bell Inn Hotel the first person I ran into happened to be a friend of my sister-in-law's – as a matter of fact he often used to stay with my sister-in-law's cousin in Birmingham. I had no idea he was here, so it was quite a surprise. He's a captain, and doing some administration work down here in the Army Pay Office. The moment he saw me he said, "Fancy finding you here," and then he asked me about my sister-in-law. But of course the Pretendant butted in. She was sort of hovering around us – you know how she does, seems to think it's part of her job, she's always underfoot somehow – so, as I was saying, she was there and I was forced to introduce her to my friend, and the first remark she made to him was, "We come from Sing Sing." You know how she's been shouting about Sing Sing ever since the evening when we first arrived and saw the rooms, over in our sleeping block, set out in a row like cells. "Six Little Maids from Sing Sing," she started singing then, and hasn't stopped since. Well, as you can imagine, that friend of my sister-in-law was very embarrassed, and before I had time to try to smooth it over a bit, Mrs Karslake, our perfect Pretendant, had begun again. "Have a drink with convict No 1," she said to him, half nudging him with her elbow, you know the way she's always doing that. Then she said, "Meet my colleague Convict Zero," and she introduced Miss Taylor to him. I wished I'd never been up to the Bell Inn. She made me feel very ashamed Mrs Karslake did, she did really. Of course Mrs Karslake isn't educated, and that's the whole trouble."

Geoffrey had got through the first course of his dinner in tune to the talk of the film projectionists. He returned to the counter and queued up for a plate of cold ham and salad. The man in front of him was slowing everything up by complaining, 'Don't like greasy pig's flesh; don't like dry lettuce.'

Geoffrey had noticed that those who had been used to a low standard of living tended to complain a great deal, and the food was almost always the target of their grumbling. Ham and lettuce were at this time almost unobtainable elsewhere in England.

'If my wife gave me this for dinner,' the man said, 'I'd kick her out of the house. I tell you straight I would,' he added. 'Kick her right out of the house, I would.'

Geoffrey decided that these kinds of comments could help a man to forget some of his former misfortunes. He moved up to get his plate while the man, still complaining, took the helping of ham and salad to his own table and ate it up very quickly with great enjoyment.

Geoffrey did not return to the group of cinema projectionists. He liked to move about because in this way he was able to hear what people were saying and so he amassed more material for his notebook. He moved on to another table, his plate of ham his passport.

A girl was saying, 'I suppose the communal life is good for us. I don't like it myself, but it does show us how other people live, doesn't it?'

A sulky woman said, 'How can it show us how others live when we all have to live the same here?'

'Oh, I don't know. Have you seen Rose's room over in Block J? She's got it fixed up all right. She's got one of them doyley things on the top of the chest of drawers with her initials all embroidered on it, and on top of that she's got her brushes and combs and a hand-mirror, with "Rose" writ on the backs of them all in scrawly letters. Just like a greeting you see on a wedding-cake; and she's got a framed photo of her boy friend—only you can't tell which one it is, because she's got two different photos, one of an Air Force boy and another of a Naval bloke. On top of her wardrobe the shelf is all full up of tinned food and biscuits from her last four parcels from home; looks like she's preparing for the invasion or something. In fact Rose has got everything in her room except the kitchen stove, and as a matter of fact she's got that, too, because there is that little stove which she's fixed up on the electric light somehow—though, of course, it is against the regulations by rights, but it doesn't worry Rose. She made us a cup of tea on it when we came in late the other night. I suppose we shouldn't have done it, really, but Rose don't trouble.'

Ysabette Jones, the schizophrenic, spoke through the conversation at the table.

'My friend, the Group Captain, was over Berlin again last week, leading a bombing raid. He said it was funny seeing Berlin like that from the air after having known it from the ground in peace-time. Of course he was a big man in business before the war; he used to travel all over the world, motoring most of the way. He always took his motor-car with him wherever he went, four-seater Packard it was. My friend the Group Captain says he is looking forward to taking me to some of these places when the war ends. He can pick up almost any language himself because he's got a good ear. Of course he knows German, Italian, Spanish, and all those already; but he says I should soon learn to speak foreign languages because I'm educated.'

Ysabette did not cease her talking; she did not seem to be

in any way discouraged, although no answers ever came back to her.

'My friend, the Group Captain, said the flak was awful when he was over Berlin last week.'

Geoffrey noticed that none of the other girls at the table troubled to tell Ysabette that Berlin had not been bombed for more than a month.

One of the girls said, 'I don't like this morning shift we're on now.'

'No,' the other answered. 'It's not like "noons", is it? When you're on "noons" you can always get all the morning posts, and you don't have to wait for your parcel from home till the evening same as we have to now we're on this early morning caper.'

The parcel from home; now here was a new section for Geoffrey's notebook. Some of these young industrial workers came from remote country districts, some of them had only seen a few people in their lives, perhaps never more than half a dozen near neighbours in any one place, at any time, and even then each person would be known to them by shape and sound, by colour and context. The 'I' was the 'I' and the 'you' was either the school friend, the neighbour, the teacher, the sweetheart, or the relative. Then all was changed suddenly; everything was set moving at a great speed. The train journey—perhaps the first—the crowded station, the factory town and the great grey hostel buildings, the work itself, carried out in silent isolated groups, never more than twenty workers in one semi-underground shed, never less than two hundred in the canteen at break-time, sometimes six hundred in the hostel at meal-times, and always seven thousand going out or coming in on shift. The journey herd, the hostel herd, the workshop herd—where even the movements of the work were disciplined down to a slow rhythm—all added to the fear and sense of isolation from the home herd.

Think back to eight years old and being Geoffrey Doran arriving at the carefully chosen boarding-school; what was there then to sustain the individual? Only the communications from home. For the young industrial worker sent here from Scotland, from Ireland, or from Wales, there was the same emptiness, time-lag, and tension; the circumstances of the world around making the sudden forced move from one set of conditions to another seem still more lurid. Well, the privileges of preparatory school had not been pleasant either; but Geoffrey had known about it beforehand – private school, then public school – bourgeois boy you had it coming to you from your birthday. National upheaval, with all its implications for the individual, was a different thing, an unknown thing, unexpected and uneasy for many of the workers here, so, for them the parcel from home was the pivot of the week. On fine days groups of girls turbanned or loose-haired walked about from sleeping-block to main building carrying, string-swinging, or clasping the parcel from home.

Geoffrey listed over in his mind the possible objects within the parcel from home – tomatoes, onions, chocolates, knitting wool, family photographs, a game or a puzzle, a postal order or some stamps, a book or some magazines, a piece of heather or shamrock, a locket, a bracelet or ring, some biscuits, shortbread, a flower in a pot, or packets of seeds to be planted in the hostel allotment, some underwear, hair slides, or a comb.

'Where's Linnet? Is she going to miss her supper, or what?'

'No, she came in and had a bite, but she went off with May – they've gone back to N Block – borrowed the sewing-machine from the stewardess and they're making a nightgown.'

'A whole nightgown? They've got a job on, haven't they?'

'Oh, well, they've got the sewing-machine, that helps. May sold her some of that pink material she was showing us the other day.'

'Beautiful, isn't it? Crêpe-de-chine, is it?'

'Triple ninon May said it was … it's pre-war … can't get it now, you can't. 'Corse May let Linnet have it without coupons. She's got a few bits left over … She was starting up a dressmaking business of her own before the war; she wouldn't have gone out to work no more … wouldn't have troubled, May wouldn't. Just worked for herself on her own, she would.'

'Bet she was fed up when she had to come here, but don't make no fuss, do she?'

'No, she don't trouble.'

'But that was beautiful material she showed us the other day. I wished I could've had some of it off her … It's true she didn't want no coupons, but she do want a price for it … all for getting her money's worth, May is … I couldn't afford it myself, I got to send money home regular. They count on it, see.'

'That's right. Don't Linnet have to send no money home?'

'Yes; but it's different for her. Her husband's coming home on leave, so she's bought herself a new nightgown. She couldn't go up to the town—there's not much time, is there, with your work and all—and there's nothing in the shops when you do go. She's ever so pleased about her husband getting a bit of leave—almost couldn't speak when she heard about it. She told me she was ever so upset when the war came between them, and she didn't know how she was going to go on without him. They hadn't ever been separated before, not a single day since they'd been married.'

'There's many like that.'

'That's true … Don't make it any less sad for them that has to go through it though.'

'I expect Linnet will move over to the married quarters when her husband arrives.'

'Yes, it seems funny, doesn't it? Can't imagine me with Jim

staying here, not in the married quarters somehow. I'd feel so strange.'

'Oh, I don't know, better than nothing.'

'Yes, but I'd feel strange … not like home is it?'

'Have they got bunks in the married quarters same as we've got?'

'No, they've got beds over there, same as in the staff block. Shouldn't fancy bunks.'

'Huh, bunks! Be all right if your feller was in the Navy, wouldn't it—like being in rough seas being in one of them bunks. Not my idea of being married, though.'

Geoffrey became aware now of the talk of four men sitting at the end of the table. The tall, black-haired man, the son of a Welsh preacher, was telling the others about his brother who had gone to Spain to join the International Brigade.

'He just went for the adventure of it, see … Didn't know what it was about, see. Mother didn't hear from him for over a year, then he landed up at Cardiff—came off a tramp steamer—had nothing left but a pair of drill trousers, rope-soled shoes, and "Madre" tattooed on his chest. He told us he had been in jail nearly all the time—couldn't stand the discipline of the Communists. That's all he got out of it—best part of a year in jail, and lost his shirt. He was pleased with his rope-soled shoes, though, and proud of the tattoo, kept pointing to his chest and saying "Madre means Mother", see.'

The older man, the one who had been a navigator and escaped from France in 1940, answered: 'That's right, Madre on his chest and Espadrille on his feet, and a year in jail—that's what you get for fighting for freedom.'

'But he wasn't fighting for nothing, see,' the Welshman said. 'He just went for the adventure, see.'

Geoffrey listened, and arranged his notes in his mind. Curious this co-educational atmosphere of the hostel—but suddenly it would disappear. That was what had happened here during meals. They shared the same table, the same food, and the same fatigue–yet the conversation of the women and the men was completely isolated, one from the other. In their talk the men and women were like co-eds sharing a bed with a bolster between them. Anyhow, Geoffrey had caught two or three conversations in one listening hour, and soon it would all be documented into his notebook. He was anxious to fatten up his notebook before Christmas.

Geoffrey wanted to ask the four men what they thought of living in a war hostel, but he'd be subtle–he wouldn't ask each one in turn for their opinion while waiting, pencil in hand, for their reply … No, he'd get talking himself, express some ideas of his own at first, and then the things they thought would come out in the course of conversation. But he hesitated. He found he had no opinions of his own–only the opinions of the masses docketed down in his notebook. The first fifteen chapter headings occurred to him. He ran through them in his mind, stopping suddenly at Chapter 12: 'The Transferred Workers'. He could cotton-on to a talk here–the talk of women workers who had lived all their lives on the outskirts of Liverpool or Manchester, women whose husbands had been called up and who had themselves been transferred here. Geoffrey cranked up a conversation along these lines: it was as if he was working out his notebook in his own words. He began in a bright tone of voice:

'I like this hostel life all right.'

The Welsh preacher's son said, 'Of course, it's good enough for food and warmth and all that, I reckon, but it's a bit too monastic for my liking.'

'Mind you, I think we miss the home comforts,' Geoffrey said, 'carpets, fires and beds instead of bunks.'

A man from the south of London said, 'How could they house and feed two thousand people if each lived in a room like his own parlour at home? The place hasn't been constructed for that—it wouldn't be practical, see.'

'You never see a real workman in England, same as we used to in France,' the man who had escaped interrupted. 'I don't know why it is, I'm sure; they all seem to be foremen or assistant foremen, or something of that. You get it here. Look at the first three rows of tables in this room—the high-up, the middle-class, and the aspiring.'

'But *you've* got a bed, haven't you?' the Cockney remarked to Geoffrey. 'You're on Time and Motion, aren't you, Mr Doran? You're in the Staff Block, surely they all got beds in the Staff Block?'

Geoffrey, talking through his notebook, felt caught out, ill at ease. The fourth man said that he would rather sleep in a bunk than in a bed. 'Bunks are all right if you know how to manage them,' he said. 'What you want to do, see, is to take the mattress from the bunk above you, or from any empty one along the passage—there's sure to be an empty room or two in the block—then you put this mattress that you've scrounged on top of yours, so you've got two then, see? They're very well made, these bunks are, the wood slopes inwards. I noticed that because I used to be a builder; they're much better than many beds are.'

Geoffrey was thinking he was not much good at getting people talking. Got quite a flair for it. He decided that it was a great mistake to wait for people to talk; that wasn't the way to do it at all. If you wanted to observe what people were thinking, the only way was to get talking yourself so that no one would feel at all awkward or self-conscious. All this God-like observation from a distance, that was bad, you had to join in to observe. He talked to the girls. He talked to the four men. He got a good hostel chapter all set. He was optimistic about it. Soon it would be well worked out, and down in black and white. It was true that here in this great communal building there was some attempt at basic efficiency. Centre heating; as many hot baths as anyone wanted; the rooms in the women's sleeping block newly painted blue and white. An atmosphere almost of adolescence, of sweetness and security.

The rooms in the men's block had a tougher distemper on the walls, but otherwise they were the same – a basin with running hot and cold water, a wardrobe, shelves, a chest of drawers, a locker, two chairs, a shelf above the basin, two towels, two windows. The rooms on the south side looked out on to the sick-bay garden, those on the north side over the hills. Each sleeping block had six bathrooms, three drying-rooms, a sitting-room and a steward's room. The residents were called in the morning; their beds made and their rooms 'done' every day except Sunday. In the main building there was a large hall, a reception desk, a shop for cigarettes, and so on, a newspaper shop, a dance and concert hall, a library, writing-room, lounge and recreation rooms; there was a small snack-bar and a cosmetic kiosk. The two sick-bays were separate blocks, well equipped with public wards and private rooms; a sister, a nurse, and two young assistants always in attendance. The communal laundry was in another block: it was rather an impressive place with its great wash-basins, hose-pipes, draining-boards, electric irons, and drying-rooms; various facilities had been fixed up, various executives engaged to carry them out. An entertainment manager, a gym instructor, a dancing teacher. A play was put on once a week. Films were shown in the assembly room most mornings and every third evening; there were concerts, dances; there was a fortnightly discussion group; a Residents' Committee meeting with elected members to meet up with the Hostel staff Committee every other week.

Geoffrey, listing over these things, contrasted them with his own private and public schools – the cold dormitory, the inadequate shower-baths, the draughty gymnasium, and the depressing stained wood of the passages and stairs which seemed to dent the rigid rules and regulations into the mind of the schoolboy. Here in the hostel there were no rules. All the ground-work of material life was ready to hand for the price of 22s 6d to 30s a week board and lodging. Geoffrey's memories went back to the boarding-school – everything uncomfortable and inefficient there; boys making their own beds and being called by a clanging bell, washing in their rooms in cold water, a hot bath only twice a week; board, lodging, and tuition for eight months of the year cost £200 a year. Why, then, were so many of the workers here melancholy-minded? Why weren't they hurrahing through the hostel all day? Geoffrey believed that through his series of astute *agent provocateur* questions he had got most of the answers. Of course it was an excellent and valuable thing that this sound basis of material life of had been set going; but who will die on the battlefield for the sake of a communal laundry – who wants to fight a war to make certain of an electric hair dryer. Existence in the hostel became arid, the irrational side of life, because not clearly understood, was not so well catered for; people searching for a more comprehensive cordiality and warmth shied away from facilities that still seemed like a sop thrown in from the outside.

'It's very nice, of course, but it's taken a war to get it – they could've given us this all the time, then there wouldn't have been no trouble like there has been. And no war now, neither!'

Geoffrey thought that although there were so few rules and regulations there still lurked fear of the institution; it was felt that at any moment religiosity might show its interfering snout; to make the most of the little leisure available needed a certain adroitness – a certain skill in the art of human existence. This technique could only come with leisure. A large percentage of the workers had never had enough leisure to know how to deal with this essential commodity. Some of the older men who had been through long unemployment were the most successful at adapting themselves to the life of the hostel—because in the 'black time' they had spent long hours in the public library.

Geoffrey was planning an arrangement of these facts for his notebook when he suddenly became conscious of the voice of Ysabette Jones.

' … Group Captain's mother gave me this flap-jack; it holds my powder and a lipstick and a comb—a cosmetic-compactum is what it's called. I told her all about how I had to leave it at the contraband hut before going in on shift, but she couldn't understand a place like this … she has white hair, and lives in a house in the country … the windows of her dining-room look out on to the rose-garden—it's wonderful when it's all in bloom …'

Now, Ysabette Jones, that was a case that couldn't be collated. Everything was planned out in Geoffrey's notebook, when in came the schizophrenic—a sort of Miss Zero on the mass observer's roulette table. The men made a move to leave the dining-hall. 'We're going up to the Goose and Cuckoo,' one of them said, 'we seen them delivering the beer there yesterday.' The preacher's son asked Geoffrey if he would be coming along. Geoffrey said that he'd be up there in half an hour or so. He went over to his sleeping block, arranged two lockers together to make a firm table, then sat down on the bed and started writing in his notebook.

The four men walked up the winding hill towards the Goose and Cuckoo. One of them said, 'Must be a good job this Time and Motion business—£8 a week and never soils his hands.'

'Must be. Is he coming along with us?'

'Oh, yes, sure to be in later. Probably writing down all we've told him in his notebook.'

'That's right. It's funny, I can tell these mass observers from a mile off. Don't know why it is. Must be the shine on their spectacles, or something of that.'

'I went to America once, you know. I was quizzed by Dr Gallup. "Do you believe in equal wages for equal work?" they asked me; and another time, "do you believe in birth control?" It all came out in the papers. "Gallup Poll: 35 per cent said 'Yes', 40 per cent said 'No', and 25 per cent said "*I* don't know"'; … I was in that larst lot.'

Chapter Five

Time Off

As soon as Geoffrey had finished his notes he left his room. He walked down the pathway with the long one-storey buildings on either side. One or two people walking back from the main building to their rooms passed him: he could see the glow from their cigarettes – some called out, 'Good-night'. It had become suddenly cold. And when they spoke, a menacing mist followed the words out of their mouths. Geoffrey took a short-cut through the field, over the fence where the barbed-wire was broken, and out into the road. Here he met Nordie, Amazon-striding along.

'Off to the pub,' she said, 'same as me?'

'Yes.'

'It's very pleasant up at the pub. There's a fire there, and some gin, and some soldiers.'

She said that several of the policemen came into the pub for drinks. 'They're quite at their ease,' she said, 'you wouldn't expect it of policemen, would you? They usually cast such a blight over everything. Funny, no one minds them a bit here. I suppose it's because they're the factory police and have no jurisdiction outside. Up at the Badminton near the factory gates the girl in the bar, the very short-sighted one with thick-lensed spectacles, is a daughter of one of the factory policemen.'

Nordie told Geoffrey that when she used to teach in a school in South-East London, she had sometimes to take some of her pupils back to their homes. 'You wouldn't find anyone associating with policemen there,' she said.

'Why not?'

'Well, you see, it wouldn't be considered socially possible,' Nordie said. 'Just something that "wasn't done" down there – fraternizing with a policeman would seem about the same as a Society "Deb" mating-up with a street walker.'

On the hill going up they passed a tree with two half-lopped branches threatening outwards. Nordie said, 'Every time I pass that tree I think it's a Home Guard sentinel.'

'What would he be doing, sitting up in a tree?' Geoffrey said.

'Oh, watching out for enemy paratroops, or something. Well, of course, I know it's only the broken branches of the tree; but I say that it looks like somebody sitting there.'

They walked on together. Nordie near Geoffrey. She was silent. There were some stars. No moon out yet. Geoffrey took off his spectacles. Twenty minutes went by. Two bicyclists went by. They got up, and went on to the pub. There was a fire, some gin, and some soldiers talking and drinking. Everything just as Nordie had said.

Girlie, the pub-keeper's daughter, was dressed in black silk. She stepped forward, in all her cylinder-shaped dignity, and invited Nordie into the parlour. Girlie had got the idea that the more grand-manner girls from London didn't like drinking in the rough-and-tumble atmosphere of the main rooms; it was her belief that 'a nice girl' like Nordie would prefer a quiet mug with the management. So sometimes after eight o'clock in the evening Girlie would go up to a new arrival and invite her back-stage. It was difficult to refuse an invitation that was so clearly considered an honour.

There were three main rooms. One with wood tables, benches, a log fire, some cedar chairs, and a photograph of the landlord in a pony-cart; and another with a sofa, three horsehair arm-chairs, a tall palm in a brass pot and an upright piano ... soldiers stood around the piano singing. The third room was much smaller than the others, two or three chairs were grouped round a gas-fire, a polished mahogany table in the centre of the room, a plush-covered sofa and two or three small three-legged tables with photographs of wedding groups in gilt frames. On the mantel piece a model ship was encased in a glass bottle. In this room a few women sat on upright chairs sipping their beer from long glasses – very silent and correct. One of them wore a hat so tall and perched that it gave the appearance of several hats one on top of the other. The landlord, in his shirt-sleeves, carrying beer on a tray, moved between the rooms and round back-stage through Girlie's salon behind the saloon. In the last a room, this silent and multiple-hat room, there was hatch connecting with the kitchen, and sometimes the shirt-sleeved landlord opened it to put forward a glass of lemonade or some soft drink that would have destroyed the symmetry of his beer tray if he had gone carrying it around the room with the other glasses.

Old Charlie sat in the first room, bringing some of the political talk out of store. The others were laughing at him. Geoffrey thought, 'It's good-natured barracking, but it's barracking just the same.'

'... without a revolutionary theory there can be no revolutionary practice.'

'Sez you!' one of the other men answered up.

'Said Lenin in 1898,' Charlie corrected.

In the centre room a hedge-cutter from the next village had come in, bringing his guitar. He was asked to 'give us a song'. He talked about the guitar as if it were an individual.

'I brought him along through Daly's wood, see. I tied this string round him and carried him over my shoulder, see. He come along all right.'

'Give us that song about the coloured man – the one they learned you when you was in Malta.'

'Ah, he won't play nothing till he's tuned, though.'

The hedge-cutter twanged the guitar strings.

Geoffrey stood in the doorway leading from one room to the other–between two schools of talk.

'Freedom is the conscious recognition of necessity, as Engels wrote,' Charlie said.

The hedge-cutter in the second room was singing out: 'My brother, Silva–hell'uva man, son' uv a gun, plenty of musc, don't push ...'

'The international proletariat will arise in their millions,' said Old Charlie; his sleep-staring brown eyes didn't move as he spoke. He drank his beer without any appearance of enjoyment–anxious to get the drink over as soon as possible in order to loose his thoughts in the next mouthful of political word-magic. 'The great ones of the earth will tremble before the might of the revolutionary masses.'

'How's your father? He's all right,' twanged the hedge-cutting guitarist from the next room. 'How's your mother? She's all tight,' joined in the audience.

'The greatest evil is Prussian militarism, as old Will Thorne darn in Canning Town used ter say, quoting old Fred Engels up in 'Ighgate ...' This had a chorus too, and as soon as Old Charlie stopped speaking the men around him chimed in with it, 'Old Will Thorne, down in Canning Town,' they said, pointing hell-wards, and, 'Old Fred Engels up in Highgate,' they said, semaphoring their arms heavenwards.

A man from a road-mending party said, 'Our foreman ought to hear some of this. Bloody capitalist, he is! Already thinking of setting up on his own after the war. As it is, he'd be as lost without his bowler hat as a blind man without his tapping-stick. He wouldn't know what to think of Old Charlie's talk.'

Old Charlie caught the last few words. 'It don't matter to me what people think of me,' he answered in an aloof manner, 'it's what I think of myself what matters to me.'

'He was a twister and a twicer,' they sang from the next room.

This was new to Geoffrey. 'What song's that?' he asked.

'Oh, that's the song they sing in the pubs when they get a bit drunk after funerals,' said the road-mender, 'most of the churchyards happen to have a pub opposite, see. They all want a drink after the interment; they soon get singing about the dead man – mostly it's that song you just heard what they sing.'

'He was a twister and a twicer!' came from the next room, 'a diddler and a shyster, but one of the best.' And then, 'How's yer father? He's all right. How's yer mother? She's all tight.'

Geoffrey moved on to the end room. Here it was all quiet talk and superior smiles. One of the men from the factory command post was sitting next to the 'pretty hare' cinema projectionist, talking to her in a low tone about his wife and family.

'Haven't been home and seen the missus more than once in eighteen months – it's a long distance, and the fare is very costly. My daughter is always asking after me; she's only five … just when she needs her Daddy most. They do, don't they, at that age?'

The fringe-curl cinema girl ate her cheese sandwich and agreed between mouthfuls.

'I believe I'd've been better off in the Forces – they don't have anything like the long hours we have, and they seem to get much more leave.'

'Pretty hare' nibbled and nodded.

Julian was slumped in a tapestry-seated chair, looking towards the gas-fire, doomed into silence; his hair clung round his forehead, giving him the dark, briny look of a creature come up from the depths of the sea.

A long-legged American girl, uniformed in a severely cut khaki jacket with a dun-coloured skirt had arrived by car;

her brown shoes were polished up to looking-glass pitch; her peaked cap was as pointed and uncompromising as her nose; her ashen hair was in a bun naped on to her neck as if silked close to a wood-fashioned dummy in a shop window. She didn't seem to be aware of the multiple-hat woman and her companions; nor did they notice her.

Geoffrey wandered through the singing room. 'How's your father? He's all right,' to the barracking boys' room. Charlie was saying, 'The dictatorship of the proletariat—Stalin believed in that, but he wouldn't have done, not if he could have seen such a lot of illiterate bastards as you all are 'ere!'

'How's your mother? She's all tight.'

The 'Guvnor' was going by with his nineteenth tray of beer glasses. Geoffrey followed his man and got his bitter.

Some of the Scottish men and women from the factory had come in and were singing now. So many were sitting on and around the piano that it had long since been silenced. There were several songs on at the same time, against each other, unaccompanied. The hedge-cutter was giving his guitar a rest—talking about it, not playing it. 'He comes from Spain, made of lovely wood he is.' Dark-chinned Donald, in check cap and tweed trousers, was foot-stamping to the song he sang—beating time with his right hand, his left arm round a girl. One of the men from the Potteries said, 'Can't understand a word he says ... Scotch is like bloody foreign language. Mind you, singing's all right in its proper place.'

'What is its proper place?' Geoffrey asked.

'Proper place is 'ere, in public 'ouse.'

The Scottish girls were singing, laughing and clinging on to each other. Suddenly one of them began to cry. She'd been discharged from the factory, and was going home to Glasgow in the morning. Her emotions panicked between two poles—joy and sorrow, North and South ... the morning special for the Highland home there ... the sudden separation from the herd here. Her friends gathered round her now, and remained, football-scrum close, in sympathy. Geoffrey could not see the crying girl any more, she had become completely obscured by her back-patting companions.

A man came in from the other room, spinning round like a leaf in a storm as he waved his arms in benign signals, but said nothing ... through the centre door, turning round, and on into the next room ... still smiling, still silent. Geoffrey followed slowly.

The pub-keeper's voice could be heard calling out: 'We're closed now,' and then again, 'Closed–Closed!' He had shut the hatch, and now could not find the inner bolts; he could be heard tapping and knocking on the door of the hatch from the other side.

The long-legged American girl was sitting on the chair next to the woman with the high hat–her own peaked cap had fallen to the ground, two tortoiseshell hair-pins had detached themselves, releasing a long strand of hair. The American girl had her arm loosely, will-lessly round the shoulder of the man from the factory command post; she was staring straight ahead, her eyes cold-blue, saying, 'Luv is a vurry fragile thing ...'

Girlie was going through the rooms with a 'Good-bye' to all, 'we're closed now–go home, all.'

Geoffrey went home. The hedge-cutter was pouring his last few drops of beer from the bottom of his glass on to the top of his guitar and then polishing the wood with his handkerchief. 'Give him a drink: he comes up lovely, don't he, with a drink?' He twanged a few notes. 'How's your father? He's all right. How's your mother? She's all tight.' He slung his guitar shoulderwards, and went.

In the last room Old Charlie was saying, 'The workers are slaves. It's the same in war-time as in peace-time, but in peace-time, mind you, it's different, in a manner of speaking.

What's labour? It's a commodity the workers are forced to sell to the employers to live! Now, what do you do when you haven't got any money?'

'Borrow it!' they all shouted back.

They paid up for their beer and cigarettes, and moved out of the pub in a body. They broke up into groups, and walked down the hill—most of them leaning a little backwards, some arm-in-arm. A man near Geoffrey said: 'You know, I take a good view of the hostel now. That's all you've got to do with these places—just get out of them from time to time, and then they seem fine. It's the same with everything, home life and all.'

There was a moon now. The broken tree branches looked more like a watching sentinel in this light, but Nordie was not there to speak about it. Geoffrey wondered where she was.

Back in the hostel there were half-a-dozen people eating bread and cheese and drinking tea in the snack-bar. One girl was telling another: 'They've got some of them new flap-jacks in the shop here yesterday. Have you seen them?'

'Yes.'

'They aren't half a price—cost nearly a whole week's money.'

'That's right. Ysabette Jones bought one for herself. Fancy her paying all that lot for a flap-jack—she's screwy.'

'Well, we know that … wonder why she never stops talking?'

'Because she's screwy, that's why.'

'That's right … no sense in what she says, is there?'

'Of course not … she's screwy, you know that.'

Geoffrey went past the writing-room, with the large word 'SILENCE' printed on cardboard over the mantel-shelf. He saw Nordie sitting there with Julian; they were playing chess. Nordie made no sign to him. It was possible that she did not see him. They were intent on the game.

Chapter Six

Work in Progress

In the early morning on Avenue B, Street VI, Julian wheeled a rubber-tyred truck forwards and thought back on last night ...

'Now that game of chess with Nordie, we got on all right because we didn't have to talk to each other; she spoke about the pub, said it was more or less as usual – the soldiers singing and the civilians cheering every song. Charlie on the political chin-wag, with all the boys jeering at him. Girlie sitting on a high-backed mahogany chair in her parlour entertaining one or two customers with careful conversation, and the Guvnor going round in his shirt-sleeves with a tray of tall glasses, giving out sly looks at the girls. Nordie said she'd walked home alone. She seemed a bit sad, as if she was in need of company but she didn't seem to mind my silence, she just got the chess-men out of the cupboard and settled down to a serious game. She seemed glad that I wasn't one of these talking fellows. I believe that's half the trouble with people – the talk between them. They have to talk because they are so afraid of each other – conversation is used as a sound for staving-off; but it won't work, and the fright still lives. Then they start shouting: no good again, so it gets to gun-fire – from shouting to shooting, but the terror looms up larger; then, all dead, and silence ... and back to the beginning.'

Julian left his truck in the special shed and then walked on and along; his rubber-soled shoes made no sound on the cleanway and he could not see his shadow on the shiny black path before him. 'Now I come to think of it, Nordie wasn't silent during the chess game last night, but she only talked to herself, which was less trouble for me. She talked about the moves. "If I do that," she said, "then he'll probably do that … but, supposing he doesn't, then he can move to there … but it won't make any difference, because I can still follow out my own scheme – it's an exchange, a bishop for a knight, nothing in it really." People often talked at cards, or at chess; it seems they can't continue the game unless they speak it out as they go along. I verbalize in my thoughts. I couldn't get on with my life if there weren't any words, if they'd never been invented. I wouldn't be able to move an inch without the words, I'd just have to stay still.'

Lofty had been walking behind Julian along the cleanway. 'I couldn't hear him, of course, and now he's right alongside. I suppose he'll start talking soon.' Lofty wore large yellow canoe-shaped overshoes, he was careful not to look down at them. He carried a leather case by its two thong handles, and walked steadily, staring straight ahead. Julian was thinking about the leather case now. 'Two foot long, six inches in width, all leather outside and inside two cardboard boxes, and inside them again there's what they call the 'Powder K' – they've even got a joke about it in the workshop. If we was to drop the 'Powder K' it would be the 'K O' for us!'

Lofty interrupted the silence with words. He asked Julian to take the powder to Shop B8. 'We walk forward together, along a long black road – powder carriers never walk alone – like a flunkey for death, sneaker-shoed Lofty waits on me now; he must open the doors; he must see that no one bumps into me while I'm carrying this case of "Powder K". It's easy to carry the case by the leather handles; they've been specially made for the purpose. It's light enough, and I've done it many times, but I mustn't be misled by monotony – not that I'm likely to slip, or anything of the kind, but supposing I caught my foot somehow and my ankle turned inwards – the way it did when I was walking up the hill outside the factory yesterday – supposing I just stumbled a bit, supposing I did that – even then, of course, I might be able to throw the whole case right over the cleanway on to the dirty; possibly it wouldn't do much damage on the dirty, you never know till you try, it depends on the strength of the explosion; but there mightn't be time to throw the case away from me; there mightn't be time for anything; then I'd be gone for good before I knew what had happened to me; and what's more, I'd have taken old Lofty along with me, poor old canoe-shoed Lofty! Of course, I've done this job hundreds of times and nothing's ever gone wrong, and not likely to; but I can't help talking these things out in my mind.'

At the mouth of B8 detonator shop Lofty held the door open for Julian. They went through, straight up to the table with the red-letter notice above it, 'Powder Only'. The table had a brown linoleum surface. There was one other box there, but it was on the other side of the white line which divided the surface in half, marking one side 'Empty'. Nothing else was ever allowed on this table at any time, neither by day nor by night.

When Lofty and Julian came in some of the girls looked up, but almost at once they turned their heads back to their work. 'Only another case of "Powder K" coming in.' The shift was almost over; it was nearing two o'clock now – the last hour. There was only one man working in this shop, that was the overlooker. Lofty stepped across to speak to him, leaving Julian by himself.

Julian stood for a few moments putting his thoughts into words, then going through them in his mind. 'Waiting for Lofty to tell me what to do next. I've got a bit of time to move around. I'll watch some of the operations in progress here; better get a bit nearer to them though.' He moved forward slowly. 'Funny, this way of dealing with detonators. I've seen it often enough, but it still seems strange and rather unreal … it's a five-girl process, and all for such a small job. I'm watching "Girl 2" now, she puts the discs on the dets, discs as small as tiddlewinks; she always picks them up and puts them on with tweezers. "Girl 3" puts them under the press, that's a sort of plunger on a horizontal bar. The end that fits the top of the det always reminds me of a cigarette-end, and you can't think of a cigarette-end without remembering what a hardship it seems not being allowed to smoke. "Girl 3" holds the det in the tweezers below the plunger and then she depresses the lever, the pointer on the dial moves around to the correct clock number … you can't say it's all done by kindness when you consider it's all reckoned up according to atmospherics. It doesn't take her long to finish five dets and put them in the box on her left-hand side; then she shuts the lid of the box, gets down from her stool and carries the box with both hands underneath – never put your hands above explosives – to the varnishing table.

'Every few minutes it happens this way: she puts the dets in the box and off she goes for her walk, a few paces every five dets. At the varnishing table "Girl 4" is waiting; she gets the dets into groups of five, fixes them into holes on a horizontal bar, and then they're all set for the dipping process. The dets go down all together into a brown bath of varnish – the horizontal bar in that frame makes me think of a child's bead-counting frame, but this one only has one bar for five beads and they're all copper-coloured dets – the silver rod rolls down within its frame and dips the dets in the varnish bath. "Girl 4" takes the rod back from its bath and puts it down on the drying mat and "Girl 5" gets going. She takes up each det in turn in tweezers and puts them in the wool-covered slot in a sloping wood plank; she rubs them back and forth with the kidstick. It seems to me that all through these processes one comes up against words that carry you way and away back to the nursery. It was quite a little while before I found out that "kidstick" didn't mean anything childish–as I'd thought at first–it's the material they're thinking of. So she gets around too, No 5 girl does, she has a bit of a walk every five dets dried. Well, I haven't seen Girl No 1 yet, she'll be doing the filling work. Lofty's still talking to the overlooker about the tear in the blackout, so I've got a few minutes before I get any further instructions. I might as well watch as wait.'

Julian walked down to the end of the shop. 'A det doesn't look much of anything–you can't hardly see it unless your sight's good–but it's got to be filled behind thick blast walls running from floor to ceiling.'

A panel of splinter-proof glass was let into the wall, and through this Julian watched the filling process. A tray of empty detonators had been passed through a slot like a pillar-box mouth. They were there now, in their tray, ready for operator No 1. Julian watched. He could not hear anything. 'It's like a film. Of course I never go to talkies because I don't like the voice sounds, but you can't hear anything from behind these blast walls; for me it's as good as seeing a silent film, quite an entertainment it is. Operator No 1 places the tray of dets on the filling machine; she goes over to that cupboard let into the wall at the far end there; she slides a bit of wooden wall back, and there's the powder in a cardboard box–six inches by about four inches, I should say that box is; it's not much more at any rate. It's funny how interested one gets in measurements as soon as you start working in a factory even when you're only doing unskilled work the same as me. I don't know why it is, I've noticed it again and again, always this working out of everything in measurements. Operator No 1 moves along so smoothly, almost as if she was dancing–and that's a lot to say for anyone during their last hour of a shift–full of life she is; don't remember seeing her before; she must have been on one of the other groups before she came here; she doesn't look English with those eyes slanting down at the corners – don't suppose she's a foreigner, though. I know what it is, she's Jewish, most likely Jewish, that's it. Those cardboard boxes look harmless enough – could be cosmetics, but when you know what's in them it's a different matter altogether. Operator No 1 is filling one of those papier-mâché things with powder now – it's quite a toy by the look of it, something of the same sort as those paper boats children float in their baths, only, of course, it's much smaller. I shouldn't think it's more than two inches by three inches. Operator No 1 carries it back to the filling machine; now she puts it above the tray – the whole apparatus is quite an elaborate affair, with its ropes and pulleys it could be a child's miniature toy crane, or something of that sort. The papier-mâché boat will move along when the whole thing's set going, and then the powder will fall and drop through into the dets.'

The Jewish girl came outside the blast walls and stood beside Julian peering through the panel. She turned a handle in the side of the wall near them both; it set the apparatus going on the other side of the blast walls, and together they watched the papier-mâché boat travelling along above the tray; when it got to the end it stopped. The paper boat with its cargo of 'Powder K', immobile at the end of its journey, made Julian think of a Chinese picture he'd once seen – it was of a boat travelling across a lake. The Jewish girl said 'Quite an old-fashioned arrangement, isn't it really, when you come to think of it – not like these modern conveyor belts and that, is it? I mean the ones that work on their own.'

Julian wanted to say something in reply, but he couldn't find the words; his thoughts panicked and he was unable to speak up in answer. It was often like this when anyone spoke to him suddenly, a wave of nervousness swept over him.

Operator No 1's coat and trousers were very white: they must have been cleaned that morning, because they were still pressed in creases. She had stopped turning the handle in the wall, but she looked sideways at it with her slant-sloe eyes.

'Like a barrel-organ, isn't it?' she said. 'All I need now is a monkey on my shoulder and some ice-creamio, and then I'd be all right, shouldn't I?'

Julian was drowning in a desperate silence. He gave the girl a sombre smile, but was unable to say anything. She looked at the sleeve of his coat. In the canteen that morning he had upset the dregs of his tea: it had happened because the man next to him had asked him a question suddenly–now there was a tea-stain on his sleeve.

Perhaps the girl was tired of Julian's silence, or resentful of his inability to answer. She looked sideways at his sleeve and said:

'Somebody's mother's not using Persil!'

Then she went back behind the blast walls.

Julian saw her take out the tray of filled detonators and pass it through the pillar-box mouth to '"Girl 2". End of operation one for "Girl 1"–and now all over again. She takes the tray, walks to wall door, opens it, takes out the cardboard carton of "Powder K", fills the papier-mâché boat, carries it over to the filling machine–but now, catches her foot, and trips ... It wouldn't have seemed possible on that smooth surfaced floor ... she's dropped the toy boat on to the tray of empty dets–a flash–that's a funny thing, as if we were being photographed at the seaside, or something ... The girl's hands go up to her face; she shouts, but you can't hear anything. I lip-read the words though. "I'm blind!" That's what she's just said, though you can't hear her; her face bleeds fast, blood runs down between her fingers over the loose sleeves of her white coat; she falls, and now you can't see anything more of her–only the toy boat remains in sight: it hasn't been broken at all, but bits of machinery are broken, pulleys and ropes smashed up, pieces of copper-coloured detonator and blood-splash ... Nothing according to plan any more, only disorder – no noise, no voices, nothing. Get quick behind the blast walls, it's near enough to help. Don't pick her up though, because she may be too badly broken – they always tell us that, not to touch anyone till the stretchers are ready for them. Running footsteps behind me – Lofty and the overlooker. I hear him saying something difficult to understand but I know what it is, he wants me to get the stretcher.'

Julian went to fetch the stretcher; he brought it back over his shoulder. Lofty said to the rest of the girls:

'She'll be all right. Go down to the canteen.'

They all know that they have to leave the shop when there's been a 'blow'. They shuffle out, sheep-like.

Julian said, 'Not my idea of "all right".'

And another laughed out once, sharp on a high note, then suddenly stopped.

Behind the blast walls Lofty and the overlooker unrolled the stretcher.

As if Julian's thoughts were taking a walk they wandered outdoors to the girls leaving the shop. He moved about behind the blast wall with the people who were here, while he escaped in mind with those who had gone.

'The second in charge will say, "Now don't none of you go spreading rumours. We don't know how bad she's hurt yet – after all, she wasn't screaming like Dot did when she lost her hand – so don't none of you go saying nothing; we don't want no one to think that Shop B8 is always having 'blows'." That's what the second in charge would say. But it wouldn't stop the talk. It wouldn't silence it in the others, nor even in her. They'd pass one or two walking up the cleanway. "There's been a 'blow' in our shop," they'd say. "In our shop there's been a 'blow'. – Been a blow – a blow."

'They'd soon get to the canteen and file in. It would look much bigger to them now; it always looks that way when it's empty. Only two or three cleaners would be there, and they'd be sitting down at tables after having finished their floor-scrubbing: cleaners glad of a rest, sitting at a corner table, chatting, sweating, drinking tea. As the girls came in the cleaners would look up at the canteen clock, the big clock on the wall, and the canteen manageress would sharp-speak out at the girls, "Ain't time for a break yet." But the second in charge would tell her; "Mr Lofty says we can have a cup of tea now—there's been a blow in our shop." The canteen manageress would answer gentle then, "A blow ... Oh, that's different . . . who is it?" The cleaners would come gathering round, anxious to hear. But the girls would stay rather quiet—move woodenly over to empty tables, and wonder about "Girl No 1". "How's she getting on now? Perhaps she wasn't so bad—it's true, she didn't scream like Dot did." Soon the sound of the ambulance bell would clang out, and a little while afterwards the next shift would come in, straight to the canteen for a cup of tea first, before starting work. They'd look into the eyes of the out-going shift, and fear would be transferred from one to the other, from corner to corner of the canteen—five hundred feet as the fear flies!'

Back behind the blast walls of the Detonator Shop Lofty put his coat under the girl. 'Important to keep her warm.'

He was very gentle, spoke softly, and the acid-edge was off his voice.

'Be careful how you lift the stretcher.'

Julian and Lofty carried the stretcher between them.

'Let's go now—take up the stretcher slowly, in step, down the road, until we reach the Rest Room.'

As they approached the place, the nurse was standing at the door. Why was it that people standing in doorways looking out seemed as uncertain as colts gazing out from their stalls? But inside the room the nurse had everything ready.

Lofty said, 'She'll be comfortable here. She'll be all right now. Must be a brave girl, she must, never made no fuss, never said nothing.'

Julian thought, 'Funny job, nurse's job, always being ready for something to go wrong – then being at your best when it does. How white the collar is round her neck, like cardboard it is – somebody's mother's been using Persil, and starch, too, by the look of it. I never knew these rest-rooms were so near the shops, only a matter of a couple of hundred yards – but a lot can happen in a hundred yards.'

Lofty and Julian put the stretcher down in the Rest Room. They waited for a little while, knowing that there was nothing more they could do. They were not aware of it at once. But it had been so for some time. Although it was not far from the Detonator Shop to the Rest Room, the Jewish girl had already died on the journey out.

Chapter Seven

Factory Tour

Consumed with secret information, Captain Quantock, the Security Officer, moved about on an errand of megalomania. The news had come through that 'a very distinguished personage' would be visiting the district and graciously taking a tour through the factory. Captain Quantock knew the Civil Service language – 'very distinguished personage' was code for King, so he did not delay before setting all the security machinery in motion.

Captain Quantock, although pleased to be in possession of news, was not completely at ease over the visit. Could everything be laid on in time? Would it be up to standard, and all according to schedule? The Security Officer travelled the length of the Administration Building, second floor from right to left, from left to right, troubling about all these problems; two-stepping through the door of this office, tapping on the glass pane of that. Galvanized by the great story, he arranged to see the Principal Clerk, the Chief Production Manager, Colonel Flore of the Home Guard, the PAD Head Officer, and Inspector Jameson. Captain Quantock had not been asked into the last Joint Production Committee meeting, but now this great story would give him the chance of a confidential chat with Whistler. The Super and the Security Officer would talk together as man to man now. Quantock could hammer out all his plans, discuss which was the route to be taken and the group to be graced. The Catering Manager would have to be consulted, so that when 'he' looked into the canteen everything would be in order. Some men would have to be specially selected and told off to arrive at work in their Home Guard uniforms, ready for the line-up. A shifting house must be made to shine and new asbestos suits drawn from the store for a few picked workers who could be relied upon to look well.

Captain Quantock went into his office; his secretary, Miss Snooper, told him: 'Twelve Irish workers have applied for exit permits. I have checked up on their records; they have all been here for more than six months since their last leave.'

Captain Quantock, preoccupied with the image of distinguished personages, did not answer immediately. He walked over to the window and looked out. A gang of builders, labourers, and telegraph linesmen were walking from the first gate into the Danger Area. Although there were over two hundred going on shift at this time, Captain Quantock did not notice any single one of them.

'You will want to talk to them, I suppose,' Miss Snooper said.

'Oh yes,' answered the Security Officer, 'I shall probably be the first person they'll speak to.'

'Oh, so you're going to interview them yourself then!'

Captain Quantock turned away from the window.

'Who?' he asked.

Miss Snooper said, 'The Irish workers.'

'Oh, it won't be necessary to see them to-day,' Captain Quantock answered, irritated at being brought back to routine business. 'Any time will do for that.'

The Security Officer turned back to the window again. He stared out again, still seeing nothing.

'By the way,' he asked, 'what group are the Irish workers on?'

'Most of them are on Group VII,' Miss Snooper told him.

'Oh, that will be all right, then.' So they would not come into contact with the distinguished personage. 'He' would only have time to see the 'new job'.

Miss Snooper moved three forms from Box K to Box L. Soon it would be time for her to go and wash before the mid-day meal. She always kept her own soap at the office. It was the tablet her aunt had given her as a Christmas present. It was wrapped in green cellophane and branded 'My Lady Glamour'.

Captain Quantock put some papers down on the desk.

'It looks as if to-morrow's going to be a real rush day,' he said. 'So we'd better make way for some of the urgent work I am expecting in now.'

He went out on the words, shutting the door sharply after him.

Miss Snooper took off her hair-net and put it away in her bag in an envelope. With her first finger and her thumb she pressed the deep waves of her hair into shape, with the palm she set the back into a careless sweep.

A tall dark girl came in, sent from the typists' pool next door to help with the extra work.

'Fancy the King coming down to visit us,' she said to Miss Snooper.

'Oh, well, it makes a nice change.' Miss Snooper took her tablet of soap out of the Sabotage file and got ready to go and wash before the midday meal.

The Administration Staff had their food in Canteen D10. It was inside the first factory gates, but just outside the Danger Area – so no one wore white suits here, all kept to their ordinary shoes. The canteen was full of typists, welfare workers, labour officers, PAD staff, nurses, chemists, entertainments managers, cinema projectionists, a doctor, one or two Time and Motion men, a CEMA party, an ENSA party, and two research doctors.

At the end of this room there was a partitioned-off pen, where the Superintendent, the Head Woman Labour Officer, the Principal Clerk, the Head of the INO (Inspectorate of

Naval Ordnance), the Public Relations Officer, Twizden, the Head Production Manager, Colonel Flore of the Home Guard, and any visiting Member of Parliament, took their lunch.

Outside on the partition wall someone had pencilled in small writing, 'Royal Enclosure, Ascot. Donkey Cup Day.' No one had troubled to rub out these words.

Captain Quantock walked through the main room and on into the penned-off staff-room. He walked in with good news; on the tips of his shoes, and sat down at Super's table.

Captain Quantock had to wait a while for his chance to score a sentence with the Super. As soon as it came, and there was a let-up in the general talk, he asked: 'What time's the meeting to-day, sir?'

Super was staring out of the window at some flower beds in bloom. He brought his attention reluctantly back to the Security Officer at the staff table.

'What meeting?' he asked.

Quantock gave a knowing look, but did not say anything at first. Super was a very subtle man, of course. He wouldn't be able to get and hold down a job like this if he wasn't. He understood most the significance of security, and no doubt he got impatient at times with men like Colonel Flore, who was always boasting about his battle-drill tactics and wasting time planting out flower-beds, which bloomed at the most dangerous moments, making a coloured landmark that could easily be seen from the air in the event of a daylight raid.

'How well those flowers look!' the Super said to Colonel Flore, 'they've grown up very quickly, haven't they?'

'Oh, I don't know,' Colonel Flore answered, 'it's not such bad soil. It seems strange to think that there wasn't any factory here at all seven years ago.'

'Yes, it's odd when one thinks about that,' Quantock said, anxious to get into the talk. Of course, he thought, a factory such as this really starts with security. Security is the foundation of the whole thing, but it is not everybody that understands that. But now the factory was seven miles in circumference and employed 30,000 workers all told, and here was Quantock himself lunching with the Super in the staff-room, and they were the only two at the table who knew that 'a very distinguished visitor' was coming to Statevale. Now that was a swell thought. Quantock looked at his notes. 'Yes, that's it. I can confirm that the meeting is at two o'clock.'

The Superintendent smiled wanly, 'I'll be there,' he said, without taking his gaze away from the flower-bed. Quantock was short of time, there was so much to arrange. A thing like this did not crop up every day, but when there was a visit, most of the responsibility rested with the Security Officer. That was it. Security first; you can't be too careful. He went out.

'What's old Quantock been talking about?' asked the Principal Clerk.

'Oh, I don't know. Belly-aching over the Royal visit, I suppose.'

Quantock's first official call was at the transport shed. He talked to the head trousered girl. 'Quite the musical comedy miss in her khaki get-up and forage cap.'

He ordered a car to take him round over the route. He hinted that he might have some special orders for them later. All the cars would have to be cleaned and drawn up for inspection the following day, but Quantock decided not to tell them too much. Of course these girls were all right; good class of girl, the straightforward patriotic type; no nonsense about them. But all the same things had to be done in the right order. No good going making bloomers and telling them about the Royal visit before the Super gave it out officially. As soon as the Security Officer had gone, the girls continued their game of darts.

One of them remarked, 'If you ask me, I think these Royal visits are more trouble than they're worth.'

One of the orderlies said, 'It wouldn't be so bad if it was like the Coronation: we came all the way up from Southampton for that—drinks all round and dancing in the streets.'

Captain Quantock went back to Admin. He ran up the steps and into his office.

'I'm just on the way to the meeting with the Superintendent. Any messages for me?' he asked.

Miss Snooper shook her head.

The Security Officer noticed the young typist who had been brought in to help. She was almost too dark to be English. He wondered if she were Irish. It wouldn't do to talk about the visit in front of her. She looked innocent, but he was far too old a Security Officer to be caught with that kind of chaff. But he said, 'There may be an announcement after the meeting that will affect the whole personnel of Statevale.'

He went out again. When he was gone the young typist said, 'I wonder what he meant. Do you think they're going to raise the bonus or anything of that sort?'

'I could do with some extra money,' Miss Snooper answered. 'It's not easy when you've got Income Tax as well as home obligations. It all seems to come at once, doesn't it? I wish they would raise the bonus; but it can't be anything like that, because Captain Quantock would have told me. I am his confidential secretary.'

The young typist sighed and went on with her work. 'Visit to Statevale by ...' and underneath this she wrote, 'Route to be taken. Arrival at factory 10 am. Inspection of Guard of Honour (Colonel Flore, DSO, MC, Croix de Guerre with Palm, presented.)'

'Perhaps they're going to give us a full week-end off at Christmas,' she said.

Miss Snooper smiled. 'It would make a nice change, wouldn't it?'

The young typist went on with her work. 'Introduction of Superintendent Whistler,' she typed out, and then she said, 'Do you think they'll present Pitcher to the King?'

She began to giggle.

'It would make a nice silly symphony, wouldn't it?' said Miss Snooper.

After the meeting was over, Captain Quantock went driving round the factory. Outside the first gates they stopped. The driver opened the door for him. He got out, stepped in again, looked at his watch, then said 'Go!' and the girl drove him back through the gates.

Immediately he shouted, 'Don't drive so fast, slow up a bit!'

He thought, 'The very distinguished personage won't loll back in a car, he'd sit upright, not bolt upright, but in dignified self-possession.' A smile froze the Security Officer's face as they passed the policeman at the Inspection Gate. He wished the man would salute. The young forage-capped driver foot-braked round the corner and drew up again at Admin.

The policeman at the first gate was staring after them. 'What's he doing, silly bastard?'

Quantock looked at his watch, walked down a row of imaginary Home Guards, allowing himself a few moments in fantasy to congratulate Colonel Flore on his decorations. Then he looked up at the Administration steps, smiled at an invisible Whistler, mouthed a few well-chosen words, and stepped back into the car.

'Drive through the danger gates now,' he said.

Outside the cop-shop two policemen were staring after him.

'What's he doing now?'

'Seems like he's off his onion.'

'Anybody would be with his job – Security Officer, huh!'

'Seems to have secured himself all right, though. £800 a year, his job's worth, they say.'

'Not bad for an amateur; and mind you, he is an amateur. Never been in no danger, Quantock hasn't, or anything like that.'

The Security Officer drove down the avenue and got out on Group IV. When he gave up his cigarette case at the Contraband hut, he put on a remote manner. What a quaint custom it was this giving up of contraband as they call it; at least, it would surely seem rather quaint to any very distinguished visitor.

In the Shifting House two attendants were being helped by three workmen. They were polishing the floor and the railing which divided the clean side from the dirty. Even the brightly painted red letters on the rail with the word 'DIRTY', they were polishing.

Quantock smiled his way out, and went on to the Section Office in search of the Shop Manager and Production Manager. The Shop Manager was becoming increasingly ill-tempered, because working on shift he had now been asked to stay over to prepare for this impending visit. It was a trouble to him to trail after the Production Manager and the Security Officer just to listen to them talking to each other.

'I saw you at the meeting, Terry, didn't I?'

'That's right.'

'Well, I just came along to see that everything was shaping all right for the visit. Shall we go round the Group?'

Quantock looked at his watch. He was most anxious to get the timing right. Together they moved to the shop where the new job was in progress. Several men wheeling trucks went by. The Security Officer saw that Julian's clothes were smudged and the knees of his suit dirty. Quantock thought,

'They must all be in clean asbestos in time for the visit.'

A young Labour Officer walked towards them down the cleanway.

'Good afternoon, Miss Robinson, excited about the visit?'

'I hope it keeps fine for them,' she answered.

The proxy party went out. They reached the shed where the eight thousand pounders used to be filled, but now the shed itself had been expanded, because they were working on a still larger bomb. A special platform had been built near the end of the shop. Two or three men were standing there and peering down into the bomb. They had 'stemmers' in their hands.

Quantock thought, 'Perhaps we shall have to explain to the personage that these are six-feet poles of specially hardened wood, which press down composition to ensure equal distribution.'

A tray of composition, faintly yellow and of a porridge-like consistency was being wheeled from the incorporator to the platform. In these few feet of space there was the atmosphere of an execution ceremony. The two men looked very hot, and their gauntletted hands seemed stained. The Security Officer made a note that they must look cool and detached on the great day. It would be wise to issue them with new unsoiled gauntled gloves.

The Production Manager said, 'Of course we're going to have new ventilators here—when we get them, that is. There was some talk about it at the Joint Production Committee meeting.'

'Oh, I see, one of the grievances ventilated!' said Quantock on a facetious high note.

The Production Manager looked dully at him without answering.

Two men with the trolley reached the platform, got hold of

the tray by two handles, swung it up to the top from where it was emptied down into the bomb casing.

'Want to go up?' the Production Manager asked.

The Security Officer shook his head. He must leave now; otherwise he might get the timing wrong.

On the way out they saw stacks of empty bombs laid down on their sides. From one of these the Security Office saw the soles of two feet protruding.

Lofty, the foreman, walked by, stopped and stared. This was a strange thing for him to do, because it was a sight that Lofty must have seen before. An empty bomb from which a pair of feet protruded could not be a novelty to a man working on this group.

As soon as Lofty saw the Security Officer he walked on. Two or three minutes later, Gluckstein, the overlooker, crawled up from the inside of the bomb. When he saw the Security Officer he started to talk about the work, and about the new job which was different to anything they had been doing last week. Gluckstein talked on at over-time rate, as if taking his technical knowledge out for a gallop.

The Security Officer was becoming more troubled about the time. He made his way back to the canteen. The canteen charge-hand in white overall and red and white cap had seen them coming. She stood silent and smiling now beside her trays of cakes and pies, ready for the next break. She had succeeded in her good-willed way in putting herself into a dress-rehearsal mood. The urn was on the bubble by her elbow, and Quantock, still existing in his 'very distinguished personage' fantasy, tasted a cup, smiled graciously, and with his other executive self, made mental notes for a special visit meal to be laid on. There was only one other girl in the canteen; she was fixing up some cinema apparatus, dragging the heavy amplifier along to the end of the room.

Quantock left the canteen by the other door through the Shift House: change shoes, once more into the car and down Avenue A, pause in front of Administration, then 'God Save the King,' three rousing cheers; salute the flag; keep it going, boys and girls …

Chapter Eight

Visit

The night-shift went off. Through the last few hours the vitality of every operative had been zeroing down. 'Can't work all night and feel as fresh as a daisy in the morning, can you luv?' Men and women were limb-heavying their way out of the factory, up the hill to the last gates and out. Two or three talked in a tired way. Others showed their fatigue through silence.

'I shall be glad to get home and have a shave.'

'I shan't shave. Go straight to bed, I shall.'

'You should have a shave, man, if you are going to see your wife in the morning.'

'I'm not going to have a shave till I've had a sleep – wouldn't trouble with shaving now, not for the King, I wouldn't.'

'The King is coming down this morning.'

'That's right.'

'We shan't see him then.'

'That's right, we shan't.'

'Our shift will miss King, our shift will.'

'Blue shift are on mornings – they'll see King.'

'Blue shift always get the best of it, Blue shift do.'

'That's right. When there's something on we're always off.'

A girl said, 'A lot of fuss they're making.'

And a woman with a red scarf wound round her head and wooden clogs on her feet, said: 'It's not often King comes down to our factory.'

'A busy man, King is.'

'Oh, I don't know. Mrs Bagaley saw King when he coom to Kindale, didn't you luv?'

'No, it was Queen I saw.'

'Did you speak to her, Mrs Bagaley?'

'Yes, I had a bit of a talk with Queen. I was working in shift-house at Kindale before I coom here. When Queen came into our shift-house it was very quiet. No-one spoke, so I thought I'd be the first to have a say; so I said, "Very pleased to see Your Majesty," and Queen asked me if I liked working here – only it wasn't here, it was at Kindale, see, in shifting-house it wor'; and Queen asked me how far I coom to work, and I told her seven miles; but I forgot one, it wor' eight miles I coom each day. An' then I asked Queen, "When will war be over Your Majesty, so's we can have a bit of peace and quiet?" But Queen didn't tell me, she only said she hoped it would be over soon. So I've lived till sixty-four now, and I've shook hands with Queen ... but I forgot one mile I when I told Queen I coom seven miles to work because it wor' eight I used to coom.'

As the night shift went out some looked up at the sky hopefully.

'Think it's going to sunshine later on.'

And others looked dolefully down at their feet.

'I see it's been raining already.'

The outgoing shift clambered up into the waiting buses. Scarlet single-deckers came down the hill carrying the incoming shift to work. Some of the Blue shift were singing. The night shift went out in their great grey buses. Some of them were sleeping.

The Blue shift staff waited in the main canteen. They were ready several hours before there could be any hope of the Royal visitors being signalled. One of the canteen supervisors said:

'The place has quite a Royal visit polish to it this morning.'

'That's right, and so have the people in it. All the girls on the group the King is visiting have had new hair sets, same as they have here.'

The men chosen to line the Royal party's route came into the canteen looking over-clean and self-conscious in their carefully pressed Home Guard uniforms. It would be a long time before anything happened; already boredom was beginning to seep through. Half-hearted conversation was battledored from man to man.

'Haven't been in here for breakfast before.'

'Tablecloths they got here, and bacon for breakfast, and girls to wait on them.'

'Not like lining up for food at the counter down on our group, is it?'

'That's right, it isn't.'

A square-faced man from the Smoke Section said:

'Distinguished visitors make such a mix-up with a working day. It's always the same. Nearly as bad as air-raids, I reckon.'

'Much worse. We don't stop work for air-raids same as we do for distinguished visitors.'

'Ah! But this is "very distinguished visitors", Joe.'

'What's the difference?'

'Distinguished only means distinguished directors, industrialists, and that … but "very distinguished" means Royalty. Distinguished means "pep talker", but "very" means "King" – that's what it comes to.'

'My young lady worked for a clergyman once. She'd been through a secretarial course, typed all the sky pilot's sermons, she did, so's he could see what he was saying in church. He was the "Very Reverend" – rural Dean, I believe he was. I suppose this is something of the same idea as that.'

'That's right. Church and State, State and Church. What a circus.'

'This bacon's all right, this bacon is.'

'I don't fancy it myself, not bacon I don't. Always seems to me like swallowing sea-water when you're going in swimming, eating bacon does.'

'When will King be here?'

'They tell me he'll arrive at a quarter to ten or thereabouts.'

'Will he?'

'He should do.'

'Suppose he'll have a bit of a jaw with Super at the start.'

'That's right ... then there'll be the parade of Home Guards for him to inspect; and, of course, there'll be more Home Guards lining the route ... that's us, that is. But he won't get on the route till near on eleven, and then I suppose he'll go to Group V.'

'Shan't see much of King, us'n shan't.'

'It'll be like those advertisements what you see for petrol – "that's King, that wor'."'

'Oh, I don't know so much, Royal cars is all slow coaches.'

After the workers in their Home Guard uniforms had finished their breakfasts and gone out of the canteen to take their places along the Royal route, the staff inside the canteen set to clearing the tables. There was not much to be done; it was quickly over. The tables were rearranged, everything was polished. It had an aseptic aspect. There was nothing to do now. From time to time some first-grade executive came officialling in to see that everything was in order. The canteen girls leaned their elbows on the long counter between kitchen and dining-hall, studied their hair-sets in small pocket mirrors, filed their nails, and took to talking.

'Will the King speak to us from the stage, the same as the ENSA compères do?'

'Yes, I think so. Mrs Franklin was here the last time the King came down, so she knows more about it than I do.'

Mrs Franklin, one of the kitchen supervisors, said:

'Yes, that's right, dear, the King will speak from the main canteen here, and it'll be relayed to every canteen on every Group. It's true I saw the King last time he came down, but it was a bit different then – the place hadn't been built long then.

Travelling to and fro was not like it is now – the men were still working on the roads, and there was only a shack where Admin is. Mrs Bennett was here with me, weren't you, dear?'

Mrs Bennett, a washer-up, had come forward to join in the general talk. She answered at once:

'Yes. Talked to me, King did. He said, "Plenty of mud you've got down here." He had a cup of tea off Maggie, made specially for him it wor' in pot, not in urn like us'n. Turned up cup after, King did – that's Staffordshire lad's trick, turning up cup is. King said, "Coom from Bissells, that does, finest pots in world coom from Staffordshire," King said. Ar said, "Hope to see you 'again, Sir," and King said, "Aye, I'll be down again when roads are built," he said, ""when you've got a bit more for me to see," and here he cooms.'

'Last time the King was here he went to Group VII,' Mrs Franklin said. 'He inspected the operations there and Super showed him a detonator and explained that a torpedo wouldn't work without it, and the King said to Super, "It's only a little thing, but it's essential in bringing us nearer victory." The Queen went to the Labour Officer's room, and she said, "What interesting work all you ladies are doing." And after the tour was over, the King was taken to Super's office up at Admin to see some of the plans. Then he gave us a few words from the canteen here. Of course we hadn't got all the loud- speakers and everything wasn't up to the same pitch of efficiency as it is now, but I believe the King had a few words with some of the workers. I know he talked to that Mrs Brownlee who's on Group VIII now – she's got seven sons all in the Services, you know – and then at the end all the Royal party got back into their cars – they were dark-blue Daimlers – and we saw them driven off and we all cheered, and went back to the washing-up.'

On Group IV in the Detonator Shop where Linnet worked, the operatives asked each other, 'What time shall we be going to the canteen to hear the King's speech relayed?'

'A message came through to Miss Robinson that we'd be going up to the canteen at a quarter to twelve.'

'That's funny. My Dad works up near main canteen, and he says King is speaking at quarter past eleven.'

'Must've got it wrong, your Dad must've.'

'When our Dick was little lad he had Coronation mug with painting of King on it—bit of fur round his neck, King had.'

'That wor' old King, that wor'.'

'I seen picture of him on post-card; it wor' bit of white cat's skin round his neck he had—shouldn't fancy it myself, I shouldn't.'

Linnet listened to her own thoughts rather than to the words of the workers round her. All her mind was on the evening. The day didn't mean much to her. Willie would arrive soon after seven. How many hours between this time and that time? Long hours, eleven all told, till Willie would get off the train. After the shift was over she'd hurry back to the hostel. She'd have time to rest, to change into her new dress, to pack up some of her things, and to move over to the married quarters. It was not easy to imagine her new dress now that it was out of sight. Getting into it would be like making a jump straight into civilian life. Out of asbestos into silk; of course she got out of asbestos each day when she went through the shifting house before leaving the factory, but she didn't get into silk. The girl next to Linnet said:

'My Dad works up the road by the burning ground near the wood, there he works. He says there's willow herb growing there, a mass of willow herb it is. Funny to think of flowers living in all this, isn't it?'

Linnet said, 'My husband's got leave. I wish I could get some of those flowers and bring them back to the hostel. I'm moving over to the married quarters this evening.'

'Flowers make all the difference in a room, don't they?' the girl said. 'Makes it seem as if you were really living there.'

'Would there be time for me to get up to the burning-ground in the break?' Linnet asked.

'You could do,' the girl said. 'Of course, you've got to go through the shifting house and that, but it shouldn't take long at this hour of the morning. There won't be nobody about; and anyhow, it's all been kept clear for the King's visit.'

'Is it compulsory to listen to the speech?' Linnet asked.

'Well, I don't suppose it's compulsory, but it makes a nice change from ENSA.'

When it was a quarter to eleven the girl on the other side of Linnet looked up and said, 'Here's Labour Officer.'

'What does she want?'

'We don't know yet; she's talking to the Blue-band.'

Between the Blue-band and the Labour Officer there was some conversation and some head-nodding; then the white-turbanned Labour Officer went out and the Blue-band walked forward to the centre of the shop.

'Just a minute, girls. Labour Officer's been in and she says we're to go to break now, as usual, and then we're to coom back 'ere for bloody 'arf hour, and then back we goes to canteen to 'ear King. Waste of time, ar calls it; but our production won't be down, cos I'll 'elp you after speech and if you don't say nothing about it ar won't.'

The girl who had told Linnet about the willow herb growing beyond the burning-ground told her now 'our Blue-band is best on Group, she is.' But the girl on the other side diluted the praise. 'Course Blue-band's safe enough 'cos foreman's in bloody 'ome Guard, so he won't come in ... they'll be swiggin' tea all morning in B8 canteen talking about speech, and thinking they're bloody 'eroes 'cos they've stood in line like bloody tin soldiers to see Royal party go by in cars.'

At a quarter to eleven the girls got going out of the workshop and down the cleanway towards the canteen. Only Linnet turned off to the shifting house. She changed out of her magazine clothes and into her grey flannel dress; she took the rubber-soled shoes from her feet and put them in a bag; she took the round flannel cap from her head and put it in the pocket of her overall coat; she hung the magazine uniform up on a hook and walked out on to the dirty-way. As soon as she was wearing her own clothes and was off the cleanway she felt free of the workshop.

Within the seven miles circumference of the factory the workshops had been burrowed down to mole depth. The trucks taking explosives to their place of export travel along internal railway lines at human level; the pylons follow the streets at house-top height. Sometimes a practice plane came hawking overhead, but soon afterwards it went swooping and circling away, so that all became quiet again. There were only a few stragglers in sight; some men tending the grass near the sheds; one or two transport drivers, and a few forewomen, labour officers, or shop managers on their way up to the main canteen, to Admin or to the Office of Works on some errand. There were seven thousand workers inside the 'Danger Area' at this moment. They could not be seen; they could not be heard.

Linnet lilted along K Street. It was a wide white road on the Smoke Section. All around and beyond there were the high hills and the unplanned woodland. A few fir-trees by the internal railway centre frowned down on the waiting freight cars; other tall trees straggled right up to the edge of the factory land as if cow-curious at the strange symmetry. The sun shone down on the valley and rayed right through the centre of the shadow of death.

Sergeant Duffy drove by, taking a couple of cinema projectionists to a canteen. A factory bus went past loaded up with girls; they shouted to Sergeant Duffy, and waved; he waved back to them, calling out, 'Bye-bye, Budgie-cage.'

At the end of K Street Linnet came to a path that wound itself around and behind one of the store-sheds; the paths spiraled up and on through the woodland to the far side of the burning-ground. Some inactive explosive was being burnt there this moment: the smokescreen went cloud-circling up some seven feet high; grey-green, blue-white smoke spread out and angry-horsed its way over the valley, blotting out the whole factory. Linnet looked up at the sky. It was clear, cloudless blue. She could hear the sound of a woodcutter's axe felling a tree a few hundred yards distant. She walked forward on fallen leaves. The blue of the sky, the sound of the axe and the warmth of the sun in this tree-tall place gave Linnet a sense of peace. It seemed to her that she had made a quick jump directly back to her home during one of those days when she was first married to Willie and he was thinning out some trees in the wood. The sun shone then as at this moment. The sky had been the same blue, and on a clear cloudless day Linnet had made her way down a path to the clearing in the wood where Willie worked, treading on leaves and carrying a basket with a napkin over it—she had carried some food to him, there on that day.

Linnet reached the place where the willow herb grew. She began to pick it quickly—she must be back at work soon. The smoke-screen from the burning-ground cleared again, and when Linnet stood up with the flowers in her hands the whole valley looked suddenly small and unreal as if it had only been mapped out and modelled in the mind; but there was no life there, although she saw the Administration building with the flag flying she could not see any of the workshops, stores, or sheds. 'That's as it should be,' she thought, 'because, of course, they're all camouflaged.' But the white streets were there, and a small internal railway line used by the workers.

It was a pity Willie would not be able to come right up to the factory and fetch her home when the Blue shift came off. She might have been able to get a permit for him to do this, but it would have taken a long time and would have been a trouble to them both. She wondered if Willie's train would be late … they often were in war-time, so there was nothing to be done but to make the best of it. She supposed that he would come to the hostel straight from the station, and everything would be the same for them both, as if they had never been separated.

Carrying the flowers with her she began to run down the path. She got back into the danger area, went quickly down K Street and along and again into the shifting house. She gave her flowers to the woman in charge.

'I got them up by the burning-ground,' she said. 'My husband's coming here on leave this evening.'

'That'll be nice for you, luv. I'll put your flowers in the fire-bucket for you and then they'll be fresh when you come off the shift. Hurry up, duck, and you'll just 'ave time for a cup of tea before you go back to your shops.'

Linnet changed back into the magazine clothes and rubber-soled shoes.

'Jest a minute, duck, some of your 'air's 'anging down under your cap—better tuck it in, that Miss Robinson's very sharp on that kind of thing, she is.'

Linnet got into the canteen three minutes before time. One of the girls waved to her.

'I got you coop of tea and meat pie. Tea's cold though, ask 'em if they'll hot it up for you.'

There was no time. Linnet drank the cold tea quickly. It made her think of haymaking and the summertime, and being at home with Willie. The woman behind her in the canteen said:

'You 'aven't 'ad enough to eat, girl. I always say to my Ted "'av a proper dinner, lad, and 'ere's tenpence to 'av it with." Young folk can't work if they don't eat. It's a lucky thing King ain't coming to this canteen else you'd faint when you saw him, and that wouldn't do, would it?'

Linnet hoped she wouldn't be feeling tired or ill when Willie arrived. She would have something to eat when she reached the hostel. Rose's mother had been staying with her last week; it was a pity she wasn't still at the hostel. It was a funny thing, really, that Rose's mother should have come from Translove way – that was only two villages from where Willie's dad used to live … They could have sat together at supper and talked things over, and it would have seemed quite like old times.

The girls got up and made their way out of the canteen towards their workshop. After they'd started work, one of them asked Linnet:

'Do you think he will be wearing uniform?'

Linnet remembered that Willie had been made a corporal. He'd written to her about it, reminding her of a picture of Napoleon which was hung on the stairs by the kitchen at the farm – it was called 'The Little Corporal' – Willie had said that it hadn't taken him very long to reach Nap's rank. Linnet answered the girl next to her:

'No, I don't suppose he'll wear uniform if he can help it. Depends how much time he's got. Of course, he has to do what he's ordered.'

'I thought he might come down dressed as an Air Commodore or as an Admiral, or something of that.'

'Who?'

'The King, of course. Who do you think I was talking about?'

Linnet didn't say, 'I thought you were talking about

Willie' – she answered instead:

'Oh yes, I daresay *he*'ll wear uniform. Sure to, I suppose.'

'But what uniform will he wear?' the girl went on. 'I know we're making stuff for the Army here, but then we've the Naval inspection side too.'

Another girl answered up: 'Perhaps he'll come in as a Colonel of the Marines.'

Linnet looked at the clock and wished it would click forward for her. Clocking-out time would take her nearer to Willie, while his train from the camp was bringing him home to her.

Labour Officer Miss Robinson came in. Her white turban made her face seem dark. She strode straight to the Blue-band. Two or three operatives looked up.

'Ten minutes before time, and we got to go down to canteen.'

'Wish they'd make up their bloody minds once for all!'

The workers went out.

Outside on the cleanway the conversation started up again.

'Funny idea hearing King speaking in our canteen when we won't be able to see him.'

'Yes. Royalty's heard and not seen. Contrary to children nowadays, Royalty is.'

The Labour Officer, walking a little way ahead, fell in with one of the foremen.

'Look at them nodding their heads together like a couple of old cousins at the seaside.'

'Like a regular Punch and Judy show, it is.'

'Talk, talk, talk; nothing but bloody talk!'

'There's been a blunder. We should have had this break some time back. The King must've begun his speech by now.'

Linnet wondered if Willie would be able to sleep in the train. It was difficult to get a seat in a train in wartime …

They said, 'We shan't hear much at this rate. The King will be gone by the time we get to the canteen.'

Linnet had a moment of fear. 'How terrible it would be if Willie went and missed his train! Still, it wouldn't do to think about that; no use meeting your troubles before they come to you.'

As they went into the canteen a voice was blaring out:

'… when I worked in't pit I was that black they couldn't tell me from coal, they couldn't. Now workers is all dressed in white, like angels, workers are—but they get job done just the same.'

Bewilderment was let loose. Questioning looks came flicker-flashing across the canteen from worker to worker, but the voice went on, giving out more sentences through the loud-speaker:

'When I was in Canada I said to my missus, "Can't 'ear what folks say for these Niagara Falls" and she said the sound of the water made her feel queer. I don't like water neither. I've got an iron constitution meself, see, so it might make it rust.'

Laughter followed the speech through the loud-speaker. If the audience in the main canteen could laugh, it was all right for the listeners in Group IV canteen to laugh too. They all went hooting out on a high note, and some started stamping their feet. Only Mrs Silas, the simpleton, spoke in a serious tone.

'Talks like us'n, King do,' she said.

One or two of the girls near her explained, 'It isn't 'im.'

'That's one thing certain, it isn't t'King.' But the voice of the distinguished visitor went amplifying on:

'You go down there, King, they told me, and talk to 'lads and lassies in war factory …'

In the main canteen the stage had been set as if for a concert. There were flowers and flags, and a piano wheeled up ready to note out the National Anthem at the end. There were two rows of clean wooden chairs on the platform. In the first row sat the Production Manager, Twizden, Captain Flore of the Home Guard, the Chief Clerk, the Chief Labour Officer, and Lyon, the Public Relations Officer; the Superintendent sat near the centre, looking as if he wished himself elsewhere; on his left side there was the Security Officer, Captain Quantock, and on the right the empty chair of the Guest of Honour. Walking up and down, and talking back and forth before the audience was a pudding-faced, check-suited, springy-heeled man with dark coarse hair and thick hands. The canteen was crowded. Only the kitchen staff behind the counter were spaced out: they stood about near the great food-heating cupboard, cross-talking to each other.

'Who is it?' Mrs Franklin asked in a steamed whisper.

'George King, same as they told us at the start.'

'Who is he?'

'Famous film star, George King is.'

'Used to be Lancashire lad before he went to Hollywood, George King did.'

'That's right. Comedian he wor' before he wor' gangster in films.'

'Plays murderers' parts, he does, in films.'

'Local boy makes bad – George King is!'

'George King! Never 'eard of im.'

'I tell you he's famous; always takes the part of big-shot gangster, he does.'

'Never seen 'im, I 'aven't. I don't like pictures with nothing but bloody guns and men chasing each other all over the place. Surely we got guns enough 'ere all day without seeing them on pictures.'

'Oh, I don't know. George King was very good actor, he was; but as he coom from Lancashire they couldn't understand a word he said when he got to Hollywood, so he always had silent parts at first. Not much talking, he didn't have, at the start, but he worn't idle, he always done the machine-gunning and that.'

'George King puts me in mind of Eddie Cantor, the way 'e goes galloping up and down the platform.'

George King was speaking out again: 'It wor' black time in Pot Banks when I went away to seek my fortune in America,' he said. 'Mind you, never expected to fall into films, but that's too long a story to tell you now, and maybe those of you who've been in blitz have got a story or two you could tell me yourselves. Of course, I've died plenty of times meself, but that wor' in pictures, that wor'. All they 'ad was blank ammunition, not the real stuff like you've got 'ere – as ' I 'eard when I was asked to coom down to talk to you. Some weeks back, it wor', they asked me. I was so scared I 'aven't got over it yet. Suppose lads and lassies were to drop something, I said.'

George King waited for the laughter to end. Superintendent smiled. Captain Flore of the Home Guard laughed silently, his shoulders shaking. There was no sign of the green-gaze of disappointment lifting from Quantock's face. Lyon frowned, thinking, 'Bloody tactless remark after that "blow" we had in the detonator shop! They should have shown me the script first. That's the worst of these spontaneous pep-talkers, they always make some blunder … suppose he'd been talking to the same shift that had the "blow", he'd have put his foot in it all right, both clogs foremost, the clumsy so-and-so …'

'Never thought I should get to know some of the big film stars I've seen on pictures,' George King said. 'I always thought I should be giving a turn once a fortnight at working-men's clubs, and making folks laugh, same as I used to; but when I got to Hollywood they made me a murderer. Fair miserable, my old woman was about that. Every day when I coom 'ome to tea she says to me, "How many you killed to-day, George," but whatever I said wor' wrong. If I told 'er I'd killed a lot, she said she didn't 'old with killin', and if I said we 'adn't got to the shooting part yet, she said I must've been in the canteen all day …'

Two policemen were waiting outside the main canteen.

'I could do with a cup of tea. How's George King getting on?'

'Still making em laugh, so we'd better stop 'ere till 'e's finished.'

'He started off by making me laugh, old George King did. When the car stopped at the gates I went straight up to ask for His Majesty's credentials, same as we have to do for everyone, even if it is the King. And, of course, I thought it was the King, seeing that we were expecting him. I heard the driver say, "It's George King," and I thought to myself, "Well, that's a bit familiar like," and then I had a quick look in the back of the car, and when I saw the suit he was wearing I was so surprised I didn't hand back his papers at once. So, up comes Quantock, interfering old bastard, wanting to see what I'm doing like … Steps up ever so smart, Quantock does … quite the Security Officer de luxe. He raised his hand to his hat; but it never got there, because old George King leaned forward out of the car and said: "Well, lad, I've coom a long way to 'av a look at you, and now they won't let me into bloody place"—fair mazed, old Quantock was! Won't do him no harm though, the bloody snob. Thinks he knows everything, he does. Fancy old Quantock expecting to see King George in Admiral's uniform, or something of that, and then seeing George King in comedian's check suit loud enough to make you deaf in both ears for the rest of your life. Looks like old Quantock hasn't got over it yet, and won't neither—not for some time, he won't.'

Cheering came from the canteen, quickly followed by the sound of chairs being scraped back along the wooden floor.

'That means George King has finished speech, so we can go in now.'

On Group IV, Canteen 3, the workers went back after the cheering. As they walked down the cleanway, Mrs Silas, the simpleton, said to white-turbanned Miss Robinson:

'That wor' King, that wor'.'

Miss Robinson answered, 'No; I'm afraid there's been some clerical mistake, that was George King, the film actor. He is one of the speakers booked by the Ministry some weeks ago, and somehow the names got confused. Of course, it's very disappointing for the whole factory when they were expecting to have a Royal visit.'

'Gave us a proper laugh, 'e did, though.'

'Gave him right royal welcome, workers did.'

They walked on to the workshop. Linnet remembered going to a gangster film with Willie in their home town, the day they'd gone in to get a present for his sister's birthday. George King had been playing the part of the gunman; she remembered it all very clearly–the day, the town, the shopping, the cinema. She often saw soldiers going to the pictures on Saturday afternoons in the town here; even when it was a fine day they queued up to see a film. She wondered if Willie ever went down to the pictures now; probably he wouldn't find much time since he'd been made a corporal. She had no clear idea of what his life was like at the present time; but, of course, she would be hearing all about it this evening. Perhaps she'd be made a Blue-band herself before long–being a Blue-band was something the same as a corporal, but more like a sergeant in some ways. After all, there was only one Blue-band to each workshop. Linnet, thinking about Willie, could only hear some of the conversation around her

'Fancy them making mistake about pep-talker!'

'Fancy them thinking it was Royalty instead of film star!'

'Took in Super and all though, must've done. He is a caution, old George King is! Wish he could come down more often though: wish he could come down when we're on night-shift: it's very slow on night-shift sometimes.'

Mrs Silas, the simpleton, said, 'It wor' King, worn't it? Said 'ed been in Canada—well, 'e *as* bin. Labour Officer said it wor' a mistake and it worn't King; but it wor' King. Thinks she knows bloody all, Labour Officer do.'

When the Blue shift went out most of the workers were still talking about the visit. A few girls from Group V, on their way home from the hostel, got into the same grey bus as Linnet.

'Came down on our Group, George King did.'

'Super showed him detonator, said a torpedo wouldn't work without it. George King said, "It's only a little thing; but don't drop it, lad, or none of us won't be 'ere to see blooming victory."'

'They showed George King rest-room, and Maggie 'ad bin taken there by the Blue-band; minor cut she 'ad, she was getting plaster put on 'er 'and, and George King coom straight in. Maggie spoke up, got 'im to write in the back of 'er coat, she did.'

'That's right, she come into shifting house and showed us her coat. There was her centre and clock number written down "LK 12 5/48" and then writ right across it "Luv from George King". She's a caution, Maggie is, know how to speak up for herself, she does.'

'Couldn't hardly get out of our canteen, George King couldn't. When he left, workers all crowded round him asking for his autograph and that.'

'Ar thought George King would be crushed when he left canteen.'

Linnet looked out of the window of the grey bus. The sky was still a clear blue; there were no clouds. She began to reckon up in her mind the hours before Willie could arrive at the hostel. He should reach the station in five or six hours, and then come straight to the hostel. She decided she would walk up the road to meet him.

Chapter Nine

Check Up

The day after King the comedian came down to Statevale it was given out, on every group, that the check-up on the identity cards had now been completed. The workers were to hand in their temporary passes to the policemen on duty at the inspection gate in exchange for their new cards.

When the White shift went out the men called out their names and numbers and handed in their cards, the policeman repeated the name and number, looked through the index files at his elbow, took in the temporary card, and gave out the permanent pass. The girls went through the same process, but they grumbled more than the men this time because they were more tired.

'It doesn't half take a time.'

'Yes, we shall be back at work before we've got out of the place if it goes on like it.'

'Number 1843217.'

'Your name?'

'Rose Waley.'

'Here you are then.'

'I wonder what's for dinner up at the hostel.'

'Whatever it is, it'll be cold by the time we get it.'

'Linnet Shore, number 1772041.'

'That's right; here's your new card.'

Old Charlie said, 'It wouldn't be so bad if they were handing out meat pies, would it?'

'Or pound notes.'

'No; that would be all right, that would.'

The man in the blue beret just ahead of Old Charlie was stopped. 'No pass for you, mate; you've got to go inside.'

'No pass for 'im?'

'*No pasaron.*'

The man in the blue beret looked round to see who had said this, and saw that it was the Welsh preacher's son; the blue beret man began to laugh, his thin bony shoulders shaking, then he went into the inspection hut. A man from Stepney said, 'I betcha they stop Old Charlie, they always stop him.'

Charlie reached the gate. 'Number 18485831,' he said.

'Your name?'

'Charles Dickson.'

'That's right. Chas Dickson, Number 18485832. You said 31.'

'I meant 32,' said Charlie.

'Here's your card, then.'

The line of workers from the Blue shift went on.

'What! you ain't been stopped, Charlie? How's that then?'

'Jameson must be falling down on his job these days; that's the third or fourth time they haven't stopped Old Charlie at the gate.'

A hundred and ninety-eight more workers went through without incident, and then Lofty spoke out his number. '6245843,' he said.

'What's your name?'

Lofty thought, 'Bluddy policeman, he should know all the foremen by sight. He hasn't got much else to do except to walk about memorizing faces'; but aloud he said, 'Thomas Loft's my name.'

'In there mate,' the policeman said, jerking his thumb over his shoulder.

'Silly sod must have made a mistake,' thought Lofty, and walked into the inspection room. A tall policeman stood by a table watching another policeman laboriously entering names, addresses, and times in a big book.

'In there,' said the tall policeman. 'The old man wants to see you.'

'What does he want to see me about?'

'About your identity card.'

Lofty knew there was nothing wrong with his card; he wondered if the policeman had been chosen for his tallness with the purpose of intimidating those who did not have any unnecessary height. Lofty was a short man himself. 'I should have been tall by rights; both my father and mother were tall, funny I should have stopped growing at fourteen, just when my father got sold up. We didn't get so much to eat afterwards; I wonder if it was anything to do with that.' Lofty smiled sourly at the tall policeman and went into Inspector Jameson's office.

Inspector Jameson seemed to be in a safe and strong position, barricaded behind his great bureau. It was an office-desk with steel-handled drawers on the right and on the left enclosing the plain-clothes policeman as if he was in an armoured car.

Inspector Jameson was looking down at some notes on his desk. The suit he wore was the same brown colour as the wood of the powerful bureau, so that Lofty had the impression that the Inspector's hands were severed from his body and he had simply unlocked one of the drawers in the desk, taken out a couple of hands, and laid them down on the smooth brown surface of the bureau. Lofty thought, 'I don't know what it is about Jameson, seems that he isn't hardly human; he makes me shiver.'

Above the head of the Inspector through the window behind his shoulders Lofty could see the workers who had gone through the inspection huts without question. At this height only their heads and shoulders could be seen. Lofty watched these industrial centaurs journeying up the hill homewards. Wondering when the Inspector would speak, Lofty wished he was with those of the Blue shift who had got away.

Inspector Jameson picked up an identity card which was lying on the desk beside him. He stared at it closely, then still without looking at Lofty he asked, 'Changed your address at all since you've been here?' Lofty hesitated. 'Not lately, I haven't,' he said. 'I did leave the landlady where I was staying at the start, but that was about a month after I first came here.'

The Inspector looked at Lofty sudden-sharp. 'Why did you do that?'

'Oh, I didn't fancy the food much, and it was rather too far from the factory for my liking.'

'Oh, so you like being near your work then,' said the Inspector. 'Some people don't.'

There was a short silence. 'What's your address now, then?'

'It's on the identity card, or should be,' said Lofty. 'I've been there a long time.'

'21 Willow Road.'

'That's right,' Lofty said. He thought, 'How did the bastard know; he wasn't looking at my card while he was talking?'

'So you're a foreman now.'

'Yes, that's right.'

'Where are you working?'

'Well, I was on Group IV—that's the Det Group as you know—then I moved over to that new job to help them out for a few days, and now I'm back in my own workshop—the Dets.'

Inspector Jameson said, 'Yes, that's it, Mr Loft. You were working for a while on the big hollow bomb group, wasn't you?'

To Lofty listening it seemed that Jameson stressed the word

'hollow', and very quickly there came back into his mind the memory of his conversation with the Labour Officer, Miss Robinson. 'One of those nights down on the Group it was, when everything was very still, moonlight it was, no one about, I went walking towards the Section Office when Miss Robinson's white turban came ghosting along towards me.' It seemed to Lofty as if in the stillness, the moonlight, and the cold air this conversation had been somehow crystallized; and again now, without willing it, the words came back and were ready to hand. '... You know, one of those big hollow bombs would hold a man's body, Miss Robinson. I often think how easy it would be to put a man into an empty bomb like that, and the next thing that would happen he'd be dropped over Germany inside the bomb. It's funny how often I think of that when I go round this Group on night-shift'; and Miss Robinson had looked at him in sudden surprise and answered, 'Now that's a good idea for a detective story, Lofty. You ought to write it. They're always troubling about how to get rid of the body after a murder in those books.'

'Well that would be a way to do it, see.'

'Yes, it would be a good idea, Lofty,' Miss Robinson had said, in her rather carefully clear voice. 'Of course I don't read detective stories myself; but my mother, who is eighty-six, reads every one she can get her hands on. She was reading one the other day about a man burning someone in a motor-car. Apparently he set it alight; there was some sort of confused identity anyhow he hoped they'd never find any trace of the body.'

'Yes, but my idea is better than that, Miss Robinson, because the body wouldn't ever be found. How could it be? It would be dropped down on Germany inside the bomb.' It was curious that this talk came back to him now, this casual conversation with one of the Labour Officers. There had been many such—but why should he remember this talk rather than any of the others?

'But the bombs are full when we drop them over enemy territory, aren't they?' said Jameson, and as he said this he looked directly at Lofty.

Lofty's senses panicked. He searched his memory for some handy sentence that would suit any occasion, something that wouldn't give his thoughts away and wouldn't mean too much. 'That's right,' he said.

Inspector Jameson picked up the identity card from the top of the desk and handed it to Lofty. 'Do you know the owner of this card?' he asked.

Lofty took the identity card and read the name, 'Matthew Reid, No 6535201.' 'No, I don't know him,' Lofty said. He handed the card back to the Inspector.

Inspector Jameson rang a bell on top of the desk. 'Proper bureaucrat he is!' thought Lofty.

The tall policeman came back. Inspector Jameson said, 'Will you bring Mr Loft's new permanent pass in, the number is 6245843—the name is Thomas Loft.'

'He's learning my name and number off by heart now,' Lofty thought.

'You'll leave your old card with us, won't you, Mr Loft,' said Jameson, and suddenly he smiled.

'I gave my old card to the copper on duty as I came in,' said Lofty. He thought, 'Jameson seems to be at his worst when he gets grinning.' When the tall policeman came back with the card, Lofty took it from him and put it in his notecase. He did all this very slowly, not wanting to appear hurried.

Lofty walked out, the men were still going towards the inspection gate.

It seemed to Lofty that the handing in of the old cards, the shuffling through the file boxes, and the giving out of the new cards was going more quickly now. Several of the men from Lofty's own group went through the gate without being stopped.

Once through the gates Lofty began to hurry in the hope of catching up with some of his mates. He got out of breath running up the hill, so he slowed down and walked along breathless and troubled about his interview with Jameson. Why should Jameson have asked to see him? He'd never done so before. It was just like Jameson to try to throw dust in Lofty's eyes by pretending that he wanted to talk to him about his new permanent pass in the factory. It must have been an excuse, because Lofty knew that there was nothing wrong with his identification card.

Oh, well, it was of no use to bother about it any more. Jameson must have been a snooper since his earliest infancy. It was not a job that many folks would take to, so if Jameson liked it let him get on with it. To hell with him.

It had been a difficult week on the group. Shortage of labour, a high percentage of men absent from work owing to 'flu. You'd got to expect it in the fifth year of the war. They were tired now. One couldn't help noticing that. They hadn't got the resistance they had at the start, but the overseer Gluckstein didn't seem to get 'flu, and he didn't seem to show any sign of tiredness. One might have known that he wouldn't. The Jew Gluckstein was strong. He worked overtime, he walked about on the group with strong quick steps. He was in with everyone; you had only to watch him to know that, in the pubs, with the workers, talking to Geoffrey Doran, the Time and Motion bloke, smiling with his white, healthy teeth at the barmaid, the pretty one who was a policeman's daughter, and always working towards promotion. Gluckstein would get himself a foreman's job before long. There was nothing to stop him, although there were plenty of men far more fitted to be foremen than Gluckstein, the stepped-up sheeny! But

Gluck would be the one to get all the good jobs; trust him. Lofty spat on the ground.

At night on the big hollow bomb group, Gluckstein had been supervising some of the screwing up of the bombs. It was quiet at nights down on the group. When it was dark and there was no moon, small lights with rubber-wheeled trucks showed up so that the lights themselves seemed to be travelling along at hip-height as if of their own volition. The big bombs lying on the ground made Lofty think of the corpses of monstrous mammals, but on moonlit nights it was all different. The trucks were like living animals then, and the bombs like whales washed up on a deserted shore. 'Bigger and better bombs', that was a phrase you often saw about.

A few days back Lofty had heard one of the Civil Servants in the canteen talking in a sham-technical sort of way about a bomb, about the blast, and how many people it would be likely to kill within a certain radius. How easily everyone had taken to this talking of death in figures. It seemed as if it was all right to kill if it was all arranged by numbers, only two or three hundred casualties, only a few thousands, or only about a dozen. Everything was all right as long as you did not know your enemy personally. We must all get down to these anonymous numbers, but supposing you did know your enemy personally, supposing there was one enemy you hated like Gluckstein, then you must be very careful, you must not do anything to hurt him.

'Well, I don't see it that way myself, surely it would make more sense to kill someone you knew. If you can drop a bomb on individuals, why can't you drop an individual in a bomb? If you can drop thousands of tons of bombs on hundreds of individuals, why can't you drop one individual in one bomb?' Lofty shrugged his shoulders. 'It makes you think, don't it?' His foot struck against a stone at the end of the road. He kicked it, and it went over. A large insect–must have been a queen ant—ran out from underneath the stone. Lofty stamped on it. 'That's Gluckstein!' Half in the grass, half in the earth, disturbed by the overturning of the stone, was a large spider. It did not turn round as the other insect, it sat quite still. Lofty stamped on that too. 'That's Jameson!' He walked on. 'You're on the big bomb group, aren't you? They're hollow bombs there, aren't they?' He went over the questions in his mind. 'But they're full when they go over Berlin, aren't they?'

A man by the name of Hopkinson overtook him. 'Evening, Lofty. I see they stopped you at the inspection.'

'Yes,' Lofty said. 'There was something wrong with my identification card. That's why they did it. My name was spelt wrong, a clerical error you see. They only wanted to ask me about that.'

'Oh—ah!' Hopkinson and Lofty walked on together in silence.

'I turn off here.'

The other one said, 'You're billeted in the town, aren't you, Lofty?'

'That's right, Willow Street, No 21.'

'What's it like there?'

'Might be worse,' Lofty said.

'Oh, ah! Coming up to the pub to-night?'

'Yes; I expect I shall be up later on.'

'Oh, ah, good-night.'

Lofty nodded good-night and walked away. In Willow Street he saw a thick-set policeman walking quickly down a road with his arm under the elbow of a little man wearing a check suit. The little man was shuffling along, though Lofty couldn't see his face, as despair was symbolized in the set of his shoulders. The policeman had the air of someone wishing to dissociate himself with the present proceedings. 'I haven't seen anything like that since I was last in Soho,' thought Lofty. 'Poor bastard. Fancy being taken off to the police-station on an evening like this!' Lofty did not know the meaning of his own thought, 'on an evening like this'. It was no different from any other evening. It was getting dark; it was getting cold—as it always did at this hour. The little man and his escort were already out of sight. Lofty squared up his shoulders, opened the door of his billet, 21 Willow Street, and went in.

II

'No 273482.'

'Name?'

'Miss Ysabette Jones.'

'All right.'

Ysabette Jones tripped into the police office. The tall policeman said: 'The inspector wants to see you, Miss Jones.' She followed him into the inspector's room.

'Good evening. I've got your identity card here.'

'Good evening, Inspector Jameson. Oh yes, my identity card; it's my old one, isn't it? I shall be glad to have a new one. It was getting very shabby; whenever I took it out of my bag it look'd shabby. So I got a nice case for it with a monogram. My grandmother gave it to me, but the card looks very shabby inside it. Every time I see it I think that.'

Inspector Jameson stared at the talking girl.

'Well, surely you know you can't take a bag down on the group—not past the contraband hut at any rate; that's against the regulations in the Danger Area. You ought to know that.'

'Oh, but I did know that. I always give it up at the contraband hut. My friend Miss Winslow's one of the Welfare Officers, so I didn't do anything that was against regulations, did I? I was not talking about what happens on work. I meant when I went to the town to have dinner at the Bristol Arms. I often do that in the evening when I am on day-shift. I have dinner there with my friend, Miss Winslow. She likes to go there, because she has always been used to proper dinner.'

The Inspector looked at the card before him, and began reading through the instructions. 'Eyes blue.' He looked at the girl and thought, 'They don't look exactly blue, but I suppose that'll pass; it's odd the way one side of her face is not the same as the other. One eyebrow is much higher, one side of the mouth more drooping. It seems as if her face has been put together like two negatives of a photograph fitted together, but one of them on the wrong side. Nose retroussé.' Inspector Jameson smiled sourly, 'That's a funny word to use. I suppose she was trying to be a bit on the cosmopolitan side.'

'Well, Miss Jones,' he said aloud, 'Would you mind just looking sideways. I am trying to check up on this description.'

Ysabette Jones turned her head to the right, but she went on talking. 'You know I've only got this job here temporarily,' she said. 'I want to be a Welfare Officer really, like my friend Miss Winslow. She'd be very happy to have me helping her down there on her group.'

Ysabette Jones had seemed to be aiming her sentences at the Inspector like fast-thrown snowballs. During the last few moments the snowballs had been going a bit wide, but when she turned again and faced him it seem as if he was the only target of her talk. 'Everybody says I'd make a good Welfare Officer,' she told him.

'Well, you would not like it really. It only means hearing other people's troubles and having to get to know all about them.'

'I like to know all about people,' Ysabette said. 'Don't you?'

Inspector Jameson felt suddenly ill at ease, so that he was glad when the talk went galloping on in another direction. He thought, 'I recognize the type; there is no need to listen to what she is saying.' He went on studying the description.

'Hair brown.'

'Would you mind taking off your scarf, Miss Jones?'

Ysabette Jones began to untie the scarf she had tied round her head, but it took her some time. It got into knots and the loop caught round her wrist. Her hair was half-pinned, half-tied. It had rather a dusty look and was untidy.

'Brown, yes that's a rough description,' Inspector ' Jameson said. 'Here's your new card, Miss Jones. That is all.' Ysabette Jones did not move away. She stood swaying on her feet. All expression had left her face as if she had forgotten the last things she had been talking about and why she was in this room at this hour. When the tall policeman came in she went sleep-walking out on his arm.

Jameson rang for the other policeman and said to him, 'Check up on the name Winslow, will you. See if there is anybody of that name on the strength; and if so, where she is and what job she has.'

Inspector Jameson, the good up-graded policeman, considered it his duty to get a rough estimate of current thought, its psychological implications, and the way it was going or might go. He had a list to hand of all the psychoanalysts, psychiatrists, social workers, and psychotherapists. He'd got their dossiers down. He had taken some trouble about this, because in his opinion they were a dangerous crowd.

'Those are some of the fellows we are going to have a lot of trouble with after the war,' he thought. Psychoanalysis was a great revolutionary movement; he knew this and considered it was his job to watch it. He had one or two textbooks here. He took one out of the shelf now and ran his fat white finger down the index until he came to the word 'Schizophrenia—split mind. A mental disorder frequently starting in adolescence and characterized by progressive deterioration and a divorce as between thought and feeling. Hallucinations are common and tend to be of a grandiose and fantastic kind.'

The policeman came back. 'There is no one by the name of Winslow in this factory, sir.'

'No new Labour Officer, Welfare Officer, recently recruited worker, or even stewardess up at the hostel?'

'No; none, sir. Not even an operative, neither male nor female. No one in the whole place by the name of Winslow, sir.'

'No, I thought there would not be,' said Inspector Jameson.

The policeman said, 'We've got a man outside here to see you. It's the two hundredth man we stopped at the gate according to your instructions, sir. His name's Gluckstein.'

'Split mind is also –' Inspector Jameson looked up. 'Send him in,' he said, 'and check up on Ysabette Jones, the operative I have just seen, and bring me back a report, will you?'

'Very good, sir.'

The policeman went out. Gluckstein came in.

'Good evening, Mr Gluckstein.'

Gluckstein smiled. 'Good evening to you,' he said.

Jameson stared at him. This chap is too damned civil, he thought; was it possible he was laughing at Jameson or somehow trying to make a fool of him? He continued with the interview.

'Have you changed your address at all?'

This time Gluckstein did not answer at once. Jameson repeated the question.

'Changed your address at all?'

'No,' Gluckstein said.

'Where are you living now?'

'Same place,' said Gluckstein, '18 Devon Road, just by the fountain in the square.'

'What's your job?' Jameson asked.

'I am an overseer on Group IV. I am in the det shop.'

'You've got some Irish workers there, haven't you?'

'There are one or two.'

'I suppose you have already formed your opinion of them?'

There was a silence, and then Gluckstein answered in an unnaturally loud voice, 'They're good workers, very good workers indeed.'

Jameson looked at the brown-skinned man before him, and wondered why he shouted. He'd often noticed this habit of shouting amongst people working in factories, the noise in the machine shops made them shout as if they had long since recognized noise as their enemy, but here in this factory silence seemed to affect them the same way. There were no machines, it was the humans that took the place of machines.

'Oh yes,' said Jameson, 'I believe they are good workers; I thought you might have some opinion on these subjects as you'd be likely to be more observant, wouldn't you, you being a foreigner?'

'A foreigner!' said Gluckstein. 'I'm not a foreigner; I'm English'

Jameson always put the same questions at this interview, but not always in the same order. There was nothing in the questions, of course; but he believed that it was possible through the answers and the way in which the answers were given, to get an idea of how the heart of the factory was ticking. In a few moments they would be stopping the two hundredth man again according to his orders. 'Stop every two-hundredth man at the gate,' he had said, 'and send him in to me. The same thing with the girls. They won't know it's by chance. They'll think I have picked them out, each one separately, for some reason. People often give themselves away. You never know what you might find out.' He decided to dismiss this man. He did not want to keep the new man waiting, because he did not want to build up unpopularity for himself. Of course the day would come when he would not have to trouble about that, because he would have more power. All the time he was working for this, but he could wait. He knew how to wait for what he wanted. 'Well, I think that is all,' he said.

Another silence. 'That's all,' he repeated.

'Can I have my identity card and my permanent pass?' Gluckstein asked.

A wave of irritation swept over Jameson; he was angry with Gluckstein for reminding him that he was being inefficient.

'All in good time,' he said. He stared down at the card, and said, 'You're very fortunate to get it back.'

Gluckstein took the two cards, and went out without saying good-bye.

The tall policeman came back. 'I have checked up on Ysabette Jones, sir.'

'Yes?' Jameson said.

'She was reported by her Labour Officer to be medically examined. It seems she can't work; she just sits staring and doing nothing half the time. And in the canteen she threw a couple of spoons at another operative.'

Jameson said, 'I thought so.' He began to smile again. He was almost pleased when he had been able to sum up a set of circumstances—a clear case of schizophrenia, just as he had thought. He understood the contemporary world; you had to nowadays if you wanted to have any influence.

Gluckstein slowed down his steps when he got out of the Inspector's office. He did not wish to show any signs of uneasiness. It was all beginning again, the persecutions which were always in his thoughts. It spread through him like a fever. All his life seemed to be like that: a recurring fever, an illness that localized itself and came out in some definite form, and after this he'd be better for a while; but at the back of his mind he knew that it would be there to happen again. It came back quite easily into his mind, the day he had asked his brother, 'What are Jews? We are Jews, aren't we? Is everybody a Jew, or is it only us? Which of the boys in our street are Jews?'

His brother had answered him at first, and then suddenly said, 'I am sick of your questions, see, I don't want to hear any more of them.'

But Gluckstein had become so preoccupied with this question that for a time he had gone about getting answers and writing them out in a notebook.

'What is the truth about the Jews?'

Charlie Roberts, a tall, fair-haired boy at Gluckstein's school, had answered, 'Oh, I don't know, some people don't like them because they work hard. They can't seem to learn to loaf about, dunno why it is.'

Another boy said, 'Jews, oh, they're the same as other folk; there's nothing to it.'

Another, a Roman Catholic, answered, 'They persecuted Our Lord, and they didn't ought to have done it. Still, He was a Jew, too, and so was all the Apostles and that.'

And another, 'Oh, Jews! They're a nuisance; they go to synagogues on Saturdays and set up a caterwauling, always having feastdays, they are. I don't see why they want to be so different.'

An older boy had said, 'They're delicate; haven't got any strength; always ill, Jews are.'

Another fair-haired boy with a turned-up nose and straight ginger hair had answered, 'I'm Jewish, didn't you know?'

An Italian boy said, 'Jews! they're foreigners.'

The child sitting next to Gluckstein in class had remarked, 'There's been a proper mix-up of people with all these wars and emigrations, and I reckon we're all Jewish by now. And I reckon either no one's Jewish by now, or else we all are. Must be, stands to reason.'

For some time after this Gluckstein had not troubled any more. There had been other interests, cigarette card albums, boxing matches, street cricket, and so on. But although he did not have to think about it, all the time the horror was there, like a leopard waiting in a dark wood, suddenly it would leap out and bare its teeth. Then when it was driven off it would run back to lie in wait again.

Gluckstein's brother enlisted and fought in the war. After the battle of Passchendaele he was reported missing and a few weeks later his death was confirmed, and one of these nights there was an air raid over London. Gluckstein was taken by his father to shelter in a tube station. They saw a woman crying on the steps. Gluckstein's father tried to console her, told her there was no reason to be frightened. He did not believe that many Zeppelins could get to London, but she shouted back at him. 'This war is terrible! Both my sons have been sent home wounded; but you wouldn't understand that, being a foreigner.' After the raid was over, Gluckstein had walked home with his father in silence.

Before the war ended Gluckstein had tried to enlist, but they had laughed at him because they could tell at once that he was under age. The same pattern had repeated itself again here, a pattern with variations. He tried to enlist in this district, but in the next town. He had taken a bus and gone on twelve miles away. But it had been the same thing. They had his address. 'Sorry, sonny; it's no use your giving us a false address and hoping to get into the Army. You fellows from the factory often come up trying to enlist. Several of your pals have been doing the same this week. Seems to be an epidemic of it. But we've got means to find out where you come from. We wish we could help you, but there's nothing for it. You've got to stay in the factory.'

Inspector Jameson had said, 'You changed your address lately?' Well, that must have been why he said it. No doubt it was down in the dossier. Jameson knew about him giving a false address and trying to enlist. Perhaps it would not be such a serious thing for another man to give a false address, but they'd be sure to stress it in his case because of him being a Jew. When Gluckstein thought back on it, he knew he was glad that his father had died before the Jewish persecution in Germany. That was all part of the pattern, being pleased when people you loved died because you knew what existence in an inhuman world was like.

Gluckstein's father had died four years before Mosley's men came marching into the East End. Once when they came down Gluckstein was standing near a young Jewish girl. She was part of the crowd who were watching, but taking no part either in attack or in defence. A swanky, smiling black-shirt saw her and shouted, 'Go back to the Polish Ghetto where you come from!' Three men rushed forward, but instantly the black-shirt was surrounded by a bodyguard of Fascists enlisted from the boxing booths. A fight started up. The Jewish girl, terrified, ran all the way home. She ran to the top of the tenement building where she had been born and threw herself down. The ambulance came. Two men who had been in the crowd that afternoon went immediately and volunteered to fight against the Fascists in Spain.

Gluckstein passed Ysabette Jones tripping along the road beside three girls from her shift.

'The Inspector picked me out from everyone; he wanted to see me specially. He didn't exactly tell me I should be made a Welfare Officer, but he hinted at it—of course that's all he could do.'

None of the girls answered Ysabette Jones. Phyllis Jenkins said:

'I like "noons" better than any other shift, because it's the only time I can go to the pictures in peace.'

'Oh you and your pictures, always going to pictures you are. I like "noons", too; not for the pictures, though, but because I can get a bit of a lie in bed in the mornings. And my mother always brings me up a cup of tea.'

Ysabette Jones said, 'The Inspector thinks they're going to give me a better job because I am educated, you see.'

The fourth girl said, 'No wonder you like "'noons", if your mum brings you your breakfast in bed. I'm staying in billets down Devon Road.'

Gluckstein walked past them. The Welsh girl was working long hours, although she had a bad industrial history. Ysabette Jones was imprisoned in her own sick mind, isolated from everyone. The other two girls were homesick, but to Gluckstein they seemed to be free because they were not Jewish. He stopped at the Badminton pub and went in to get some cigarettes. Two or three of his workmates were there and two coloured American soldiers. The barmaid was saying, 'You come from O-ee-O, and you from Massershoesits.' The man with the hair that fitted close to his head like an astrakhan cap said, 'It's Ohio and Massachusetts.' The barmaid shook her head, 'O-ee-O and Massershoesits, that's where you come from,' she said.

The close-curled coloured man said, 'No, mam, Ohio and Massachusetts.'

Red-haired Tom from Group IV said, 'Obstinate, ain't she, mate?'

The other coloured man laughed loudly, slapped his knee, and answered, 'Sure she is.'

'I'd like to see your country,' said red-haired Tom, and a dark-haired miner said, 'I wouldn't mind going over there myself.' Welshmen are very fond of travelling.

'It must be swell,' said the barmaid. The laughing coloured man answered, 'What could be sweller?'

'Do you like it here?' one of the girls from the detonator group asked, and both coloured men answered together, 'We like it fine.'

Gluckstein leant up against a bar drinking down his pint.

'Have you got twenty Players you can let me have?' he asked the barmaid.

'I think we can manage that,' she told him. He put his hand in his pocket for half a crown and handed the coin over to her. 'Here, what's this?' she said in her good-natured way, 'You trying to Jew me down or what?'

Gluckstein looked at the coin, found it was a florin, said, 'Sorry,' and handed her four more pennies, then he went out without finishing his beer.

'What's the matter with him?' asked the barmaid.

'Expect he's tired; works on our Group, he does; overseer he is; one of the best fellows we've got there,' said red-haired Tom.

The Welshman said, 'Good fellow is Gluckstein, not like some of the foremen he isn't. Very profligate some of the foremen are.'

The three girls, followed by Ysabette Jones, went walking homewards. Ysabette turned off to the hostel. The other three went on towards Devon Road. Phyllis Jenkins said, 'Dai might be coming up to-night.'

'Working late is he?'

'Yes; he's never sure when he can get away now. I'll write my name in the road so's he can see we've been this way.' She took a piece of white chalk out of her pocket.

'You can't write your name in the road, it'll take up too much room. Just put your initials.'

'All right,' Phyllis said. She chalked her initials across the road, "P J". 'I wonder what he'll think when he sees that.'

'Think you're daft, most likely.' They walked on.

When the last two-hundredth man was stopped at the gate and brought in to see Inspector Jameson, it was almost dark. The questions went through Jameson's mind before he spoke them out. 'Changed your address lately?' That was always a good question to get people rattled. 'What Group are you working on now?' Jameson always liked to see a flicker of fear through men's eyes. You knew you were getting somewhere then.

'I hear you wanted to see me?'

Inspector Jameson looked up suddenly, startled. The man opposite him with his coat collar turned up was H D Whistler, Superintendent of Statevale. Inspector Jameson found himself forced to think fast. He said, 'Oh, I am very sorry to trouble you, Mr Whistler, I hoped you'd have time to call in, but I didn't want to disturb you. I heard that you'd lost your dog.'

'Pitcher?' said Whistler. 'No, he's all right; he's up at home.'

'Oh, I am glad to hear that, sir. It must have been a mistake then. One of the policemen down by the other gate told me. I don't know where he got the idea from. I didn't think the little fellow would get lost. Always keeps close to your heels, doesn't he?' Inspector Jameson coughed to give himself time to think up another sentence, then he told the Superintendent that he'd been going through the checking up of the new issue of identity cards and permanent passes. 'I arrange to stop every two-hundredth man, sir, and have a chat with him just to see how things are going on.'

'Is that really necessary?' asked Whistler.

'Oh, I think so, sir. I always like to have a friendly chat with some of the fellows to get to know them, and then of course we do get some tricky customers down here in war-time, you know. Bound to.'

'Oh, well, that's your province,' said Whistler. 'I don't have to interfere with all that. I've got enough on my plate already.'

'I expect you have, sir. I think everyone has got their new cards and passes all right on the Blue shift now, sir.'

'Good-oh, good-oh,' said the Superintendent. He hurried out.

Jameson sent for the policeman on duty outside and asked him if he knew who had just left. 'The two-hundredth worker you asked me to stop,' the man answered.

'That,' said Inspector Jameson, 'was the Superintendent, Mr Whistler himself. Have you seen Super before?'

The policeman was a slow-thinking man. It was the first day he had been up at the inspection gate. Until now he'd been on another group four miles away.

'Yes; I have seen him before,' he said, 'but I have never seen him without his Burberry and his dog. He comes in at all hours. I have never known him go out with a shift before.'

The two other policemen waited in the small room. 'Jameson's still on at Davies for sending Whistler in to see him. Wonder what he's saying.'

'Oh, he'll go on at him for hours. You know Jameson when he gets started. Must be in a terrible temper by now.'

'Yes; I shouldn't like to be Davies. But, mind you, it must have frightened old Jameson to have found himself face to face with Super.'

'Yes; he can't put on airs and show off in front of Super, can he?'

'Expect he wishes he could, though.'

'Wonder what he's saying to Davies.'

'Expect he's letting himself go. Shouldn't like to be Davies. Wouldn't do for him to have too much power, would it? Never know what he might be doing.'

'That's right. But he won't get much out of Davies. Used to be a miner once, Davies was. Welshmen are very independent, Welshmen are.'

Gluckstein walked down Devon Street; when he was nearing No 18 he saw the mark. It was the same mark he had seen in the East End years earlier. It was chalked in white on the road.

'P J' – Perish Judah.

It was getting cold. Damp too. It often started to rain at this hour. Gluckstein touched his forehead. Two drops of sweat fell on to the back of his hand.

Chapter Ten

Snowed In

The Red shift coming home from night work walked into breakfast at eight o'clock. The White shift were on 'noons' now, the two till ten work-day; they breakfasted with the Blue shift. Although they all came in together, it was easy to tell the White shift workers from the Blue because of the fatigue furrowed into the faces of the night workers.

As soon as the night workers reached the hostel they went over to their sleeping blocks to wash, but soap and water could not wash away their tired look.

Miss Robinson, the Labour Officer, had walked over to breakfast early from the staff sleeping block. She sat at one of the long wooden tables watching the workers come in while she jammed her bread and drank her tea.

As they went up to the counter to get their food, a man from the Blue shift told the others, 'It was snowing when we left; we were lucky to get back when we did; it's coming down fast now.'

One of the girls from the White shift said, 'Weather don't make any difference to me. I never notice what sort of day it is; I can't understand why folks are always belly-aching about the weather.'

Linnet of the Blue shift came and sat down at Miss Robinson's table. She had a cup of tea in one hand, a plate of bacon in the other; she put them down on the table, did not say anything, ate and drank very slowly, and stopped every now and then to stare window-wards at the falling snow. Miss Robinson remembered that Linnet was the one whose husband had been on leave; she was the girl who had taken the willow herb home from the factory, gone into the town to get material for a new dress, and moved over to the married quarters.

'Well,' Miss Robinson said, 'I suppose your husband's gone back now?'

'Yes,' Linnet answered. 'He's gone back.'

'Never mind,' Miss Robinson said. 'He's sure to be getting some more leave soon, and you'll be seeing him again. What do you think of the married quarters here?'

'It wasn't any good, Miss,' Linnet said. 'It was as bad for him as it was me; we couldn't do nothing.' Linnet returned to the eating of her breakfast: tea, bacon, tea, bacon. Her meal card was on the table beside her; the unused coupons across one corner read, 'Breakfast, Breakfast; snack, snack.'

Miss Robinson said, 'Perhaps it was being in a strange place that upset you both. Everything would be all right if you were back home in your own surroundings.'

'I don't know,' Linnet said. 'Once everything's wrong it don't go right again. Once you've been separated for a long time it's not the same; even our own home would seem different to us now. I don't know why it is, but nothing seemed to be right with me and Willie.'

Nordie and the hare-like cinema projectionist came to the table. The projectionist was protesting; but Miss Robinson, preoccupied with personal problems, did not listen, nor did Nordie; but the girl went whining on in a thin voice, needing neither the stimulus of agreement nor of disagreement. 'I was showing a film in Canteen Eight Four when our Superintendent came in and told me to move the apparatus back a couple of feet; it got the whole thing out of focus, and made me feel a fool. I'd had difficulties enough already with the shop stewards collecting the dues, and then someone turning on the light in the kitchens, then Mrs Karslake coming in at that moment was the last straw –'

Miss Robinson wondered if the White shift would be able to get to work before the snow became too heavy.

'– and Mrs Karslake never likes anyone to get any praise,' said the cinema projectionist. 'She went into Canteen C7 and asked if I'd been in there, and one of the canteen girls said, "Oh yes, I've seen her, a very nice-spoken young lady, wearing a brown head-scarf," and Mrs Karslake said, "Nice-spoken; then it can't have been any of my girls"–now I don't mind how hard I work, but I do like to be recognized for what I do –'

After breakfast, the Blue shift went back across the snow to their sleeping blocks. Most of the White shift stayed in the main building all morning, some sang to the thumping accompaniment of a piano in the assembly room, others listened to the radio in the recreation room, wrote letters, got books from the library, played cards and dominoes, bought stamps, cigarettes, and newspapers, or sat in the café talking, drinking tea, and staring out at the snow; and every now and then one would say to another, 'Wonder if we shall get to work in this; it's coming down very thick now.'

After the midday meal they were ready to go out on a shift again. The buses drove right in to the hostel gates; the drivers got down and went stamping about complaining, and saying they wished everyone would hurry into their places. 'The journey won't be a treat in all this anyhow.'

The voyage to Statevale by bus through snow took three times its usual time. A mood of silent gloom came down on the minds of the travellers; none of them talked till they had descended from the bus, gone through the inspection gate, and got into the Danger Area. Then they looked around them, and began to speak about the strangeness of Statevale under snow.

'Doesn't it seem closed in, just as if it had got smaller since yesterday?'

All along the cleanways men were working with large wooden spades clearing away the snow; some of the workshops were shut, most of them were still snow-covered.

'Gawd, looks like our workshop's gone, doesn't it?'

'Yes; looks like it never had been there, doesn't it?'

Some of the shift house women had not arrived, and those who had been working on the last shift were talking about it. 'You see, dear, we shift house workers have been here since the start of the place, and we knows what we're about; we remembers the bad snows of three years ago, and how we didn't get home for two days; so you can't blame those that haven't managed to get here, can you? – I wouldn't have come myself if I hadn't been here already.' Most of the outgoing shift house workers started back for home. 'Got to get Dad's tea this evening'; or, 'There's the children to put to bed'; or 'No one to see to things at home if I'm not there.' Volunteers were asked to work in the shifting house. Two canteen workers came in; some unskilled workers were sent to work in the canteens; many of the workshops were short of their right numbers; some of them were shut. The snow started to fall again; it grew dark early, but everywhere there was an atmosphere of friendliness.

Miss Robinson went round the workshops on her group. She thought, 'It's wonderful what a change in routine can do.' They were singing already; the singing usually started up at night, but not at such an early hour. In Workshop IV3, one girl said to another, 'Want to go to the lav, duck?' The other answered, 'Don't mind if I do.'

This conversation was carried on in the mood of one man asking another to have a drink at a nearby pub. The women were not allowed to walk along the cleanways alone at night. Soon the two set out together on the expedition, first to the lavatory. Then one would say to the other, 'I've got a bit of a cough, I think I'll go to Nurse.' They walked on together to see Nurse; they talked to her about the snow; a girl was lying on a sofa in the rest room, having fallen off the cleanway and twisted her ankle–they talked to her about the snow. Then they went to wash their hands at the Ablutions; the Ablutions woman was a large, home-like woman, welcoming, shaped like a sugar-loaf. They talked to her about the snow, too; then they wended their way back along the white cleanway.

When they got into the workshop again, the Overseer said, 'How can we get on with the work with you two away all the time? There was several who wanted to go and couldn't.' The two girls returned to their work, saying to each other, 'I expect Blue-band wanted to go off herself,' and 'That's right, thinks she knows bloody all, Blue-band does!' And from the journey out down the cleanway, the conversation, the return, and the argument with the overseer, was all a convention, a routine recognized and agreed on by workers, overseer, and Labour Officers alike. Without such conventions the monotony, the fatigue, and the nature of the destructive work itself would have made existence impossible.

Before the ten o'clock break Miss Robinson went round the workshops saying that the Super would speak to them in the canteen. At ten o'clock in the canteen the Security Officer's voice came through the loud-speaker first.

'Now, boys and girls, some of you may have noticed that there has been a spot of snow round here. Unfortunately the bus drivers have noticed it too, and they won't be able to make it. Only a certain number of the night-shift will be able to get in, and there won't be enough buses to take you all home, so that I'm afraid you'll have to make up your minds to stay here. We will make you as comfortable as possible, but those of you who are married and worried about their children at home had better see their Labour Officers. They'll get through to the nearest police-station for you, where volunteers from Scouts, Guides, and WVS are waiting to take messages. In the meantime I wish you all good-night, sleep well, and dream of a white Christmas. Oh, wait a moment, the Superintendent wants to speak to you.'

The Superintendent said, 'Mr Quantock has just explained all the facts to you, so that I have nothing to add except to say I am sorry and it can't be helped. Some of the night-shift are coming in now. Of course we will get you all away as soon as we can, we hope, in the morning. All supervisory staff are staying on. Thank you very much. Good-night.'

Complete silence, then chatter-yapper all over the canteen. 'He said some of the night-shift were coming up, so there must be some buses available. Why can't we go back in them?'

'Because there aren't enough, same as Super said.'

'He don't say much, do he, Super don't. Not like old Quantock is he? Full of talk old Quantock is. Security Officer – talk about careless talk. Seems old Quantock would talk himself silly if he was given a chance.'

'Yes; that's right. I like Super, very quiet, Super, isn't he?'

'Yes; they say he's a very clever chemist, Super is.'

Two women from the shift house were completely absorbed in the arrangements for the evening. 'I must get back to the shift house now, because Mrs Judd will want to come up and have a cup of tea.'

'I expect we shall have a busy time with all them young girls sleeping on the floor.'

'They'll be bringing blankets up from the surgery like they did last night when we were snowed in. Came up in the ambulance, blankets did.'

'Yes; I've got to see to all that in my shift house too, because my workers are contact workers. We shall have to keep our blankets separate in the morning. They wouldn't be able to go down in the ambulance with the other blankets, our blankets won't – all covered in yellow powder they'll be.'

'I'll be going up to see Labour Officer first. I must have

someone to go round to my house. My Billie, he's a good lad he is, sixteen years old now, he'll look after the little 'uns as much as he is able; but he's on early turn, and that means getting up at four in the morning to get to pithead. So who's to get the little 'uns off to school, I'm sure I don't know.'

Some of the night-shift came in talking about the snow. They said there hadn't been many waiting at the bus stop. It had been difficult to get the buses up the hill. They had to walk a good part of the way. Some of the men had taken their socks off and left them in the shift house to dry. Others had got extra pairs with them.

Lofty singled out the men who were wearing their shoes on their bare feet and sent them back to the shifting house to dry them. 'If you haven't got another pair of socks with you, wait till the ones you came in are dry, and then put them on before you come back here. Can't have any of you getting rash when there's no call for it. Use your loaf, will you.' He shrugged his shoulders. 'It's like looking after a lot of blooming kids.'

Lofty said to the White shift, 'I know it's the time for you to go off now, but we are short of workers for the night. So if some of you want to help us out a bit you can.'

Most of the men and girls said they'd work till the first break. Ambulances came down to the shifting house with blankets. Food vans came up with pies and chips, steamed puddings, and custards. The canteen supervisor said, 'My, we're grand to-night, chips and that. The girls will be pleased. Fine feed they'll have, first break.'

He started to make a cup of tea for the van men, who were cold. Presently one of the policemen came up and spoke to a van driver. 'You've left the door of your van open, mate; someone might get hurt. You ought to be more careful.' The policeman stayed for a cup of tea and someone said, 'He's quite civil for a policeman, isn't he?'

Most of the White shift were working with the Blue shift

now, but those who had chosen to sleep had gone down to the shift house. Some of them were able to get stretchers to lie on. Linnet was one of those. She supposed that the snow would keep them inside the factory for two or three days, and now she was glad about this. Here inside the Danger Area she felt secure and safe, certain that she could have no news of Willie, so that it seemed that neither good nor bad could touch her at this moment. She had not slept these last two nights, and did not expect to do so now. Above the scrubbed benches a few clothes were hanging up, and some blue and red scarves. Everything was very quiet and clean. It was very warm in the shifting house, and within five minutes Linnet fell asleep.

In the canteen at first break the White shift workers and the Blue shift were singing. It was the first time they had worked together. 'Always thought Blue shift were lazy and untidy, never cleaning up after their work; but now it seems like they're not so bad. It seems like they're the same as us.'

They were short of canteen workers, and Lofty went behind the counter to help. 'Funny, isn't it, how Lofty keeps going – don't know how he does it. Don't seem to get tired, do he? He's from London isn't he?'

'Yes; that's right, cooms from London Lofty does. When we was having fish and taters one night same as we are having now, he coom in and asked for fish and chips. He didn't know it's fish and taters 'ere. He thought taters was boiled. Funny, wasn't it?'

Some of the women from the White shift were helping Lofty, and some from the Blue shift. The Shop Manager came in, tired and blinking. He said he had been sleeping for two hours in his office; it had made him very tired.

Two projectionists came in and put a cinema show on the screen. It was a short singing picture about the sea. Some of the operatives in the canteen joined in the singing, and others called out, 'Doesn't half make you feel cold seeing the sea on a night like this and people bathing. Good thing it's only a picture, isn't it?' One of the men went up to the cinema projectionists and said, 'You got a Mickey Mouse for us?' She said, 'No, not to-night.' He said, 'We had Mickey Mouse here on the screen one night, chased by Pluto he was.' He pointed to a hole in the black-out curtain at the top of a side window. 'See that,' he said. 'Well, Mickey went through that hole he did, followed by Pluto, and we ain't never seen him any more.'

The Shop Stewards went round with their bowls of cigarettes. No matches were ever allowed inside the Danger Area, smoking was only allowed in the canteen half-way through the break. No cigarettes could be taken outside the canteen. The men and girls put their pennies in the large bowl and took out one or two cigarettes. The first man lit his from the lamp in the centre of the canteen. All the others lit their cigarettes from each other. A man from the Blue shift came up to Rose Waley of the White shift and lit his cigarette from hers. Another man from the Blue shift standing near-by said, 'There's five hundred of us in this canteen. All of them have cigarettes, and yet he has to go right across the room and light his from you. He's the Sheik of the Blue shift, he is.'

A lame man limped up on to the stage and sang two verses of 'You Can't Change It.' At the end of the song someone shouted out, 'The war will soon be won now we've got the White shift working with us.' And someone else shouted back, 'That's right; then we'll all be on the dole again together.'

The girls went down to the shifting house talking and laughing, arm in arm through the snow. 'Well, we've stayed on and done a long shift this time.'

'Yes; at least this snow will bring us a bit of bonus this week. I'm saving up for my home. £25 we've spent on covers for the front room alone. It takes a lot of saving up for, £25 does.'

'Yes; you can't save much out of what you get, even with bonus and all, when the Income Tax, Insurance, Red Cross funds, and Trades Union dues have come off.'

When the girls got down to the shifting house, most of the stretchers were already occupied so that those who came in late slept on mattresses and lilos laid in rows along the floor. They were parcelled up in blankets, pleased and happy about the change of routine. 'We may have to stay here for another day and night. It was like that when they had the snow before.'

'Yes; Mrs Franklin was telling us about it.'

'Never cleared up for two whole days and nights she said it didn't.'

Linnet woke up and looked round her. It seemed to her now as if she had returned to the time before her marriage with Willie. She listened to the girl next to her talking about the evening. 'And we was all singing in the canteen at first break, workers and staff and all. I've never seen anything like it, and the foreman went behind the counter and helped serve out tea with Miss Robinson and the shop manager, too, from Group V – regular bastard they say he is, all those who have anything to do with him. But he was all right to-night. You wouldn't have known he was a shop manager. And our foreman told us about the Italian food they used to send round to his Mum when they lived in Soho, all Italians they are in Soho, don't speak no English nor nothing. The volunteers have gone down to clear away the snow from the trucks on the internal railway. Ted's gone and Gluckstein, and two or three of the Staffordshire fellows, and that little Welshman and Old Charlie, and that fellow they call Julian, the one with specs, and that man in the blue beret, don't know his name, though, and one or two others. Don't envy them their job – they'll be wet through as soon as they start. Funny, isn't it, here, all night sleeping in the shifting house. Seems as if you feel quite safe away from home obligations and all. Right away from the war and that. Funny, isn't it, seeing as we are right in the centre of the Danger Area; don't seem sense, do it? It looked beautiful when we come down, all snow everywhere, clean and white. Curly picked up a handful, so did Phyllis Jenkins. The men was working there too, cleaning away the snow on the cleanways. Working by the light of lanterns they were, with large wooden spades, seemed like spoons or ladles, or something of that.'

As Linnet listened, bits of her conversation with Willie filtered through her mind again. 'You look well.'

'Yes, you look well, too.'

'Heard from Mum lately?'

'Yes, she's all right.'

'What does it seem like being a corporal, Willie?'

'Oh, I don't know, not so bad.'

And then the evening in the hostel over there in the married quarters. They had talked like strangers with a kind of growing dislike and resentment creeping up until it was all about and around them. Willie and she had looked at each other like animals–distrustful, afraid, and on their guard. The conversation of the next day came back to Linnet.

'What time's your train, Willie?'

'It leaves at ten o'clock, that ought to get me back in good time.'

'Oh yes, there isn't any hurry.'

'I expect you've made a lot of friends round here, Linnet.'

'Oh yes; the girls on my group are the ones I get to know best, of course. You do, don't you, when you've got to work with people, and share some of the same sort of troubles and that.'

'Yes; it's the same with the fellows in my unit.'

'Yes, I suppose it is. I wonder when the war will be over, don't you?'

'Yes, everyone wonders that, don't they?'

When they went up to the counter to get some food Willie said, 'I didn't know they had men as well as girls living here in the hostel. I thought it was all women. Who's the man with the dark glasses?'

'That's the chef. Austria, they call him. He's Austrian, you see; he's been in a concentration camp.'

'Poor fellow. There are some like that working near us. They're in the Pioneers.'

'Yes. When does your train go, Willie?'

'It don't leave till ten o'clock; plenty of time, isn't there?'

'Yes, plenty of time; no hurry at all.'

'Will they let you go to the station, Linnet?'

'No, Willie; I'd better not do that. I've got to be on shift later.'

'How far do you have to go to work then?'

'Oh, it's only a few miles. We go down in the big buses, see. We've got to be waiting for them at the crossroads. If you miss one you might not get another.'

These words came back to her; but they made no a sense, neither then nor now. It was all part of a fight against the growing antagonism which they had feared would strengthen in silence. Linnet had thought, 'If only the hour of his departure would hurry.' It did not seem as if it would ever come round. She had walked down to the cross-roads with Willie, and then when the bus came waved him good-bye. He had said, 'My train don't go till ten o'clock, but it's best to be in good time. It don't do to rush yourself, do it?'

When Willie had gone she had been glad – glad to be silent and not to have to talk any more. The forty-eight hours had been a waking nightmare, and after it was over and Willie had gone back, there had been hours of work and mealtimes in hostel and factory canteens. It was very strange, this regular taking of meals within the framework of deep despondency.

But now it seemed to Linnet that she had travelled some distance away from this uneasy encounter with Willie. Sleep and snow separated her from this unhappiness. She listened again to the talk around her.

'Sleeping here in the shifting house reminds me of the days at my Mum's when we was little 'uns, six brothers and four sisters, and we used to sleep in rows like this. Of course, two lots of twins we was, and that's what made us all so near the same age, see. That's the good time, isn't it, when you don't have to trouble much about anything. You don't have any time like it again, not after you're fourteen and got to go to work and that.'

'It was funny to-night in the canteen when Maggie and Miss Robinson were serving out tea together. Maggie was much quicker at it than Miss Robinson. They brought up some of that tinned food for us. Some of the invasion stores I expect it was. Tinned chicken and that. If we can have it when we're snowed in, why can't we always have it? Funny, wasn't it, all them people singing and working together – the Blue shift and the White, Labour Officers, operatives, canteen workers and all. They were all laughing and seemed happy. Funny when you think of what we're all here for, and how we're only making things to kill people. It don't seem right, do it?'

'No; but it would be all right if we were working here for something that was for all of us.'

'What sort of things?'

'Oh, I dunno; gramophones, perhaps, and food, clothes and musical instruments, furniture perhaps. I don't know, just something that was for all of us. You know, things you can use and things that you need, instead of things that just destroy themselves and everything around.'

'Oh yes, that would be all right, that would.'

'Did you see Mr Doran come in?'

'That's the Time and Emotion man, isn't it?'

'Yes, he didn't sing with the others, did he?—just looked through his spectacles.'

'Always writing in his notebook, isn't he?'

'Yes, writes his life away, he does.'

'Wonder what we shall do to-morrow; wonder if we shall get back to hostel.'

'We're on noons; wonder what we'll do in factory all day if snow is still coming down.'

'Don't matter though, do it? Don't have to keep to time, do we?—even though we're on noons we can do a bit of overtime if we've a fancy for it.'

'Perhaps they'll have volunteers again. If they do that, I should like to work in the kitchens.'

'I wonder if they've got a message up to my Mum.'

'Our Mum don't worry about anything, our Mum don't. Whether we're in or out, she don't trouble.'

'Wonder what they're doing up at the hostel.'

Linnet listened for a long while to the talk. It seemed to her that her unhappiness was not absent but had been moved a little distance from her as if the story were still there but happening to someone else. She did not know when she ceased to listen to the talk around her and fell asleep.

Chapter Eleven

Snowed Out

The second day of the snows the café in the hostel was kept open extra hours, but it was not licensed and this caused some grumbling. 'I don't see why they can't have drinks here, treating us like we were a lot of blooming kids.'

A girl from the Red shift, wearing a green scarf round her head, said, 'Well, they did try that, didn't they. Sort of club it was, and you could get beer and that; but one evening there was a dance, some of the fellows got drunk and broke the place up, so that was how the licence got took off again.'

'I bet the pubs were pleased. They don't want to lose our custom.'

'Funny, wasn't it, about the fellows getting drunk. My Dad says he don't think much of a man who can't hold his drink, nor I don't neither. But it was funny about the fellows breaking the place up. Most times when they drink more than they can stand in the pubs they start talking about their wives or their mothers, sentimental like, so that it makes you feel sick. There was one like that up at the Greyhound the other evening. He was on about his mother and how he'd buried her in a little church at the foot of the hill; and then he carried on about his wife and how he'd married her at the little chapel round the corner. Then he got mixed up, and it was his wife he'd buried in a little church, and his mother he'd married in the little chapel. Then one of the other fellers said, "I suppose you mean you was at your mother's wedding in the chapel round the corner?" Of course that started up a fight, and then they was both thrown out down some steps and into the street. Very dark it was at the time, and bitter cold, too, but after a bit the other man came back and had some more drinks. And soon he was no better than the first man, because he started up about his wife being the best little woman in the world, and then he came out of the Greyhound, same time as we did; and when we were walking up the hill out of the town he was still on about his wife and saying he was not worthy of her, and all the time he was talking he was trying to put his arm round Rose. Fed up she was. Can't blame her, can you?'

'No; there's many like that.'

Nordie came back from the counter with a doughnut on her plate. Two Pioneer Corps soldiers in battle dress came in, one blond and talkative, the other dark and silent. The blond soldier sat down at a corner table, a girl on either side of him. The brun soldier sat opposite, staring as if nothing could shake him out of his mood of melancholy. The girl who had been talking about drunks said now, 'I wonder how those two met up with those fellows. They're from our shift; but the fellows they've got with them are foreigners, aren't they?'

'Yes,' Nordie said, 'Pioneers. Kind of refugees, aren't they; same as our chef, Austria.'

'Course their camp is only about half a mile away; but it must have been tough walking in this weather.'

Nordie drank her tea, removing a book she had perched up against the cup. Mrs Karslake, the Film Unit 3 Supervisor, came and sat beside her.

'Puts me in mind of Lyons Corner House, seeing you reading a book like that. I always did that when I went there, leant my book up against a teapot. There's nothing I like better than a good read, when I've got time, that is. But it isn't often I do have the time now. I have had a lot to do getting out the reports about the films for the Head Office. I have tried to telephone through to the girls at the factory, but I can't get any answer from them. Do you think the wires are down on account of the snow?'

Nordie answered, 'I expect so; but there is nothing to be concerned about. They have got plenty of films to show, so they're sure to get on all right. Mrs Teglar will tell them which canteens are still open. She can help them out, can't she?'

'Mrs Teglar—I don't think much of her. She thinks herself high and mighty just because she's one of the Labour Officers. Last week she asked me to go up and see her. But I did not choose. I let two days go by before I went into her office. And there she was, sitting behind her desk. She asked me how the film shows in the canteen were going, so I told her, "We're showing the films that are sent to us, the films we've been told to show by our Head Office." And she said, 'Well, let me know if there is anything I can do to help you, Mrs Karslake. I will be glad to do so if there is anything you want." Huh, I suppose she thinks I shall go crawling to her any moment anything goes wrong. Well, all I can say is, she's mistaken.'

'Oh, I don't know,' Nordie answered. 'I expect she was only trying to help.'

But there was war within Mrs Karslake. 'They try to trip me up, I know that; but if they think I am going to crack up on the job, they're wrong. I am going to show the films I've been instructed to show in the order they're to be shown; and if anyone thinks they could do the job better than me I should like to see them try, because I know they couldn't do the job any better.'

Mrs Karslake was afraid of invisible enemies—the Head Office, the Ministry, and so on. She did not seem to be sure who her employers were, but she felt that they had smiling faces. 'You're doing a grand job, Mrs Karslake, you carry on.' But that was not all. They weren't only smiling faces. They were also wild animals lurking behind trees ready to spring out suddenly. 'We're not satisfied with the way you are running this unit, Mrs Karslake.' From behind their blinkered eyes came sly looks. 'We have had good reports from the Admin about the films you're showing,' and then suddenly the creature would change its shape again and become tall and menacing. 'We hear there has been a lot of trouble, and you cannot manage your staff. Can't you use tact; be more discreet, can't you?' A shout, a whine, a threat, an identity card and a couple of forms, this was Mrs Karslake's idea of officialdom. 'You see,' she told Nordie. 'the girls have been down in the factory twenty-four hours now, and they don't look like coming back. How do I know what they're doing while they're snowed in there? Most likely they're not showing the right film in the right canteen; most likely they're getting in wrong with the Labour Officers and with the shop stewards. I don't understand now about the Trades Union movement. Is it very powerful?'

'Yes, of course it is,' answered Nordie.

'Oh,' said Mrs Karslake, 'I wonder what my girls are doing down there. You can't rely on them.'

'Have a cup of tea, Mrs Karslake, and don't worry any more about it.'

Nordie sighed deeply in weariness. There was nothing she could do about Mrs Karslake; she could see no way to smooth out the antagonisms, and the fears.

'To my way of thinking,' said Mrs Karslake, 'it's always safest to do exactly as you are told.'

She stirred her tea and looked down into the cup with a slight smile.

'Then they can't blame you if anything goes wrong, can they? In fact they've got to blame themselves for doing things in such a ham-fisted way, haven't they?'

The blond snub-nosed Austrian was telling the girl about his life in the Pioneer Corps.

'I had a stripe once,' he said, 'but I losted it for being late into the barracks.'

The more the blond talked, the more the dark, hooked nose brun became melancholy. Blond said, 'We had wonderful quarters last year—splendid place it was, central heating, hot and cold running water; but they sent us away to where we are now, and they gave over the whole shooting to the Italian prisoners that are living there now. Damn bloody rotten shame, wasn't it?'

Three girls from the Red shift lolled on the chairs near the window looking out. 'Not much to see outside, is there? Nothing but snow, snow, snow.'

'Yes; you get fed up being cooped up here.'

'Yes; it wouldn't be so bad if so many of the Supervisor Staff hadn't been snowed up here too. I mean they're always organizing our recreation and that.'

'Yes; two or three of the fellows from Block K have gone up to the Goose and Cuckoo.'

'Gone up to see Girlie, have they?'

'Yes; shouldn't fancy it myself in this weather. It'll take them near an hour to get there, and then they'll lose their way as like as not.'

The blond pioneer told the others about the time when they had a day off. 'We got our pay on Friday, so they allowed us to go off on Thursday. We had no money at all, and all our day off was arid and dull because all what we had was poverty. The Commanding Officer did it this way from spite.' The young hostel manager came in to ask if anyone wanted to come into the assembly room to sing or recite or do a comic turn. 'It's a sort of talent-spotting competition,' he said shyly. He wore grey flannel trousers, a high-necked pullover, and rope-soled shoes. A few of the people from the café followed him out.

'Free and easy, isn't he?' remarked one of the girls. 'He's our warden here.'

'What is "warden", please?'

'The man who looks after the residents of the hostel. This is the hostel, and we are the residents. Well, you know the pictures you saw in the reading room when we first came in, you said they were reproductions of French Impressionists. Well, he hung them up on the wall, at any rate he arranged for them to be hung up there so as we could see them, and he allots the allotments, books up the concert parties that come down, gives out the library books, and kind of gingers up the residents so that they start their own concerts and amateur shows. He does it all in a quiet way. Diabetic he is, discharged from the Army. He's no trouble to us at all, so everything was all right at the start when we only had him: but now they've brought in another entertainments manager and a games instructor–gymnastics and that. It's all this idea of welfare. We'll be welfared down to nothing if it goes on like it.'

Mrs Karslake continued nagging at Nordie. 'You see, I told Mr Lyons about the girls being so difficult and about how they seemed to resent my authority. I thought he might have a word with them himself. That's what I was told in my instructions–"the Cinema Unit is in touch with Mr Lyons, the Public Relations Officer on site"–you see, I was only carrying out my orders from Head Office, but of course Mr Lyons went and rang up Head Office himself, and they sent a letter to each of the girls asking them to sink their peace-time prejudices. You know the kind of letter, a real telling off, all set out in snooty sentences. So of course the girls thought I had complained about them, and ever since then they've been worse. They've been proper bastards to me, those girls have.'

Nordie looked dully at Mrs Karslake. 'I shouldn't worry about that.' Then she thought, 'How odd it is that I should have to say "I shouldn't worry about that" when I really mean "I shouldn't worry me about that.'

'Well, I've done everything I've been asked by Head Office and still it isn't right,' said Mrs Karslake. 'I'm going to see if I can get through to those girls on the telephone now.' She went.

Nordie read her book. She was sorry silent Julian was snowed in at the factory. It was only six miles away, but the snow stretched out the distance and there was no means of communication for her. The café became more noisy, people were gathering in little groups—some arguing, some quarrelling.

A patrol man came in. He leant up against the counter, and in a little while he said to his neighbours, 'There's a fight going on outside.'

'What sort of a fight?'

'Oh, it's Mad Jess again. It's all over that foreman fellow, proper soft about him she is. The other girl has been made an overlooker, and Jess was waiting for her to-night; told her she knew how she got her Blue-band.' The patrol man sank his voice, and turning to the melancholy brun pioneer who had come to put two cups down on the counter, he said, 'Jess told her she were made overlooker for the same reason as others; she said it was for ——ing in the air-raid shelter.'

The face of the foreign soldier did not lose any of its sadness. He listened politely to the words of the patrol man, acknowledged them with a ceremonious little bow, then, still in a mood for profound melancholy, he put the teacups down on the counter.

An MTC girl in khaki battle-dress said, 'Couldn't you stop the fight?'

'Me?' The patrol man looked back at Battle-Dress. 'Me stop two women fighting! No, you wouldn't catch me attempting nothing of that. I'm not on duty till eight o'clock.'

It became clear now through the conversation of the patrol man, the MTC girl and the woman at the counter that the fight was still on outside. Twenty or thirty people moved towards the back of the main building. Outside, the twelve long, low, grey sleeping-huts overshadowed the centre path, and here two black splodges circled and shouted, clawed and slapped, crouched and sprang at each other. The man in the blue beret walked by, stared for a moment, then spat in the snow and walked on. All the others stood stolid, watching without speaking, but the two women were not silent.

'Don't suppose your mum was no better than she should be neither. Don't suppose your dad's name's on your paper. Don't suppose your mum never got a good look at him.'

Jess did not say so much as her opponent. She said, 'You leave my mum out of it.' She clawed at the other woman's clothes so that a sleeve came out of its socket. She clutched at the enemy's hair and wrenched out some strands, and then she shouted three times in a loud voice. 'Bloody bastard!' And all the time twenty or thirty people stood silent, stolid, and lifeless as snowmen. Then a big square-shouldered man from Dorset shouted, 'Pack it up, girl, I'm sick of this: it doesn't seem right women fighting.' He went up to the assailants, and quick as two cats' paws in play gave each one a tapping blow over the ear. Several of the women watching in the snow called out, 'Bloody coward, hit a woman, would you?' They all moved forward towards him, menacing and fast-footed. He ran. Some of them followed, but soon the strong man from the South was lost to sight in the snow.

The two women stood shivering and dispirited in the cold air. The patrol man gave the sleeveless girl his coat. 'Better take this, it's getting a bit chilly now.' He was anxious for everyone to go back into the main building. 'I shall be on duty soon,' he said uneasily, 'and I don't want no trouble here during my watch.'

After supper in the main building Nordie noticed that the Welfare Officers, Labour Officers, and MTC girls who had not been able to get to work were now attempting to give everyone something to do. 'Discussions, lectures, concerts, games, or something of that sort. It doesn't do to let people just sit about unoccupied and only thinking of their own troubles.'

Some of the ex-unemployed men had gone into the library to get themselves some books, and now it seemed as if they were on the run from the Supervisory staff. Nordie saw several speed past in the passage that led to the exit door behind the assembly room, as adroit as birds avoiding visitors in an aviary.

In the reading-room Nordie sat down beside a heap of out-of-date shiny papered magazines lying on a table. These had been sent up by some of the local residents who had received a circular saying that any books and magazines would be welcome. Half a dozen of the front pages of the top copy were missing, so that Nordie saw, staring up at her, a group of people who had been photographed sitting on a beach wearing long shantung trousers, coolie hats, silk shorts or patterned handkerchiefs; almost all of them were disguised in large-size smoked glasses.

A man Nordie did not know, but whom she had seen waltzing Girlie round one Saturday night at the Goose and Cuckoo, was tearing the pages of the magazines and making them into spills. He sighed over the snow and the Supervisory staff. 'It's a pity so many of them have got cooped up here. You don't notice them so much on ordinary days; they go to work themselves then and leave folks alone in their off-time; but now it seems as if they can't stop organizing, funny isn't it. They're all supposed to be educated people. Haven't they got any resources in themselves, or what's the matter with them? 'Course I came in here to get away from all that. None of the

Supervisory staff wouldn't dare to come in here and ask us to join in a discussion group, sewing bee, talk on gardening, spelling class, or anything of that.' He pointed up to the large placard over the fireplace, the one word 'SILENCE' was printed on it in big black threatening capitals against a white background. 'That'll scare them off all right. They'll take notice of that because they put it up themselves. Official it is, so we ought to be safe here.'

Nordie started to make some spills too. On the first one she read 'Mrs Lombard-Pringle has a host of friends. She was still flushed with victory when I ran into her the other day, brogued and tweeded on her way to the country after having won the scavenger prize of the previous evening. "All the items were so easy, my dear," she told me. "We had to collect a hair from the moustache of a policeman on point duty in Piccadilly Circus, the wing of a cold chicken from the Savoy kitchens, and a toy limousine from the arms of a sleeping child. It was thrilling, I only just got to Gracie's a few minutes before Twigs Fitzgerald and Hunchie Pargrave."' Nordie looked at the date at the top of the paper—May 1938. A mass of snow slithered from the roof, hit the ground and turned to slush. Two men came in and settled down by the fire to a fierce discussion on the training of whippets.

'Mind you,' said the man Nordie had seen dancing with Girlie, 'folks don't always know what to do with their leisure. Seems as if they've got to first get their leisure before they can learn how to use it; but look at those two women out there to-night. Don't seem right women fighting like that. It don't seem as if they're human. When you come to think of it, it's not civilized, is it?'

Yesterday's paper was still lying on the table. Nordie noticed two captions—'ALIENATION OF AFFECTION CASE': 'HEIRESS SUES SISTER-IN-LAW FOR TEN THOUSAND POUNDS.'

Mrs Karslake came in. 'The Welfare Officer from Group III has asked me to put on a show. We've got the two films we brought up here. I'm quite willing to put them on, but you are next on the rota.' Nordie shook her head, and pointed to the 'Silence' notice. Mrs Karslake went out again, leaving the door half open. A little man with a pale coal-pocked face sitting at one of the writing-desks turned up his coat collar. Girlie's dance friend under-toned to Nordie, 'You see that bloke there by the writing-table? He plays chess with a mate of his, all by correspondence he does. I seen what he writes often. Can't understand it though, myself. All numbers and letters it is.' He tore out another handful of pages from the shiny papered magazine. 'The warden left these here to make spills, but he hasn't had time to do it himself so we might as well help him.' He tore a page in half, and then folded it carefully into four. 'All saves matches, don't it?' Nordie looked down at her page. It had a photograph of horrific hominids porpoising on the beach at Honolulu. Mrs Lombard-Pringle was there again, and underneath the photograph was written the words: 'Off again! Mrs Lombard-Pringle overtakes the sun.' In the top left-hand corner of the page there was a small printed clue to the time of the year–January 26th, 1938. Nordie remembered it–the date of the fall of Barcelona.

Chapter Twelve

Internal Railway

The men who had volunteered to clear the internal railway tracks went walking forward in black oilskin suits. They moved silently, slowly, over the snow without speaking; the engine was just outside Group V, but the trucks were still in the Danger Area, covered with tarpaulins over wooden planks. They had the look of a long line of military coffins, but it would be some time before the cortège would move off. The volunteers worked by the light of lanterns to an orchestra of sounds: spades hitting against steel spokes, the grating of the wheels moving slowly over the cinders put on the track, the high-pitched whistle the engine gave out when the driver let off the steam, the diminishing impacts of truck buffers, and the squelching scrunch of the men's boots sinking down into the snow.

After an hour the air-raid siren sounded out; the first few notes were set going a second or two later on each group so that the warning wailed over the valley like a brutish part song. After this, whistling, hammering on the truck wheels and more shunting of the engine, and then a voice, 'Shut up, they'll hear us,' and an answering voice, 'Don't act so soft, how can they hear three thousand feet up and travelling at four hundred miles an hour!'

'More likely Inspector Jameson will hear us. He isn't interested in nothing but snooping about listening to what other folks say.'

The man wearing the blue beret walked out from behind the engine; he had taken a broken bit of plank from under one of the tarpaulins. In this snowscape with sounds, the figure of the blue-bereted man with the jagged piece of wet wood seemed so strange that several men stopped working to stare at him; the gunfire started up, drowning all other sounds, and when it stopped the minor music of hammering on wheels was continued again; the man in the blue beret threw the bit of wood away and went to help the driver and fireman to start up the engine. After an hour, the men got the last truck out of the Danger Area; ten minutes passed, then the all clear sounded out.

When the relief party came up the men walked back. They went into the boiler-room to get their clothes dried. Julian noticed that Mathew Reid, the man in the blue beret, was not with them. The snow started to fall again. The man in charge of the boiler-room had one hand missing. He wore a sort of stocking over it—it was his right hand. His gold-rimmed spectacles were fastened behind his ears, and he had a habit of looking sideways and downwards as if to evade some painful sight. He had found a piece of rope and slung it across the room between two pipes. The men took off their oilskin coats and put them down on an empty bench, hung their trousers up along the rope line, then walked about in their vests and underpants. They were glad of the warmth, and glad the air raid was over.

'Never seem to fancy being in this valley when old Adolf's Loofter Wafter's overhead.'

'Well, he's gone now, so you've got no cause to grumble. Come to think of it, I shouldn't fancy being up there neither with this barrage what we've got now.'

The man in charge of the boiler-room said, 'Make yourselves at home, mates.'

The men went to their jackets to get out their cigarettes, but the snow had got into the pockets, turning the tobacco to pulp. Dai, the Welsh miner, had brought his cigarettes in a tin. He handed them round. 'I like to see a fire. Up at the hostel we've got a good heating system, but only one room with a fire. It seems that folks can't settle till they get near a fire.'

The men took off their vests and underpants now, and hung them up to dry beside their trousers along the rope line, then they sat down on the benches. The fires burning in the bunkers made a sound like a flock of birds overhead, with wings fast moving against the wind. Sometimes the coal, stored in giant bins at the back of the bunkers, shook itself down and resettled in its place with a shudder.

Several of the men leant against the wall with their eyes shut, resting. On the journey over from the internal railway Julian had thought he could fall asleep like a tired traveller in the snow, but now he was wide awake as if the warmth of the room had brought him to life. Here in this herd of naked men resting with eyes closed, only the man in charge of the room was dressed.

One of the men opened his eyes to light a cigarette. 'Look at Old Charlie, he's still asleep, isn't he?' Another man answered without opening his eyes, 'Yes, he must be asleep. We wouldn't half have some political talk if he was awake.' The man in charge of the boiler-room said, 'I'm not interested in politics.'

Julian did not hear the answer because he slipped over into unconsciousness, and when he woke up he could hear a voice speaking out a story. At first he did not know where it came from, and it seemed that it was part of the sound of the fires and that the words were coming out of the boilers. It was the man in charge, dressed in overalls, who was speaking. 'We were in the South at that time, and we soon became aware that things around us were changing. These changes forced themselves into my mind. I wanted to paint pictures then, and didn't want to trouble about anything else. I was living amongst peasants, and I supposed they, too, had hoped for peace; but it was not possible as I see it now. Most of the peasants were poets too. There was the work in the fields in the daytime, and at night that other life—the talking over the table, the food and the wine, and then the sitting out of doors and the music of the words, sometimes singing too. I suppose it had been coming our way all the time, but suddenly we were all in it. There were only a few of us, but the one I remember best was the leader, a young fellow—four or five years older than me he must have been then—rising a twenty-two. He had thick hair, very strong hands, and a way of walking with a swing the same as you see sailors walking, and he used to talk a great deal of the future, and of how things would be better and people would love each other instead of hating each other. One of my friends who used to carry the despatches to the town was killed, and after that I was the one chosen to carry them. Soon after the sun went down I used to set out secretly, and run by night with the messages. I thought it a fine thing to do then, and I didn't suffer the loss of my friend so much because it seemed as if he went with me. It was not long after this that we found ourselves fighting in the town behind the barricades.

'There was a fellow with us who was always cleaning his gun—very proud he was of this gun, treated it almost if as if it was a piece of wood he had carved himself—and he used to talk too, because he knew all the political stuff and could quote all the speeches. Once when we were told we might have to wait behind the barricades for three days he got restless. Finally he couldn't stand it. I saw him rush out suddenly into the streets shouting and shooting upwards at the houses where he knew the enemy were. It seemed as if he knew exactly where to aim and that was all he had been thinking about these last weeks. Of course there was no hope for him, and we couldn't do anything except wait. He had a bandolier slung round his shoulders and he went on like that, shooting and shouting; and from the windows the enemy shot down at him, and every now and then he would be hit and his body would jerk back with the impact of the bullets against it. But he never stopped, just went on shooting, and the blood came spurting out of his body the same as wine had come out of a cask that I had hit once when I was practising shooting in the fields beyond the village. Soon I saw this boy standing in his own blood, but still reloading his gun and shooting upwards. Then he put his hand up to his bandolier and found it empty, no more cartridges, and suddenly he fell down dead. I suppose he'd been dead, in a manner of speaking, for some minutes with all those bullets in him, but it seemed as if his fanaticism had kept him going.

'When I thought about him afterwards I decided that he was just a man with a gun behind an idea. It should be the other way round by rights, but it wasn't so with him. He'd just got it wrong. I didn't see this so clearly myself at the time: it was difficult sitting there behind the barricades with that fellow dead in the street and knowing that something of the same sort might be happening to us soon. The hours went by very slow. But a few of us survived, and there were several more fights.

'Some time later we heard there had been a successful march on the city, and after this we never took any more interest in it. It was over for us as soon as it became a success, because we knew we shouldn't have to do any more. We went back to our work in the villages and in the fields.'

Julian looked round the room, and saw that two or three of the men had opened their eyes and were listening. They did not say anything. The man in charge said, 'When I'd seen a few more pictures and understood something more about it, I got to know that I should never be a painter, not a real painter you understand. I learnt to work with my hands instead, a carpenter I was for a while.'

Julian had a sense of being free of all effort. No striving, no wish to say or to be anything. The censor of his mind came down over the awareness of his surroundings – silence and sleep. He re-awoke on the words: 'We lived in workers' flats there. They were the best buildings I've ever seen. Of course it was more civilized in central Europe. I had become a member of the Trades Union, and thought I was beginning to know what it was all about. That morning I woke later than usual. I had put on my shirt and trousers in a hurry, went out and waited for a tram; but I waited a long time, and it didn't come. Then I realized that the trams were not running. That was how I knew it had begun. So I went back to see the leader, a very learned fellow he was, middle-aged and with a great gift for seeing all sides to a question. His hair was a bit on the long side, so that he seemed to be looking out of a sort of iron-grey cage. He was slow-speaking and thoughtful, but he never hurried and never seemed to get upset. We met down in the cellar of the workers' flats; planks had been laid over the rifles and coal on top. The rifles were new, and they were still covered with grease when we got them out. We knew there was a pile of sand in the courtyard, so we decided we could use this to clean the rifles. Several of us got over there and got working on it, but it was very slow. The fellows were inexperienced and some of them got the sand down the barrels. I thought the job would never get done.

'Before we had finished a lorry came down the street full of men. We didn't know whether they were ours or theirs, and two or three of our fellows went to look. The lorry was followed by an armoured car. We knew then soon enough, because they shot our fellows dead. The rest of us flung ourselves against the wall, and then we went back round the courtyard like so many nervous crows. Our men did not want to let us in at first, but we hammered on the door and they opened it a bit. Then we ran in and took up our posts. I was on the first floor of the building. We had got a machine-gun fixed up there; we waited beside it, looking down on the armoured car, beetled out there in the street. No one did anything, we waited to be told what to do, our minds full of questions. Had we got the Post Office? Had all the electricians come out? I supposed our leader was in agreement with all the other leaders on our side so we waited for some signal.

'Suddenly guns got going on the other side of the city. We took this as a signal for the start and began to shoot too. It did not take more than twelve hours for them to make our place uninhabitable. The women and the old people knew that they would have to surrender. Already it seemed a miracle that we had managed to hold out so long. Each of us was beginning to suspect that our leader had not come to any real agreement with the other leaders on our side. Their liberty of thought got in the way of their decisions, and tripped them up when it came to action. When it was dark, some of us were sent down to the cellar to look for a way out. I suppose they picked on me because I was young and a foreigner. Our leader did not know what to do. He did not want to leave the men under his command, but he wanted to get out so that he could continue the fight. He thought, just as we did, that the battle had succeeded in all other parts of the city. The men persuaded the leader to go along with us, but when we started on the journey out I saw that he was not with us after all, so I suppose he stayed with the others and changed his mind again.

'I heard afterwards it had been about the same thing everywhere. Nobody knew anything, nobody acted at the same moment, and yet at one time we had had it all in our own hands. We started out on our journey through the sewers. We had to climb down those iron ladders underground. The rungs were so far away from each other that I started thinking that all sewersmen must have very long legs. I got out in the end, of course, otherwise I should not be here now. I had been shot in the right hand, but I had tied a bit of sheet round it and made some sort of a bandage. It took a long time to get out, and all the time I was thinking that this journey through the filth was not worth it, and those that stayed and got shot had the better bargain. One fellow was drowned, and another one died from loss of blood before we could get him out. It was a funny thing, really, because he did not seem to be very badly wounded at the time. But after some hours I did come up on the outskirts of the city, otherwise I should not be here now in my boiler suit, talking to all you fellows in your birthday suits. But it was a hell of a journey. When I landed on the far side of that city I hadn't much life left in me, and I thought how I had gone in a social democrat and come out a sewer rat.

'Soon after this I was looking for a job. People were saying that there weren't any jobs going any more. It's true that there weren't any in England; but I got into France and began working in a restaurant, washing up. It was very long hours, underground, and very dirty. Foreigners were supposed to get a permit to be employed, but I knew I should not have a chance of doing that. The proprietor didn't ask any questions, because he couldn't get Frenchmen to take these sort of jobs. When the Spanish war came along, I saw a chance to get out of it. We were nearly all foreigners working down there in that restaurant. We thought it would be quite a change to see a bit of daylight, and we all joined up with the International Brigade. But this time I never got into any sort of action because I was in one of the groups that were arrested on the frontier and put in prison in Perpignan. The others all got out after a few weeks; but my hand got poisoned, this same right hand. It started to swell up and had to be amputated, but I was very well looked after. It was the time of the Popular Front, you see.

'A French doctor took me into his house and did everything he could for me. He thought I was sacrificing a lot to come and fight in Spain, but he misunderstood it somewhat. Because it was mostly bad times that had brought me to the frontier. But his ideas were all organized, and he could only see me as being the same as himself. I told him that I had promised myself to keep out of politics and that I was fed up with ideological battles. But he didn't believe me. Anyhow, I was not much use to anyone after my hand had been amputated, so the French doctor took my place. I don't know just how he managed it, but he got into Spain all right on some sort of fixed-up passport—of course we all had those. I heard afterwards that he had been killed. I came back to England myself and managed to get a few odd jobs until the war came; but there you are, I am not interested in politics myself, same as I told you.'

The clothes were dry now. The man in charge of the boiler-room walked over to the line to look at them. Some of the vests were tied by the neck with string. He cut them down like corpses, and they collapsed on the ground. The men started to dress again. One of them said, 'It's right what you say about politics in a manner of speaking, mate. Politics are not what they purport to be, of course. We know that, but it don't make no difference to the fact that you've got to fight against Fascism wherever you find it.'

Another answered, 'That's right enough, you don't have to study it at all. You hate Fascism, you don't like school, it's the same thing; it comes natural like.'

The man in charge, looking through his gold-rimmed spectacles towards the ground, said, 'I'm not interested in politics, never have been. Of course I admit, mind you, that politics have overtaken me. Right from the start it's been like that. I always seem to have been in some place when there was a flare-up.'

Julian said, 'Yes, that's it. If you have the fortune to get into the field of events you can move forward with them; but it doesn't last long. Most men turn off in a direction they never intended. The words get in the way.'

The man in charge came back to the hanging clothes. He cut at the line with his left hand, and the rest fell to the ground in a heap. When the men were dressed, they walked out. Gluckstein got blinking into the sunlight first. He began to think again of his own attempts to get into the fight against everything he hated, but each time it was the same story, somehow he was kept out of it all. He walked forward fast over the snow. The others followed him without hurrying. 'Seems anxious to get back to work, that bloke does.'

'Who, Gluckstein?'

'Yes, he's one of the best workers we've got, even though he is an overseer.'

'He's a good fellow, Gluck is.'

'We can go down to the Group and get a bit of a wash. It seems funny waking up already at your work. It saves a lot of time though.'

'It was a sweat working on that internal railway last night.'

'Yes; we'll have it all to do again to-day, two or three feet of snow has fallen since we were there. It must have come on to snow again early in the morning.'

'Didn't get no colder, did it, not in the boiler-room?'

'The man in charge likes to talk, don't he? Telling stories, wasn't he?'

'Yes, strange sort of good-night stories for grown men.'

'Anarchist, isn't he?'

'No; he's not interested in politics. Didn't you hear him say so?'

'No; I was asleep most of the time. Seems as if I didn't have nothing to worry about surrounded by those fires and the air raid over and the snow outside. Slept like a child, I did. Don't know why it was. Suppose I was tired.'

'Must be lonely for that bloke in the boiler-room.'

Chapter Thirteen

Writing Home

All the snow and slush had gone from the ground. All the shifts were working again on time. In the evening, Mary Smith, a transferred worker, aged nineteen, stopped at the stall in the main building of the hostel and bought a pen, some ink, and a twopenny exercise book. She put a scarf over her head, walked over to her sleeping block, and sat down to write a letter to her sister. She headed her letter: Room 24, Block D, 3 Statevale Hostel.

'Dear Jane, – I said I would write again and tell you how I was getting on when I had found out more about the place. I've never been much a one for writing letters, but now I've been here a whole week, and I feel as if I want to write. It's very strange here, not a bit like I expected. I don't think there's anything else quite like it. The hostel is a big place, almost like a small town. There's one long building and twelve or thirteen long low buildings – all grey. When we first got here I thought it was the factory. I am in one of the sleeping blocks now. My room is like a cell, it's got two bunks in it; but I am alone at present, so I'm lucky. But they tell me when they get more crowded they may have to ask me to "double up" with someone else. I think of asking Linnet to share my room with me. She works on the same shift, Blue shift they call it. Her husband's been on leave for forty-eight hours, and she moved over to the married quarters, but he only stayed one night. She's back in the room next to me now, but she has not been in to talk to me like she used to. She seems sad somehow. I don't know why it is. It's supposed to be better when you are married, but it don't seem to be no better – at least not when it's like Linnet and her husband. I saw them at supper, and they seemed like strangers.

'At the moment I am sitting on my bunk writing at a little wooden table. It is a kind of cut-out cube with a space for keeping your books in. They've got them in all the rooms, but I went and got another one out of an empty room down the passage and put the two together, so that it makes a good table to write on. The window looks out on to the allotments, and I am going to have one next week. You might as well be really rural while you are about it. I've been washing my stockings in the basin, and have hung them out on the window ledge to dry. There's the laundry, of course, the same as I told you, but somehow you feel shy of going there at first. A girl in Room 23 told me she didn't want to go over there because she a was afraid her clothes wouldn't seem as good as some of the others. Shame, isn't it? But in these days of coupons and that, those that used to be so well dressed don't seem to get so much chance to come it over you socially as they used to. I've been noticing that the men aren't as shy as the women about the laundry. They often go over there and wash and iron their own things. Of course one or two of them have been sailors, so they've always done it.

'I pay 22s 6d a week for my board and lodging; but of course I have to get myself something in the factory canteen too, and then there is the bus to and from work, 1s 6d a week it is, which is not so bad I suppose seeing that the factory is five miles away. There's a big dining-room in the main building, and you go up to the counter and get your food and take it to any table you want. There's a chef dressed all in white standing behind the counter. He wears dark glasses because his eyes have been hurt. They call him "Austria", and the girls in the kitchen say he's always kind and thoughtful. They say he's been in a concentration camp, but he never speaks about it. Must be sad for him living amongst a lot of strangers.

'Our shift, the Blue shift, is working nights now. We start at ten in the evenings and get home to early breakfast. About the work: Well, I have been in the training section learning safety precautions. The stewardess used to call me in the morning when I was on Day Shift. There's hot baths at the end of the passage here, and after we'd been in to breakfast we go down to the cross-roads and get the bus – a great lumbering thing it is. There's a policeman standing at the first factory gates. He's a tall fellow, and he's got a revolver in what they call a holster. It gave me quite a shock when I first saw it, but of course I am used to it now. All the factory police wear these revolvers. They say it's an imitation of Woolwich where they were all armed too. The policeman, whose daughter works up at the Badminton, that's a pub, told us that if the factory were attacked by the enemy his instructions were to challenge three times and then shoot. But he said, "I don't think a German paratrooper would give us a chance to challenge him three times." Well, the bus lumbers us down to the next factory gates; it's quite a way, and on a great grey road with hills on either side into the valley. We go past Mr Whistler's bungalow, he's the Superintendent. I've only seen him once, walking back from work he was wearing a raincoat. He looks quite young. When I saw him he was throwing sticks for his dog Pitcher to fetch. He threw two at once in opposite directions just to get his dog diddled, so the poor brute didn't know which way to run. He laughed like anything, Super did. He hardly seemed like a full-grown man standing there in the road laughing at his dog. But they say he's a very clever chemist, regular back-room boy they say he is.

'So, as I was telling you, our bus stops near the inspection gate and we get out and go through. Sometimes we're stopped and asked a question, or searched, but I haven't been yet. Inspector Jameson used to be at this first gate: he was not liked. I don't know why it was, one of the fellows told me that Jameson had a Power bug, another said he was an arch type of snooper; but I don't see that Inspector Jameson could have been much of a danger, because he wasn't allowed to do anything outside his duties. Well, we shall never know now, because he got killed two days ago—accident they say it was, but I don't know so much. Once we've passed the factory inspection gate we see a square building in front of us. It's used for Administration, Admin they call it. It looks like a country house, only it's grey and camouflaged, and Super has his office there, and the production managers and some of the PAD—that stands for Passive Air Defence. Then the head electrician is up at Admin and all kinds of clerical staff, and there's a bit of lawn in front of it with a flag-pole and the Union Jack. We walk down to the left, past what we call the Cop Shop, that's where the policemen are. Then after this there's the Registration Office and the Office of Works. Of course they call that the Office of Twerps, same as you'd expect. When you have got through the next gate you are inside the Danger Area, as it's called.

'There's long streets, and the pylons overhead that make everything seem so straight and thought out, and then there's avenues, as they call them, all marked with their numbers; but you see some grass along the sides of the avenues and there's grass over the mounds of the workshops, too, and buses travelling about taking workers from one place to the other. "Budgie cages": they call them, because the girls, the very young ones, are called "Budgies" here. And then there's the internal railway with trucks of explosives travelling about, and the sidings, and the canteens, and the shifting house where you've got to go to change your clothes before you can walk along the cleanways. Straight rubber composition paths, cleanways are, between the workshops, all black and shiny and soft to your feet. We're in a valley, you see, with the hills behind us, and our factory is seven miles round and has 30,000 workers. Of course they're not all on at the same time, because there are the three shifts:—the Blue, the Red, and the White, and there's the clerical staff and the Managers and the Time and Motion men, that they call Time and Emotion men. But still there are 30,000 workers all told. It makes you think, doesn't it.

'Before I go into the shifting house I walk down to the Group and stop at the contraband hut and give up anything that I am not supposed to take with me. The contraband hut looks like a loose box, a sort of stable I mean, with a half-door and the contraband keeper himself leaning over the top like a colt. He knows everyone on the Group. I suppose he knows them most by their things: their cigarette-cases, packets of snuff, lighters, and that. Of course he always knows the girls that go out with American soldiers because they have Lucky Strike cigarettes, and he knows the ones that have boys in Africa because they hand in those cases with pictures painted on, but the contraband hut man says that all these cases are made in the Midlands, and he knows the man that makes them and sends them out to Africa. The first inspection, where Jameson used to be, as I told you, is for anything you are carrying in a bag. I suppose they think you might have a bomb or something with you, but it is not very likely, is it, that you'd take a bomb in, because it would be as bad for you as the others.

Then I go into the shifting house and change into the asbestos suit, white trousers and coat, and a round cap on my head—kind of comical. When I first saw the fellows dressed like this I thought they all looked like convicts, but you soon get used to it when you are dressed the same way yourself. After a cup of tea in the canteen I go into the ablutions, and nurse is standing there with a tin of cream—ever such nice cream it is, though some of them don't like it. You put it all over your face and round the back of your neck and hands and rub it well in, and then you put the powder on top—dead white it is. It's difficult to get some of the girls to use it, and they tried to tell them with posters that they looked like Madonnas, but a lot of them said, "We don't want to look like bloody Madonnas," but there's some rouge in a little saucer and we can use that, too. Then we go down the cleanways in our special shoes and into whatever workshop we are in. Of course there is no need for me to do this, because I am still in the training section and the powder we are working with is not explosive but French chalk.

'My training workshop is just the same as the real ones, only we have got a lot of notices up on the wall: "This is the right way to do it, and this is the wrong way." Of course I can't tell you what we do, or what we're filling, but the first time I saw it all I was reminded of how we used to play shops when we were kids, filling up little boxes and handing them backwards and forwards to each other. We're all working class, on my shift at any rate. You hear that all kinds go into the industry, but I have never seen them except for some of the Labour Officers who have been to college and got degrees.

'There was a girl on our shift who pretended she'd been educated and all her friends were group captains. Ysabette Jones her name was. She was always talking, seemed like she couldn't stop, but none of the others ever took any notice of her. One of them told me she used to sit at her bench just staring, not doing anything. Then she threw a couple of spoons over one of the girls in the canteen. She didn't do it for any reason. She said afterwards she didn't remember anything about having thrown the spoons, and it was because she'd been bombed when she lived in London and hadn't heard from her boy who was a group captain. They've sent her away now, the doctor said she wasn't well enough to work. He said she had a split mind or something; and it seemed she hadn't got a boy at all, didn't know any group captains, had never been in London, and had no friends. She used to talk about a Miss Winslow too, on the supervisory staff, but we haven't got anyone called Miss Winslow in the factory. Ysabette Jones used to talk a lot about her family too, but we know now that she was an orphan brought up by her auntie who works as an office cleaner at a bookmaker's somewhere in the North, and she wrote to the factory saying that her niece's name was not Ysabette at all, that she had never been "right" and always been known as Crazy Liz. There wasn't any truth in what Ysabette Jones had been telling us. She made it all up. Funny, isn't it, what folks will do. Anyway she's gone now. It was funny, wasn't it, how she got in. I suppose she just talked her way in same as she's talked her way out now.

'After a few hours' work in the morning we go down to the canteen for a first break. Of course I know the canteen very well now. I have been working there myself as a volunteer – that happened when the snow came and we got stuck in the factory, had to stay there for three days. Lofty, the foreman on Group IV, was helping us serve the dinners, and one of the shop managers came up and helped, and Miss Robinson, our Labour Manager. They were the same people we'd seen every day, but they had always been like strangers. And then suddenly it seemed as if they'd all been brought up in the same street, workers and staff alike. Funny to think that something like a fall of snow could do that; but of course it didn't last, and now the snow's gone we're back to where we were. There was an air-raid warning while we were snowed in. It was the first time I'd heard the siren ringing out suddenly in the quietness, knowing we were in the Danger Area. I was doing a bit of kitchen work in the canteen when we heard it. I felt sorry for those who were out in the snow there, by the internal railway. It seems as if you feel safer when you're altogether indoors, though of course those working by the internal railway were better off than the men in the magazine.

'But it wasn't so bad in the canteen even with the air raid, and all because everyone seemed so friendly. I don't know why they can't be like it in ordinary times; but then they're so busy thinking of their place in the world and how to hold down their jobs and the bit of importance they've got just as if they're living under a kind of crust they've baked over themselves—and then a bit of danger comes along and it all cracks, and they're just ordinary and don't trouble any more. It seems as if some people can't even speak to their neighbours until they've been bombed to blazes. I can't understand it myself. We carried on cooking and making tea in the canteen, and it wasn't long before the Raiders Past sounded out.

'But the next day when they'd cleared away the snow, down by the internal railway near the hill, they found Inspector Jameson. He was dead. They can't make out how it happened. None of the engine-drivers know anything about it, though they say the brakes jammed several times, but they didn't see anything in the snow and they couldn't hear during the raid. There were several of them on duty at different times, and some volunteers helping as well. It was all a bit of a muddle owing to us being snowed in, not like ordinary times, but they all say the same thing. I never saw Inspector Jameson, and now I never shall, but it does seem a strange thing that he was the only one to get killed in the air raid, and not by enemy action neither. They say his head had been struck by a piece of wood and that he might have got hit accidentally by one of those planks that prop up the tarpaulins over the trucks.

'The men who were clearing away the snow from the internal railway lines got wet through, and they went and dried their clothes in the boiler-room. There was a man on our shift they call Julian, a good-looking fellow. The Contraband Hut man, who knows everyone, says that this

Julian had come back from Dunkirk. It was a terrible time for young fellows Dunkirk was, and after this boy had been discharged from the Army he was sent to work here. I saw him wheeling his truck along the cleanway the first day I came. I noticed him because he has very clear eyes staring straight ahead, and he looks as if he was talking to someone all the time – and that was the strange thing about it, because he never spoke. At first the other fellows were angry: they thought he considered himself too grand to talk, but after they knew what he'd been through they didn't trouble any more about it. Well, the night of the snowfall he was in the boiler-room drying his clothes – they were having a bit of a jaw, politics and that, when he came out suddenly with a whole sentence. Gluckstein, the overseer on our group, told me about it later in the canteen. He said it seemed like they were all equal and untroubled in their minds at the time, just sitting round the fire talking like kids at bedtime, but it seers funny, doesn't it, spending an evening in a boiler-room. I shouldn't choose it myself.

'A lot of things happened during the snowfall, the air raid and all that about Ysabette Jones, and Inspects: Jameson getting killed, and Julian getting his speech back. That wasn't the only thing that the fall of snow caused: there is a fellow called Geoffrey Doran working on Time and Motion, lives here at the hostel. He wears spectacles with those horn-rimmed glasses and looks kind of comical, and he always carried a great notebook with him everywhere he went. Well, it seems he was working on one of these mass observation capers, but he was doing it on his own, writing down all what the workers said, and what they ate and how much they earned. Only he thought no one didn't know that he was doing it, but of course they all knew it from the first day. Well, what happened to him doesn't sound much, but it almost finished him off. On the second night of the snowfall we were going up to the main canteen—it's by the big surgery near Admin, just outside the Danger Area, because we'd volunteered to work there in the kitchens. There was quite a lot of fellows going in, engineers and some of the storekeepers—it's what they call a dirty canteen, being out of the Danger Area, which means that you can wear your own clothes and your own shoes—but just as we were getting near it we saw Mr Doran come rushing out and he began digging in the snow with his hands and then kicking it like a mad creature. I didn't recognize him at first, his spectacles were broken, and he didn't half look in a state. I thought he'd been fighting, had a fit, or taken poison, or gone off his rocker, I didn't know what to think. Well, we found it out afterwards. He'd lost his notebook, and from the way he acted it seemed as if his reason had gone and his wife and only child and all. But it wasn't anything, more than that he'd lost his notebook. There was a mass of workers observing him.

'The snow cleared, and we came back to the hostel. We envied the workers that had been left up there, because we thought that they'd been having a nice holiday but they all looked sour. The holiday was all right, but some of the supervisory staff had got snowed-in at the hostel with them, and it had all been quarrelling and regimenting and welfaring. It seemed to us when we came back from those three days snowed-up at work that we came back from a place where people were acting like grown-ups to a nursery with a lot of blooming kids rushing about. But they had one bit of news for us. It seems that some medals had been sent down as a reward for industry. They do that sometimes and they give out OBEs—what the workers call here "Other Beggars' Efforts"—but there was one left over, and no one knows how it happened, but it was down to go to Ysabette Jones. She's the one that's scatty and been sent away now. Of course it was a clerical error.

'There's a cinema girl here called Nordie, shows films, she does, in the canteens: she used to be a journalist. I asked her once why she didn't write about the factory, but she said, "There's no story there." I don't suppose there is, neither. The way you know people at work is different to ordinary life. It is jagged and uneven, not just straightforward like in a storybook. This girl Nordie's been a school teacher too, educated girl she is. I don't know whether the war will be over before you have passed your examinations, Jane, but I do hope you'll get to be a school teacher same as Mum wished. They'll be needed.

'Well I've told you all I can remember about my first week here in case the war goes on long enough for you to get sent to one of these places yourself, then it won't seem so strange to you. It would be funny if you came here and got taken on in the welfare with me amongst the operatives. Even if you did, you'd only see a bit of it. There's no story there, one can't know it all. How can one—with thirty thousand workers, some brave, some sad, some stupid, some clever, and others just kind of comical. But all I've found out so far is that you've got to like them all, because if I hated any of them I'd feel I hated everybody.'

Musical Chairman

'Of course it gets very monotonous sitting here dealing with forms all day. You don't see much life. I do like a bit of life myself.'

These were the words of my colleague clerk at the Labour Exchange. She was a tall thin girl settled into a routine mood of despondency. Although we sat next to each other at high desks I do not think she would have troubled to talk to me if it had not been for her interest in my Aunt Amabel.

'It's funny,' she said, 'I should never have thought you were connected with the stage, somehow you don't look like the type. When I heard you were Amabel Corvo's niece you could have knocked me down with a feather.'

My colleague's adolescence had been coloured by her admiration for the musical comedy actress; now that she was grown up she did not make any attempt to free herself from this gallery-girl attitude to all actresses.

'She must have seen some life.'

'Who?'

'Your Aunt Amabel.'

'Do you think so?'

'You bet.'

This was the sort of talk that battledored between us on week-days at work. On Sundays I was free and did not think about the Labour Exchange except on those afternoons when I took a train to one of the Home Counties and went to tea with my aunt.

Amabel Corvo, after a prolonged success, had retired from the musical comedy stage. She had bought a country cottage, and at colossal cost had it modernised inside and old-worlded out.

My aunt's days did not vary much. She had a mid-day meal prepared by the Breton cook whom she had brought back with her after visiting France, then she spent the afternoon in her garden followed about by short-legged dogs and long-haired cats; sometimes she carried one of the Persian kittens in a kind of sling scarf round her neck, but this impeded her movements and made useless the large flower-basket which she took with her whenever one of the gardeners told her that any particular part of the garden was in bloom. When it rained, Aunt Amabel moved back into the cottage and settled herself fatly before the fire in her expensively ingle-nooked but inaptly furnished centre room. Here the walls were well plastered with the signed photographs of famous men, theatre posters, and pictures of Amabel herself in various musical comedy roles. Heavily framed looking glasses seemed to increase the size of the room and stuck in the corner of one of them was a stamp-sized snapshot of the last rich stockbroker my aunt had married.

My colleague at the Labour Exchange took two forms from the IN basket and moved them over to the OUT basket. 'You see,' she said, 'it was my ambition to become a musical comedy actress—like your aunt.' She sighed. 'The life would have suited me,' she said, 'but there you are, it wasn't to be. When I grew up, I grew up too much, as you might say. I got too tall. They told me that no man would want to play the lover opposite me because I should dwarf him.' She gazed palely out past the half-open door towards the jellied-eel shop. 'Men don't like being dwarfed when they're playing the lover, do they?' She had two Bomb-damage forms in her hand. 'I wonder how these got in here,' she said, and filed them carefully in a green file. 'When I was a kid I used to keep an Amabel Corvo book,' she said. 'Every time I saw a piece in the paper about your Aunt Amabel I cut it out and pasted it into my album. Half the crowned heads in Europe were after her or so it said. I remember there was a bit in one of the Sunday papers about that young Prince who was supposed to have given her some of his royal jewels. I wonder how she got him to do it. Quite a feat, wasn't it, when you think how few foreigners are free-handed with their money.'

Listening to this talk was a trouble to me. I had to switch my mind from the well-established widow maintaining a simple country life at colossal cost to the past-time pin-up girl of a million high kicks. Besides this, my own image of my aunt's public and private life did not coincide with that of my colleague's. In our family, Aunt Amabel was not approved. If it had not been for the money my mother would have had nothing to do with her at all, but, as my father was fond of saying, 'The cost of living is high and the cash is hard to come by.' These sayings of his were like milestones on the road to quarter-day when I would be given a fourpenny bus-fare and sent westwards, once more, to my aunt's dressing-room with a request for the money for my mother's rent in arrears and my father's season ticket to work in advance.

My aunt always received me kindly. She believed fondness for children to be a straight hit to the hearts of her public, but the success or failure of my mission depended more on the kind of company she was keeping in her dressing-room at the time; sometimes she wanted to appear open-handed and generous, and then my mother got her rent, my father his season ticket, and I enough money to keep me in sweets and cinemas for a month. But at other times, Aunt Amabel wished to show that she had a sense of the value of money, then there was nothing for my father or mother, and I had to walk all the way home, a complaining chorus echoing on through my mind: 'What a bluddy shame! She could at least have given me my fare back.' I tramped on, trying to find short cuts through the ill-lit small streets. 'She could at least have given me my fare back. What a bluddy shame!'

But it was a long way back in memory to my aunt's dressing-room from the Labour Exchange where I now worked, and I was sorry that my colleague was always shunting my thoughts back and forth over that furrowed ground. I had only had this job for a fortnight and was still uncertain about it, but the chief officer often told me not to worry. 'You'll soon get into the routine,' she said. 'Ask Miss Simpkins anything you don't understand. She'll be only too pleased to help you and put you on the right road.' Miss Simpkins was my pale-eyed colleague clerk, and I did not find her so free with the answers to all my questions because she was more interested in the films and the stage and the romantic haze which hovered over my Aunt Amabel.

I knew that the Local Appeal Board session was being held at the Labour Exchange to-day. I knew that the room the visiting board used every fortnight was a little way down the road in another building, but all this week that room was being re-painted and so we had lent our Juvenile Interviews office for the hearing of the Hardship cases. I asked Miss Simpkins about the Local Appeal Boards and instantly a light of exasperation flickered into her pale eyes. 'It all comes up through the Essential Work Orders,' she said. 'You've got it on your PL 103 leaflets and your EDL 64. You know the form an employer has to fill in if he wishes to terminate a worker's employ. ED 336, isn't it? And, as you know, the worker has to fill in ED 337 if he wants to leave. In each case it's the same. They've got to state their reasons and then the forms go up to the National Service Officer and he takes it up; well, sometimes one or other of them appeals against the National Service Officer's decision, on the grounds of hardship or something of that sort, and then it comes up before the Local Appeal Board—it may be an employer appealing against a decision or it may be a worker pleading extenuating circumstances or hardship, an invalid mother at home that has to be looked after, or a deaf auntie or something of the sort.' Her voice tailed off.

'But what happens at the Local Appeal Board?'

'Oh, there's a chairman. He's usually a retired magistrate or barrister, and there's the employer's representative and the worker's representative. They sit behind the Board-table; and then the clerk—in this case that's George, the old lame porter—has the case papers ready for them and when he's given a copy to each of the three men and let them look through it, he opens the door and calls the case in and they—the case, that is, and perhaps a parent or something—sit up to the table opposite the Chairman and answer his questions and they discuss it a bit, and then, if the Chairman thinks there's hardship and his colleagues agree with him, he usually recommends that the National Service Officer shall reconsider his decision.'

My colleague picked up a whole handful of forms and began rearranging them in alphabetical order. She drooped over her work as if her extreme tallness was a trouble to her and then, afraid that another question might come to her out of the silence, she said suddenly, 'There's not a lot in them.'

'In what?'

'The Local Appeal Boards. It's just people coming in and answering questions and going out again—just people and talk, the same as we get here every day.' In a little while she told me that she was going to the pictures during her lunch hour. She explained in detail how she managed this. She would go straight to the cinema and then come out half-way through and get a sandwich at the snack-bar down the road; then to-morrow she would do the same thing the other way round—'snack bar first and film second, see. Like this, I usually manage a whole picture in three mornings.' She began putting all the papers on her desk in a neat pile; she did this with a desperate briskness. 'I like to go to the pictures and see a bit of life,' she said, and was gone.

Now that my colleague clerk was off to the films for a bit of life I had only the empty desk to keep me company. I sorted out some of the papers which, I had been told, 'fell to be dealt with' in this capacity or that. It seemed to me that further from real life than the artificial languages of Esperanto and Ido was the language of Civil Service-oh. I took a sandwich from my own high desk and began to eat, first pushing aside some of the forms and thinking, 'They'll fall to be dealt with' when I've finished my lunch.

Half-way through my second sandwich the chief officer came in. She told me that old George had been taken ill and had collapsed suddenly. 'Just after the sixth case, it was,' she said. 'It's his heart, you know.' And now there is no one to give out the case papers, call in the appellants and get the tea at half-time.'

Something seemed to be expected of me here, so I said, 'What a shame!"

'Yes,' she said, 'The Chairman has come all the way here for this session and now look what's happened.'

'It's a shame, isn't it?' I said again.

The chief officer agreed with me and then she asked me if I would mind doing the work of clerk to the Local Appeal Board for the rest of the afternoon.

I put my sandwiches away in the top of the high desk and followed the chief officer to the end of the Labour Exchange building into an almost square room with green-distempered walls and one window at shoulder height. There was a long table in front of this window with three chairs behind it and three squares of blotting-paper on it. The centre square was the largest and in front of this there was also a large unspillable inkpot and a tray of pens and pencils. This was the Chairman's place. Exactly opposite on the other side of the table there was another wooden chair – the appellant's place. There were other chairs in the room, too, some near the table, some by the wall, and one behind a desk in a corner of the room – the clerk's place. The room was impersonal, but it did not have the depressing atmosphere of a court. It was all set for the session, but the Board was out to lunch.

After the chief officer had explained my simple duties, she smiled and went out. I began to read through some of the workers' statements on the case papers. Worker's statement from a Cypriot aged sixty-three: 'I thought Snitchfield was a suburb of London and said I would journey thither with pleasure, but now I learn it is many miles distant and means taking trains to arrive thence. I do not know the English language without my nephew to translate the words. He lives at home with me, is sick of the lungs and like to die. He has only me to succour him –'

A middle-aged man, grey suited and Homburg hatted, came into the room. He took off his hat, put it down on an isolated chair near the wall, and shook hands with me in a formal manner; then he stood with his back to the fireplace and talked out into the centre of the room. 'You know,' he said, 'we always try to talk things out with the people who come to this Board. It's not in any way a court, you understand. We like to get them to tell us their troubles.' He handed me a cigarette from a flat metal case and then lit it with a square metal lighter. 'Now that's a thing you don't often see,' he said.

'What?'

'A lighter that lights.'

After this there was silence between us which soon became awkward.

'Do you ever get any rough customers?' I asked him.

'Oh yes, sometimes,' he answered. 'But not like those we got in the last war. Why, I can remember men who thought nothing of picking up a heavy inkstand like this and pitching it through the window.'

'They did?'

'They did indeed. Mind you, there are many cases of hardship, and even the National Service Officer isn't infallible. Of course it isn't easy to sift everything out and to decide what's hardship and what isn't.' He put the inkpot back beside the large centre square of blotting-paper and said, 'But you'll soon see yourself how the Local Appeal Board works, and when the Chairman comes in he'll tell you all about himself.'

'I thought you were the Chairman.'

'Me? No, I'm the employer's representative. The Chairman's a barrister by profession; very clever man he is. But I thought as you'd come all the way from the Ministry down here you'd like to get to know as much as possible about it.'

I said that I had been very interested in all he had told me, but that I did not come from any Ministry and had indeed never been inside one. 'I'm a clerk from the Labour Exchange here,' I said. 'I've come in for the afternoon to act as clerk here because old George is ill.'

'Oh, we were told that some young woman from one of the Ministries was coming to sit in at one of these Boards. She was going to write something about it, I believe. Perhaps it's the next session she's coming to.'

Now that it had become clear to us both that he was not the Chairman and I was not the ministerial executive, we both felt as out of touch as two people who happened to be sitting next to each other on a bus. Grey-suit sat himself down behind the boardroom table and began writing some notes in a little book he had taken from his pocket. I sat by my desk in the corner of the room and read through the case papers again. 'Worker's statement: I have been treated for nerves and dismissed the light rescue service. My wife has just had another child. He has been operated on for cleft palate and hair lip. He is going on all right now, but the wounds are still open. I have been directed to a reconstruction camp up north, but think I should stay at home and look after my wife and child for a bit. I am a miner and used to being underground. What can I do at this building camp when the gaffer tells me to shin up buildings? I ain't never been used to that. Why can't I go down the pits again, same as I used to before the bad time come –'

Then in came Councillor Higgins. He was the worker's representative, a round-faced man wearing a brown suit, hatless and frowning. The employer's representative introduced us. 'From the Labour Exchange, are you?' said Councillor Higgins. 'I knew it well when I was unemployed. I thought I should wear away the wood of that counter with resting my hands on it, but those days are past now, aren't they?'

Then in came the Chairman.

He wore a black coat and grey-striped trousers and he was humming, some musical comedy number it was, and this trivial buzz buzz beneath his breath did not match up with his Roman head and judicial air. But for all his greyed-up hair and down-drooping eyes he took such sprightly steps from door to boardroom table that his pince-nez, dangling from a knotted silk string, danced a gallows jig against his black waistcoat. Again the introduction was gone through and again it was explained that I stood proxy for Porter George struck down with sudden heart attack.

As I looked at the Chairman it seemed to me that I had seen him before, but there was no answering look from him. The three men took their places at the table. I laid a copy of the case paper before each bit of blotting-paper. I abandoned the idea of having met the Chairman elsewhere. It was improbable. I thought, 'After all, I do not move amongst magistrates.'

The employer's representative on the Chairman's right and the worker's representative on the left studied the case before them. The Chairman read it out like a litany. Miss Margaret Day, aged sixteen, working at Robert's Telephone Company, wanted to leave her employ because she was anxious to learn to be a telephone operator. She believed that she had been engaged on the understanding that she was apprenticing herself to this trade, but now she found that she was wasting her time with clerical work of the most petty kind. She believed that she should be allowed to leave to find herself more important work. This was her case and it was clearly set down in neat, carefully spaced, well-punctuated sentences.

The employers had their statement too. 'The girl was on essential work and it was their opinion that she should stay in her present employ.'

The Chairman stopped reading, looked over his pince-nez towards the door, and said, 'Would you ask them to come in, please?'

Three came in.

A thin, grey-faced, severe-suited woman personnel manager wearing a brown hat haloed to the back of her head showing a widow's peak in the parting of her hair, she had an efficient but exasperated woodpecker manner which made it clear at once that she considered it all an interruption and a waste of time and regretted having to come to the Local Appeal Board session in working hours.

The employee's father was a thick-set, white collared man suffering from a sense of strain and injustice. He was conscious, too, of being a salaried man and not a wage-earner.

Bolstered between the two salaried executives was the wage-earning appellant, a lumpy sixteen-year-old girl, ill at ease in the encounter between parent and employer. She slumped in her chair silent and stolid while questions and answers were being exchanged across the boardroom table.

First the protest of the parent:

'My daughter wants to leave her firm. She doesn't get much work on the switchboard although she was given to understand that she was being employed for that. She wants to do more useful work than she's doing now. I should think my daughter's appeal is just the kind Mr Bevin would approve. Why should my daughter go on doing unessential work just running errands and addressing envelopes when the messenger girls at the firm where I work myself are all leaving and going to essential jobs? If they can release them there, why can't they release my daughter here? It does seem unjust. Your daughter, Mr Chairman, is probably at boarding school still, learning languages, studying economics, and fitting herself for this better world that we're going to have after the war. My daughter wants to learn to be a telephone operator and I think it's right to encourage her' – he smiled – 'seeing that she's so smit on the switchboard,' he said.

Then the explanation of the personnel manager:

'We can't afford to lose an employee at the present time. This girl's on essential work. We're a scheduled firm. The girl's learning a job and we pay her well. Mr Bevin says we're to keep our workers. What are we to do? We're only obeying regulations.'

And then a slow summing-up talk from the Chairman:

'Your daughter, Mr Day, is on essential work. She's part of the war effort. Perhaps the firm for which you work can afford to let their messenger girls go. The firm that employs your daughter evidently cannot do so. It is of no use to attack us because of the Government's laws. What we think and what Mr Bevin thinks may be two different things, but we are not here to discuss that now. Robert's Telephone Company, for which your daughter works, is a scheduled firm. The country cannot afford to have workers moving about at will now. Your point about my own daughter being educated at a boarding school is not relevant because I have no daughter. I am sorry I cannot recommend your daughter's transfer to another firm. Thank you for coming up here to see us. Good afternoon to you.'

Mr Day had been rather impressed by the assured manner of the Chairman, but a sense of injustice was still jangling behind his brain. He said, 'Well, thank you, Mr Chairman, for listening to me so patiently. I know how busy you must be. It's not that my daughter's unpatriotic, you understand. It's just the contrary. She's only too anxious to do all she can−more than she's doing now. But it does seem a shame that she won't get a chance to improve herself. However, there it is. Thank you all the same. Good-bye.'

The personnel manager did not say anything. She was thinking, 'Of course the girl could have gone over to the production side. The firm wouldn't have had any objection to her working on the assembly bench, but she wouldn't want that, not in her present mood. She'd know that her parents would think it a bit of a come down. It's a problem, but I don't know what they're beefing about. The girl won't have to go through the tough time I went through myself−years of apprenticeship just picking up the bits of knowledge I could about the job on the way. That was a hard struggle and no mistake about it.'

They got up to go. The girl walked between her father and the personnel manager. She was embarrassed and ill at ease, wishing to disassociate herself from the present proceedings.

The three went out.

The Chairman said, 'Nothing much to discuss about that case. Very straightforward, isn't it?'

His colleagues agreed in silence. I took away the case

papers and substituted others, then I went outside and asked case eight to come in.

Case eight was a girl. She wore a brown suit; her hair was dark brown and fell in straight sad lanks except where it was dented back by a kirby slide. Her skin was brownish, too, so that her eyes seemed more pale than her face.

A well-dressed young works manager with the look of a wide boy came in and sat down beside her.

The Chairman said, 'You're Mary Langton, aren't you?'

'Yes.'

'You're fourteen years old?'

'Yes.'

'You're working at Messrs Taylor and Bexley as an assistant secretary, aren't you?'

'Secretary,' she said – 'I don't think I'm a secretary.' She looked puzzled. 'I answer the telephone sometimes and go through the card index.'

The Chairman began to read the girl's statement aloud: 'I want to go and work in a factory. I sit all day in this office with nothing to do. I get so *very* bored. I want to go and work in a factory.'

The chairman put the case paper down on the table before him and looked at the works manager as if attempting to intimidate him by staring. 'Who are you?' he asked.

The wide boy answered up immediately, 'I'm the works manager.'

The Chairman asked the girl if her parents were coming up to the Board. 'They might be able to help us.'

'Dad works on the railway,' the girl answered. 'He said he would come up to-day, but it's a goodish way.'

'What about your mother?'

'Mum works too,' the girl answered.

'Why are you so anxious to leave your present job?'

'Nothing to do,' the girl answered – 'nothing whatever.'

The wide boy works manager chipped in here. 'I've brought a list of her duties,' he said. He took a piece of paper from a thin metal cigarette-case and handed it to the Chairman.

The list was read out: 'Answering the telephone, filing letters, card indexing, invoicing, making the tea, taking messages, tidying the office.'

The wide boy said, 'I asked Miss Willis, that's the head clerk, and she said the girl had plenty to do and had no cause for complaint. I don't know what the trouble is—honest I don't.

The Chairman looked at the girl. 'What is the trouble?' he asked.

'I want to go and work in a factory,' she said. 'I don't like the office where I work. I get sad there; I am unhappy there. I want to go and work in a factory.'

'We can't afford to lose her,' the wide boy said stubbornly.

The girl looked desperately from chairman to councillor.

'I want to go and work in a factory,' she said.

The Chairman said, 'But we're only trying to help you. We're trying to think what's best for you. How do you know what it's like working in a factory? You might be much more unhappy once you got there?'

'I know I wouldn't be unhappy,' the girl said.

The employer's representative turned to the works manager.

'You do realise that this girl is only fourteen; she's a child.'

'We have to take what we can get nowadays.' said the works manager.

'Yes, but she's a child,' the employer's representative repeated. 'There's no compulsion on children of this age. I think this is the saddest comment on the war that has come my way yet.'

The works manager shrugged his shoulders.

The Chairman said, 'This is a case for the Juvenile Department: I don't know why it has come to us at all. It should have been sent straight to the Juvenile office. Perhaps she could have a talk with Miss Langton and find out what the trouble really is. I shall recommend her leaving the firm if necessary, but the Juvenile Officer must find out what is wrong first.'

I was sent out with a message to the Juvenile Officer and when I returned the lank-haired girl and the wide boy works manager had gone.

'I kept the case hanging on longer than usual,' said the Chairman, 'because I thought it might give us a clue to the trouble. I didn't like the look of that works manager at all. A nasty bit of goods'–he shook his head–'a nasty bit of goods,' he repeated.

Case nine came in next. Case nine was a young man. He wore a speckled grey belted overcoat; he had no hat, and he came in alone, walked straight up to the table and sat down opposite the Chairman. I saw by the case paper that he was not yet twenty, he looked older.

The Chairman said, 'You state here that you are appealing against being directed to the North. You say that you will not be able to earn enough money to pay three rents. How do you make out that you have to pay three rents, my lad?'

'I have to send money home to my mother,' the boy said. 'She lives in the South. You see, I was directed from there to London in the first place; then I'd have my rent up North where they want to direct me, and my rent for my lodgings here in London.'

'But you can give those up.'

'No,' the boy said.

The Chairman looked down at the statement again. 'I see you state, "Housekeeper expecting a baby." What does that mean?'

'It means that my young lady is expecting a baby.'

'Are you the father?'

'Yes, definitely.' The boy took a note-case from the inner

pocket of his overcoat. 'I've brought the medical certificate.' He handed it over to the Chairman.

'How old is your young lady?'

'Twenty-two next March, she is.' He was silent for a few moments, then he said, 'I found her some lodgings at last. We've been there a few weeks now. They're not bad lodgings.'

The Chairman asked the boy if he was going to get married.

'We can't. She's married already to someone else.'

'Who's been supporting her so far?'

'I have.'

'I see she's not going to have her baby for some time yet. Can't she work at all in the meantime?'

'No, she can't; she's been ill. It's not long since I fetched her back from hospital.'

'I see you've been earning good money for your age. How do you manage that?'

'I'm semi-skilled, see. I went to night school and took a technical course. It was hard work, but it was worth it.'

'Well, my lad, when you're sent away I think you'll have to give up your lodgings in London.'

'I got to keep them on,' the boy said. 'I got to look after my young lady. I can't leave her destitute, can I?'

The Chairman said that he did not think the circumstances exempted the boy from re-direction. 'After all, my lad, you'll be called up for the army soon, won't you?'

'Yes, but the army's different. I'm expecting that, but I can't afford three lots of lodgings now, and I think I ought to stay at home and work in the firm where I'm employed now till I do get called up.'

'Well, my lad, we'll discuss your case in your absence.'

The boy slowly buttoned up the belt of his speckled grey overcoat, then he got up and walked towards the door. 'Shall I be let know soon?' he asked.

'Yes, in a day or two.'

The boy went out, and again the three men were alone for the conference. Councillor Higgins shook his head sadly from side to side. 'Ah, a bad business altogether, poor boy.'

'Yes,' the Chairman said. 'He's thoroughly involved. Of course, it wouldn't be so bad if she wasn't married.'

The Board conferred. They did not think there would be any possibility of recommending that the boy should be allowed to stay in London. While they were still discussing this, someone came in and said that Mr Langton had just arrived.

'Mr Langton. Who's he?' said the Chairman.

Councillor Higgins remembered that Langton was the father of the fourteen-year-old girl who wanted to work in a factory. He was the railway man who was to come up from work to the Local Appeal Board.

'Oh yes, tell him to go and see the Juvenile Officer. He'll be able to help them. I'm glad he's managed to come up here to-day.'

I called in the next case. Then I heard Councillor Higgins say, 'Here's a crowd,' as the girls came colting in three abreast. They were all from the Frizz Frozz Electrical Company and all appealing against three days' suspension. After them followed the works manager, but a long way after, stepping sedately, smiling slowly, taking a chair near the wall at some distance from the girls, and then sitting down, legs crossed, silk socks showing, and an expression of confident calm blanded across his face.

All the girls were under seventeen years old. The eldest, Florence Whitaker, had written under the heading 'Worker's statement': 'I don't see as how we should only get seven and six bonus for doing the same amount of work. We got ten shillings bonus before. That's all I've got to say.' The youngest girl, Ivy Jones, had written: 'The production had gone up from six thousand to nine thousand. In view of this, we are of the opinion that the management are not within their rights in reducing the workers' bonus.' The other girl, Dorothy Davy, had written her statement in pencil and without punctuation: 'Florence and Ivy refused to go on the packing bench Mr Harding sent them home there was a row because they took us off the bonus and never told us nothing it do seem a waste in war-time it do really.'

The three girls were all silent and all sulks at first, then they all spoke at once.

The Chairman, looking down at the case papers, singled them out by name.

'Now, Florence, I see that Mr Hardy –'

The works manager stopped smiling down at his socks to look up and frown at the Chairman. 'Har*ding*,' he corrected.

'I see that Mr Harding says, "Florence Whitaker refused to work on the packing bench, and when asked to do so she used bad language."'

'I never used no language,' Florence answered.

'That's right. She never used no language,' Ivy said.

'Never used no language, Flo didn't,' Dorothy echoed.

The works manager smiled in a knowing way, but kept his silence.

'Well, in future, Florence,' the Chairman said, 'you must be more careful of your conversation in the workshop. Now I read here that you refused to work on the packing bench. Is that true, Ivy?'

'Well I don't know about refused,' Ivy answered. 'It was agreed that we were to have a bonus of ten shillings and when they went and reduced that to seven and six we said we were going to see Mr Harding about it. I hadn't got into my overalls then; we'd just come to work, see, and as it turned out, it was just as well I wasn't in my overalls.'

'Why?'

'Because Mr Harding comes busting out of his office and sent us all home.'

'That's right,' said Florence. 'We was all suspended.'

The Chairman turned to the works manager. 'I see that all these young ladies state that their bonus was cut down although the production had gone up. Is that true?'

'In a sense that is correct,' Mr Harding answered.

'Why was that?'

'Because our own contracts had been cut down. The way it was we had no choice but to decrease the bonus.'

'Did you explain that to your employees, Mr Harding?'

'No, but I would have done if they'd come to me in the proper manner.'

'Have the workers got their own Trades Union representatives?'

'No, I don't want no Trade Union in my shop.'

'Well, then, how can the workers come to you in the proper manner?'

'That's what my Dad says,' Ivy chipped in.

Florence's finer treble took up the argument: 'Mr Harding's always on about production and us never missing a minute of work. Regular theme song it is with him, yet he sends us all home for three days. Me sitting at home waiting for Mum and Dad to come in from work isn't helping the war effort much, is it? There's not a lot of sense in it.'

'Not a lot of sense in it,' echoed Dorothy.

'Now, Mr Harding,' the Chairman said, 'I suppose it didn't occur to you to suspend the girls for one day and instead of three?'

'If the same happened again, I'd do the same,' Harding said, obstinately.

Ivy said, 'I suppose you'd sack us if you could.'

'Knows he can't. We're on essential work,' said Florence.

'Ivy and Florence,'–the chairman stared at the girls through his pince-nez–'Ivy and Florence, we will you please address your remarks to the Chairman only. You're not here to talk to the works manager.'

'That's right. We see enough of him at work,' said Florence.

'Far too much,' added Ivy.

'Now, Ivy,' said the Chairman, 'when Mr Harding sent you home what did you say?'

'I told him we was tired of all this chopping and changing and fed up with being bamboozled.'

'She was most abusive.' The works manager spoke in a distant voice as if he disdained to remember the exact words.

'She didn't say nothing out of the ordinary,' Florence interrupted.

'Nothing out of the ordinary,' echoed Dorothy.

'Well, Mr–er–er –'

'Harding,' prompted Councillor Higgins.

'Mr Harding, if you have no Trades Union representatives and take a bonus on and off without telling the workers why, you're bound to have trouble, aren't you?'

The works manager still smiled down at his socks and said nothing.

The Chairman told them they could all go and he would discuss the case with his colleagues. The girls stampeded out and Mr Harding, the works manager, walked slowly after them.

As soon as the door shut it seemed as if the room had become strangely silent. The scratching of the pen-nib on the case paper was very loud as the Chairman wrote, and when he stopped and started to speak his voice sounded slow and weighted with gloom. 'Of course,' he said, 'this kind of case could all be settled in the workshop. It should be really. You can't blame the girls with no Trades Union representatives and that superior-looking works manager. I should have used bad language myself if I had to see much of him. I think that the girl—let me see, what was her name?—oh yes, Dorothy Davy—she should be given the wages lost for her three days away from work, but the other two are not entitled to that in view of the fact that they did use bad language. Well, then, let's get on with the next case.'

I handed the next case papers to the Chairman in the centre, to the employer's representative on the right and to the worker's representative on the left; this was as automatic a work now as being a nippy at Lyons and putting food before mealers at marble-topped tables. But I became aware again of a sense of having seen the Chairman somewhere else, in other circumstances, in a different mood. Thinking of this, I missed hearing the first few sentences he read out from the case paper before him: '... Montagu Smith has several times asked to leave the factory and been refused permission to do so. Ten days ago, after being sent with a message to another firm, he took the law into his own hands and did not return. He has not been back to work since, although several times told to do so.' The Chairman coughed, then, like a man on the march changing step, went on as if against opposition. 'Let's see what Smith says about it. Ah, here it is. "I do not want to continue work in this factory as I wish to work in a dockyard, the country being very much in need of more shipping." Well, we'd better get Smith in now.'

As soon as the door was opened they came in. First Mrs Smith, herding three small children. They all took their places on the chairs by the wall and looked straight ahead of them as if they were at the cinema. The Chairman said 'Oh, good evening, Mrs Smith. I see you've brought all your children along with you.'

'No,' she answered; 'I've left the two younger ones at home.'

Montagu Smith walked in then. He was a small boy with straight dark hair and slow-moving brown eyes. He carried a check cap in his hand, did not speak, and stared at the Chairman in a thoughtful and serious manner.

'Now, young Montagu Smith,' the Chairman said, 'come and sit here and tell us what the trouble is.'

The boy did as he was asked, still staring straight at the Chairman.

'Well, my boy, I see by this paper that you are fifteen years old. You are fifteen, I suppose?'

The boy nodded.

The Chairman found it difficult to put the questions. He was disconcerted by Montagu's manner of looking at him and he would have found it more easy if the boy had looked older, but he was so short for his age that he seemed more like a studious, neat ten-year-old.

Through reading the case paper carefully again and questioning Montagu's mother the Chairman got to know that the boy could not accustom himself to the long hours and the sameness of the work. He got tired early each day and wanted to go away.

The Chairman turned to Mrs Smith. 'Any trouble with him at home?' he asked.

'No,' she said. 'Always been a good boy at home, Montagu has. He minds the younger ones for me when I go out to do the shopping and that. Never had no trouble with him.'

The Chairman had this habit of humming under his breath when he was tired, amused, slightly embarrassed, or ill at ease. He started this again now, but I could not pick out the tune. Mrs. Smith quietened the younger child who had got off his chair and begun hopping up and down first on one foot and then on the other and finally jumping both feet together.

The Chairman said 'Your son, Mrs Smith, had been working in a scheduled workshop. Do you understand the meaning of the word "scheduled"?'

Mrs. Smith answered, 'Yes. Scheduled means it's got to be clean and have food and the welfare and that.'

'Well, it's true that a scheduled firm does have to comply with those conditions, but being scheduled under the Essential Work Orders also means that an employee cannot leave his place of employ without the consent of the National Service Officer. The worker is deprived of his right to sell his labour at a higher rate, but also he is no longer liable to dismissal without a thorough investigation into the causes, and he is guaranteed the right rate of pay for the job. You understand, Mrs. Smith, that the Essential Work Orders affecting both workers and management have been put into operation in order to prevent the unnecessary turnover of labour at this time when production is so vital to the whole war effort.'

'Yes,' said Mrs Smith; 'but how do it all affect our Monty?'

'Well, your son Montagu has run away from work and been directed back. An adult would be liable to prosecution but we don't prosecute juveniles.' He hummed quietly to himself, searching in his mind for some more words. 'I understand, Mrs. Smith, that your son went to the Labour Exchange some months ago and asked for a job. He said he had left school now and wanted work as soon as possible.'

'That's right: he did. It was just after his Dad had been sent overseas and we needed the money very bad.'

'Well Montagu,' the Chairman said, 'your mother depends on you a great deal. Your father's in the Forces now, isn't he?'

The boy nodded his head, still staring at the Chairman.

'Your schooldays are over now, Monty. Don't you think you could give the factory another chance?'

The boy shook his head.

'Now come along, Montagu, your mother looks up to you as the wage-earner.'

The boy still stared, but now he nodded his head again.

The interview was over. Mrs Smith hustled the younger children to the door; the smallest one went rabbiting along in little jumps. Montagu followed them check cap in hand, heavy footed and silent, the principal bread-winner in a family of six.

None of the three men spoke for some time. The Chairman wrote on the case paper, the scratching of his pen-nib harsher than his humming, but now I was able to pick out the notes of the song. It was an old musical comedy number called 'Do, do, do what you've done, done, done before, Baby.' I wondered if the Chairman knew the words of the song he hummed.

The employer's representative said, 'Difficult to believe that boy's fifteen, isn't it?'

'Yes,' said Councillor Higgins. 'Small for his age, wasn't he? Didn't seem above fifteen at the outside, did he? Mind you, I can sympathize with him easy enough because I was bread-winning myself when I should have been scholarship-winning by rights.'

'Very taciturn type of boy, wasn't he?' said the employer's representative. 'Not like those girls, was he?'

'No, he wasn't,' answered Councillor Higgins. 'They had plenty to say for themselves, hadn't they?'

The Chairman said, 'Couldn't we have a cup of tea now? I think we deserve it.'

His two colleagues agreed, so I set out on my errand down the long passage to Mrs Wayland's cafeteria over the way.

There was a long queue waiting at the tea counter. I got an oxidized metal tray and took my place behind two women with shopping baskets; it was clear from the conversation that one of them had been to the Local Appeal Board.

'We 'ad a bit of dinner early before we come up. Our Maree's case come on the larst just before the Chairman went to get hisself some grub. It took ever so long with the questions and that, 'ardship cases, they call them. I don't know what I should 'ave done if you 'adn't come up after and helped me with the shopping and that; it's not easy in a strange place.'

'Can't get the stuff now, can you?' the other woman answered.

''Course, Maree told the Chairman herself that she wasn't trying to shirk the war effort, nor nothing of that, but it would be a help to her if she could be transferred to a factory nearer home. That's why she wanted me to come up with her see. She said, "You tell them, Mum, about me having to change busses twice on the way and having to do all the shopping, and about Fred being on a special diet and him working on the railway and not being able to help much in the house because of only having one arm. I know it all see, but I don't know how to put it to them. You can tell them better than wot I can, and then they'll give me a transfer to a factory nearer home."'

'That's right,' the other woman answered. 'Never was much of a one for talking, Maree wasn't. Not like you, is she? More like her Dad, isn't she?'

For a while the two women were silent, seeming to withdraw into their mood of fatigue, and then Maree's mother said, 'The Chairman asked if we couldn't have Maree and Fred to come and live with us so's I could help with the shopping and that, but we haven't got no room for them seeing as we have to look after Mother.'

'Needs a lot of care, your mother does at her age, doesn't she?'

'I don't know why the Chairman said that. Even if we got a new place with room enough for Maree and Fred it would take us so long to find it with the housing shortage and all, that the war would be over by then.'

'Shocking rents they're asking now, aren't they?'

The queue inched onward towards the food counter. I

thought about the cases and how individuals could be contorted by circumstances. How strange it was that a boy of nineteen was not considered old enough to have a family, but a boy of fifteen was not too young to keep one.

'Mind you,' said Maree's mother, 'the Chairman was very well spoken and all that, but he said he couldn't see the hardship. He said he always did his own shopping hisself.'

'Yes, but he don't work a nine-hour shift and have all the housework to do as well, do he?'

'The Chairman listened to all we had to say. They tell me he does a lot of this work. They say he don't never make a mistake in law nor nothing of that, but he told Maree he couldn't recommend her transfer, said he couldn't see where the hardship lay. Funny him saying that, wasn't it?'

'Don't they 'ave no women as chairmen?'

'No; he was a man, the Chairman was.'

Soon I reached Mrs Wayland's food counter. A cup and saucer for the Chairman and for Councillor Higgins and the employer's representative, some sugar twisted in a paper in each saucer, teaspoons, a white corrugated milk-jug, a metal hot-water jug, an earthenware teapot, four plates, four knives, four slabs of bread and butter—I counted it all over carefully and then went out. I passed the two women; they were sitting down at a table now. 'It do seem a pity Maree won't get her transfer, don't it?' one said to the other.

When I walked back into the boardroom the idiot was there. He did not look at the Chairman; he stared slantwise towards the door. He had been fined for refusing to fire-watch; he had written letters of abuse to the Labour Exchange asking for his unemployment money and again refusing to fire-watch. Now his brother, who had brought him up to the Local Appeal Board, sat at the end of the room and answered up for him. The sane brother wore a tweed suit and bright checked tie. 'You see, when my brother was discharged from the army his wife was given this note saying she'd have to be responsible for him.'

'Thank you, Mr Calloway.' The Chairman took the note and read it through quickly, then passed it on to his colleagues. I had put the tea-tray down on top of the desk in my corner of the room. I was very careful not to make any noise because I did not want to upset the unsound appellant, but the idiot did not look in my direction; he kept his eyes fixed down to that part of the floor that led under the door.

'I understand you wrote a letter to the Labour Exchange asking for your unemployment money,' the Chairman said, but the idiot made no sign of having heard. His brother answered for him, 'Oh yes, he can write quite well.'

'But he can't fire-watch?'

'Well, he went and signed on, but then he came back. Ran all the way home, he did.'

'Is he afraid of air raids?'

'No; he doesn't seem to be afraid of air raids at all. It's people that he seems to be afraid of.'

The idiot's hands began to shake.

'You see,' the idiot's brother said, 'the fire-guard officials came round to see him. He got into an awful state. I'm afraid he'll attack them if they come round again.'

'If he does that, he's likely to get a punch on the nose one of these days, isn't he?'

'Very likely, but he's not responsible for his actions. He doesn't know what he's doing, you see.'

'Can he answer, do you think?'

'Yes, I think he can.'

'You feel that you can't do any fire-watching at all?' the Chairman asked the idiot. 'Not up to it, eh?'

The idiot's shoulders began to shake and then he answered abruptly all on one note, 'What I can do I will do.' After this the idiot began turning his head quickly from side to side;

his shoulders and hands did not stop shaking. His brother looked at him and said 'Shh, shh!' making a slow downward movement of his hand as if to calm an animal that is jumping round its cage.

The councillor and the employer's representative were as still as statues, now; a painful expression seemed to be caked over the councillor's face.

'Do you think this will all be settled soon?' the idiot's brother asked. 'I've had to bring my brother all the way up from Acton four or five times over this fire-watching. I work in an aircraft factory myself and I lose a lot of time, you know.'

The Chairman nodded and asked the idiot one more question, 'Are you working now?' The Chairman repeated the question, but the idiot did not answer. 'All right, Mr Calloway, your brother will get complete exemption from fire-watching, of course.'

Mr Calloway got up. 'Come along,' he said to his brother and then more gently, 'Come along, Laddie.'

He led the idiot to the door, but before they reached it the idiot spoke up suddenly, 'I'm working,' he said. 'I keep a little store at home.' Then he repeated more loudly and more quickly, 'I keep a little store.' His brother led him out, but as he went away along the covered way we could hear him shouting, 'I keep a little store' over and over again until the words went running into each other—'I keepa little store I keepa —'

The councillor shivered, but the expression on his face relaxed. 'It's easy to see he's not normal,' he said.

'Poor fellow,' said the employer's representative. 'He ought never to have been brought here. Someone must have slipped up a bit when they sent him up all the way from Acton.'

The Chairman, who had been writing notes on the back

of the case paper, again said suddenly, 'Well, we could all do with some tea now.'

I brought the tray forward and put it down on the boardroom table.

'Bread and butter, too,' said the employer's representative. 'I was getting quite hungry.'

The Chairman took off his pince-nez and stared down at the oxidized metal tray. 'So was I,' he said.

While the three men were drinking their tea Councillor Higgins asked the Chairman if he thought the Essential Work Orders would be carried on after the war.

'I should think so; for a time, at any rate.'

Councillor Higgins said, 'Of course, it would come in as a kind of counter-blast to unemployment. It can be very hard on workers sometimes.'

'The Essential Work Orders are all right if they're taken in the right way,' said the Chairman. 'It's the beginning of planning.'

The employer's representative said, 'Employers can't dismiss employees just as they please. That's a bit of a revolution in itself, isn't it?'

The Chairman said, 'Of course, it's very difficult to fit some people into the system, but in war-time an effort has to be made.' It was clear that he did not want his colleagues to get away with the conversation. 'Most people want to work. I know that it is not generally admitted, but my experience has taught me that it is so. People want to work in war-time and peace-time, too.'

I sat in the idiot's chair, poured out more tea, saw the reflection of the Chairman in the metal tray, and listened to him lecturing on about designated craftsmen.

The Chairman seemed to be choosing this time to take his technical information out for a run. The other two men did not seem to be listening to him; they knew it all off by heart already.

After I had got the cups back on the tray and piled up the plates I put the last case papers before the three men. The Chairman said, 'Now here's a curious coincidence; it bears out exactly what I've been saying. This man's appealing against dismissal: he says the employers are trying to get rid of him because they say he's too old. Well, he's younger than me according to this. Ask him to come in.'

I went out with my metal tray of cups. I went into the waiting-room and told Joseph Hudson that the Board were waiting for him.

He had thick white hair and very bright blue startled eyes as if he had just come from a dark place and was seeing the sea for the first time. Joseph Hudson went into the boardroom and I went on to Mrs Wayland's cafeteria, because there was no queue there now I got back within a few minutes. As I came into the boardroom the Chairman was saying, 'Now no one wants to stop you doing your bit, Mr Hudson.'

'Huh, that's what you say,' answered Joseph Hudson. 'They've been trying to sack me for being too old, haven't they?'

'How old are you, Mr Hudson?'

'I'm just turned sixty. Of course I know I look more because my hair's white, see.'

'Illness, I suppose?'

'Illness? No; it's what they call an idiosyncrasy. My son's just the same and he's only twenty-six. Just looks as if somebody's mother has been using Persil on his head—white as a table-cloth, his hair is. Illness—I've never had a day's illness in my life except when I was in prison, in Spain that was, but that was the treatment we got there. Fascist prison, it was.'

This gave the Chairman his chance. 'Surely, Mr Hudson, you find there's more freedom here.'

'Course there is. That's why I went and fought against the Fascists in Spain. Mind you, we were all volunteers. The Fascists beat folks up with rubber truncheons, give them castor-oil, and then shoot them like dogs or send them to concentration camps. Now, under democracy, so called, same as we've got 'ere at the present time, you never know rightly where you are. Proper muddle, it is. Which is better of them two? It's obvious, ain't it?—the latter. That's why I come up here to this Appeal Board. Under Fascism there wouldn't be no appeal board, so seeing as we've got the machinery, we might as well use it so's it don't get rusty.'

The Chairman was disconcerted. Hudson had got away with a long speech. He hastened in now with his 'Yes, yes, Mr Hudson, but there's no need for you to get upset.'

'Upset,' said Joseph Hudson. 'I'm not upset; it takes a lot more than this to upset me.'

The Chairman told Joseph Hudson that he had all the facts that were relevant to the case. It would be discussed and Mr Hudson would be told the result.

The white-haired man went out. As soon as he was gone the Chairman sighed and said, 'A very troublesome type, that last fellow.' He looked through the case paper again, frowning over it. 'Well, I think his case is quite clear. We recommend his immediate reinstatement at work.'

The employer's representative said, 'Do you think they had some other reason for dismissing him? He may be quarrelsome or something of the sort.'

'He may be, but they don't say so. In this statement they definitely give his age as their grounds for dismissal. They know they are not within their rights in dismissing a man who wants to work and is fit to work, and their not troubling to come up here to-day tells very much against them. It is clear that in a case like this the worker should be reinstated. Are you all agreed?'

They said they were all agreed. The session was over. The Chairman thanked me for taking the place of porter George. The employer's representative said 'I don't know what we should have done without you.' The councillor commented, 'Must be a bit of a change for you from the usual day's work. Well, one never knows what one may be doing next in war-time.' Then they all three went out, grey-suited employer's representative, brown-suited councillor, and the pince-nez, humming, black-coated Chairman.

I tidied up the room, pulled the black-out curtains across the window, and then took my way back to the Labour Exchange.

My colleague clerk was at her high desk. 'Did you get on all right?' she asked me.

I said I had got on all right.

'Mind you,' she said, 'I shouldn't like that sort of work myself. I like something with a bit of life in it.'

As she said this I began to think about Aunt Amabel and a supper-party on the stage after one of her successful last nights. I had been sent up with a message from my mother. I was watching from the wings. Amabel was talking to the man on her right, talking with persistence, stopping only to sigh, to look at herself in a small mirror she always carried, to drink some champagne, or to shiver and draw her fur wrap more closely round her shoulders. The man had to leave the supper-party before the end; he passed by me in the wings. Either he was more tall and square or else his white starched shirt-front made him seem so. He was humming to himself, but he stopped for a moment to mutter, 'Poor Amabel. What hard lives these girls have! What hard lives!'

As I thought back on the supper-party of the stage and the Hardship cases of the Local Appeal Board, it became clear to me that it was the same musical Chairman.

Soldiers' Chorus

The train took a long time to leave London so that the soldiers looked at their watches several times before it started. At last one of them said, 'Seems as if they've forgotten us.'

His friend answered, 'Wot you worrying about, Jack? We're still on leave, aren't we?'

'Well, not my idea of leave, sitting in a railway carriage waiting for it to move off.'

The boy near the window pushed his cap to the back of his head; his hair was damp-curled close and low on his forehead with sweat. 'I don't trouble,' he said. 'We'll start soon enough,' and at this moment, as if in answer to a signal, the wheels began to grate round, the train took itself backwards, forwards, and then backwards again, the soldiers were jolted against each other and shuffled back into their places as we went out of the station. They sat staring at their boots.

'"This is a smoking carriage, so I'm going to smoke in it."'

A calf-faced boy said, 'Go on,' and Jack went on:

'I took out a bottle of beer, see –'

'Did you say good 'ealth to the old couple?' asked a more mature soldier who had got in with the last lot.

'Oh no, I didn't like to be as rude as that.'

'There was some girls in my carriage,' said Calf Face. 'Such a crowd, we were all sitting on each other's laps at the finish. We was reading the newspaper and these girls kep' on saying, "Ere, don't turn over yet; I ain't finished the last page yet."'

'I was lucky, too' said the more mature soldier. 'I had a very pretty little nurse in my carriage.'

The long-legged man who was married sighed. 'I put on my "civvies" larst week,' he said. 'Collar and tie – looked quite decent, I did, cuff links and all.'

'Do you wear cuff links?' asked Jack.

'Yus.'

'Do you?'

'Yes,' Dark Eyes answered modestly. 'I've got one or two nice sets of cuff links, and my mother give me another for my twenty-first birthday larst week.'

'Well,' said Jack, 'I think a bloke wot wears cuff links takes as long to dress as a girl does.'

'I seen *Life's a Picnic* wen I was on leave,' said Calf Face.

'Good, ain't it? but the trouble was I couldn't laugh as much as I wanted, see, because I'd got my young lady with me.'

'I seen Ted Summers in *All Aboard*,' said the married soldier.

'He's orf again; we've almost seen that show with him by now.'

The married soldier smiled in his good-natured way. 'It was fine, though.'

Calf Face croaked out, 'Bless them all ...' but stopped abruptly to ask, 'Can we get a drink wen we get there?'

'Too late at the King's Head,' said Jack. 'But I bin in there later by the side door to play the piano.'

The jokes jerked round the railway carriage again. 'Can you play "God Save the King" yet?' and 'I suppose you play with one finger', and also 'Did you learn by correspondence course?'

'I can play most stringed instruments,' sad the mature solder. 'Can't play the violin, though,' he added in a sad voice.

Dark Eyes asked, 'Have you heard any more about that rumour?'

'Wot rumour?'

'About us going abroad.'

'That's not a rumour,' said Jack. 'It's true.'

'Where we going?' asked Calf Face, his eyes wide open.

'As if we'd be told that.'

'We'll know soon enough.'

'Isn't that just life in the Army?'

'When I was in the Army in 1890,' improvised Jack, 'we did have a time down in Poona.'

'We did have a time beneath the moon-a,' said Calf-Face. The train drew up at the last station. It was difficult to get the door open.

'These local trains are not worth going in; they're not really,' said Jack. 'Might as well stay at home.'

Someone gave the door a kick; it opened suddenly. The men got out on to the platform. They heaved their kit-bags on to their shoulders and started down the country road.

Soon it was no longer possible to tell which was Jack, which Calf Face, Dark Eyes, the married soldier who had played the invisible violin, the older soldier or the one with sweat on his forehead. They were a group singing in time to their steps. To the travellers in the dim train the words of the men marching came back, 'We don't know where we're going, but we're on our way.'

Exiles in Conversation

When I saw Miss Mallins she was dressed to go out for a walk. She stood on the landing of the second floor looking down on the people in the street below. She had not troubled to take off the black unbrushed hat or that speckled anonymous raincoat which she wore without any spirit of hopefulness. When she saw me coming out of my flat she told me what I already knew.

'Air-raid warning,' she said.

We watched together from the window. At this early stage of the air war on London people did not know what they should do at the siren sound. There were stories of casualties in other districts, but so far no bombs had fallen on ours. There was a restlessness in the street life below us now; everyone put on a different manner as if they had suddenly found themselves on the boards of a stage. Some ran to shelters, others looked up at the sky, several strolled along taking no notice of the activity around them, and a few, perhaps as a protest, exaggerated this indifference to the point of strutting absurdity.

Miss Mallins was the young woman who lived in the flat on the floor above me; the few words we exchanged had always been an effort towards a polite sound without meaning, like a pair of Prussian heel clicks. But now the event of an air raid made Miss Mallins more talkative in the way that some people suddenly give themselves over to conversation in a cinema or a circus.

'Like a lot of ants, aren't they?' she said.

There came into my mind the various ways in which the street passers-by were not like ants – they were not organised, did not build anything and often bumped into each other. In all these ways they were not like ants.

'I have been up north,' Miss Mallins said. 'The air raids there are very bad; the internees feel that they have no protection against this sort of thing. You see, my friend Dr Heinz is a diabetes patient, but even on the plea of ill-health I can't get him out of the camp.' She sighed. 'I suppose Dr Heinz is one of the worst diabetes cases in the world. I've written to everyone about it, but it's all so slow.' At this moment a grotesque-looking Gothic creature sped along, crouching on a steel steed, fast followed by a second and a third. 'Canadian Despatch Rider Motor-Bicycle Corps,' Miss Mallins said in her well-informed voice and then let her talk gallop on down the long, bitter northern road of internment camps. 'You see, Hansi, Dr Heinz that is, sleeps in a ward with twenty other men; he has to drink from the same cup as the tuberculosis patient and there is only one nurse to look after them all.'

A man was unharnessing a horse in the street. He arranged the cart before the horse, to protect the horse against the bomb. 'And when I asked the medical officer about Dr Heinz,' Miss Mallins told me, 'he answered very roughly, "Don't come here trying to hustle me. I know all about the Heinz case." Well, later on, I was walking in the internees' yard with Dr Heinz himself and I said, "Look Hansi, there he is, the round-shouldered man, the medical man. He has your case in hand; you must know him." And Hansi said, "Not I — never set eyes on him before in my life."'

As the bitter words of Miss Mallins' talk dripped into my mind I realized that now she had switched the subject on to some elementary nursing examinations which she had passed, but, she said, in spite of these high marks chalked up to her she still could not get a hospital job. I asked if it would be possible for her to get work as a medical helper in an internment camp. 'Well, I should hardly care to do that,' she answered. 'It's very dirty in those places and there are so many people speaking no known language. No, thank you.' The key-sounds of her voice reminded me suddenly of a retired naval officer I had heard talking out some weeks back, 'Intern the lot,' and then on the upwards shout again, 'Intern the whole lot; that's what I say.'

Miss Mallins looked down on the street below. 'The buses go on running just the same, don't they?' she said.

In the ground-floor flat of this small building there lived the widow of a clergyman. 'She can't be there now,' Miss Mallins said, 'because if she was in she would come out' and at this moment the All Clear sounded. We smiled each other good-bye and Miss Mallins wrapped her speckled raincoat more closely round her and went down and out for her walk.

I did not see Miss Mallins again for some time. I worked in a hospital at nights and in the daytime we no longer troubled to leave our own flats for air-raid warnings. But when I did see Miss Mallins, the anonymous grey coat had been discarded and she wore instead a red overcoat and her black hat had been brushed and brim-twisted into some Spanish-rascal attitude. She was paying a man who had brought flowers to the door. There was another carrying fruit and a third had queued up with clothes from the cleaners. Miss Mallins said, 'Can you lend me half a crown?' She looked at the ledge where the letters were left. There was one addressed to me from abroad. 'Would you give me this stamp?' she said, 'Dr Heinz collects stamps. He used to have more stamps than anyone in the world. You know I've got him out of the internment camp. He arrives to-day—by a fast train. Thank you for lending me the half-crown. Do you mind about the stamp? Hansi will be pleased.' When she went up the stairs she was singing and carried in her arms fruit, flowers, a blue-patterned dress from the cleaners and somewhere among all this the foreign stamp which we had torn from my letter.

On this evening I was not on duty at the hospital. Outside

there was the insistent orchestra of gunfire, and above me the footsteps of Miss Mallins as she walked about her flat; sometimes when the door opened I heard voices. There were four separate voices, that of the husky-toned, quick-talking man who seemed to have something that must be told against all interrupters, then the carefully-spoken German woman's voice anxious not to miss anything she said herself. I did not hear the third voice very often. It agreed in German, not harshly, but these gentle monosyllables came into the talk very seldom. Miss Mallins' voice chimed in sometimes, like an early cuckoo, with 'Oh, Heinz, really,' and 'My dear Hansi.'

Soon Miss Mallins' walking ceased. The treble of inner life was almost muffled out by the bass of barrage gunfire outside. The voice of Dr Hans Heinz got through. 'Ve are all going down now,' he said, and I heard them running quickly along the passage and down to the ground floor.

The door of my room was broken open suddenly. I shut it, but in a little while it was broken again. It was difficult to believe that the blast of still distant falling bombs was swinging the door inwards because these interruptions seems more like the malicious moves of some poltergeist existing only in a ghost story of a haunted house heard at second hand. But the door opening did happen, and because it went on happening I followed my neighbours down into the ground-floor flat.

We were six people in the sitting-room of the clergyman's widow. Miss Mallins had brought two rugs and a thermos flask filled with hot coffee. There was also the German refugee woman, dark eyed and eager smiling, the Czech soldier in British battledress, lonely without language or country, and Dr Hans Heinz, who was talking like a wound-up machine that must not stop until the spring of obsession has all uncoiled itself. This continental conversation piece was centred by the clergyman's widow with her blonde hair plaited and falling before her shoulders to her waist as if she was a character from a German fairy-tale, but when she spoke, it was in cathedral-town tones. She said, 'Oh, do come in; we are quite a happy little gathering here.' But the people sat there in the room looking interrupted, sunk in secret obsession, or melancholy. Clearly this was no time or place for happy looks. The home-learnt English of Dr Heinz was on the run around internment camp life as if he had to get the words about this second persecution out into the room. 'And I tell you the man next me answered me, "But I'm afraid I don't speak Cherman; I am landing only yesterday from Austraillia." "Vell then, Mr Schmidt," I am asking him, "how long are you living there in Austraillia?" and he is answering me back, "Forty-seven years." You see, as soon as he is getting back to the Motherland he gets popped quick into internment camp. Fonny, vasn't it?'

The German woman did not listen to Dr Heinz and she did not speak either, but hugged to her own heart the wish to say a great deal. She waited for the trapeze of talk to be swung to her so that she could catch it and sail away on some specialised subject, but big blond Dr Heinz had the conversation well in hand. 'Then there was another internee who was komming to the Kommandant and telling, "I have very bad neuralgia here," and all the time touching his knee and asking also, "Vot iss konsumption?" and telling, "I have that too, bot it was a disease I forgot about till now."'

Mrs Clergyman-widow walked about offering us biscuits. 'Won't you have a wee bickey.' The Czech solder without words took one each time, bowed from the waist and began his melancholy munching. The German woman refugee said 'Thank you, no.' Dr Heinz talked on and around the biscuits and all the time the enemy aeroplanes continued their hiccough-humming overhead.

Sometimes as Dr Heinz talked, the Czech soldier pointed upwards sad-smiling and said, 'Not all clear—German bombers.' Miss Mallins looked towards Dr Heinz often; her face never lost its expression of loving patience. The silent Czech seemed to know the stories now by voice inflexion and the clergyman's widow walked with her biscuits, hoping through them to interrupt Dr Heinz and to save him from saying something which might reflect against the British. 'Well, after all,' Mrs Clergyman-widow said, 'these things are very sad, but, of course, we had to be careful. We must win the war, you know, and then you can all go back as free people to your own countries.'

'Never, believe me, never these poor refugees will be getting back into their own countries,' said Dr Heinz.

'Why not?' Mrs Clergyman-widow's voice went up as sharp as defensive fists.

'Because there will be so many forms to be filled up,' Dr Heinz answered. 'Even in the internment camp we were always filling up forms. After the war it will take many years, just filling up forms. You will see—just filling up thousands of forms.'

Mrs Clergyman-widow did not say anything, and the Czech soldier, who had no words for refusal, took a biscuit again and began to munch with his front teeth like a disappointed horse.

When the outside sounds became dimmer we began to troop back upstairs, promising Mrs Clergyman-widow to return 'if things got serious again later on'. Dr Heinz heavy-footed his way up to Miss Mallins' flat in tune to his own talking. The German woman and the Czech hesitated, uncertain what they should do. They did not know Miss Mallins well; they had been asked in to make a gay dinner-party, to welcome a refugee back from internment. Now the lateness of the evening had overtaken the guests. Outdoors there was the gunfire and aeroplane hum; indoors the stale welcome, so they were glad when I asked them in. The Czech stood by the drawn curtains of the window of my room listening as intently as a musician interpreting music, and telling us in German the story of what was happening. 'You see,' the woman said, 'he knows it all from France.'

The noise of brute warfare which kept us awake, in these early days, was the same sound which also finally tired and sent us to sleep. I lay on the bed in my room; the door into the sitting-room was open and the fire was on. The Czech soldier sat in the arm-chair. 'You see, he can sleep anywhere at any time,' the German woman said. 'He got used to that during his journey from Prague.' She rested on the sofa herself and talked in a quiet tone to the Czech soldier in British uniform. From time to time I heard a thudding sound which I supposed, at first, to be bombs falling in the district, but each time it happened the German woman said 'So. Miss Mallins walks again.' Miss Mallins, possessed by an inconsequent love, liked to walk about and wait on the lazy-limbed and energetic talking Heinz, the collector of stamps who was one of the worst diabetes cases in the world.

Early in the morning the German woman came into my room and woke me up. 'It has just gone all clear,' she said. Because she should have been in her home at curfew time I wrote a note saying that she had stayed with me owing to the severe air raid. She was childishly pleased at getting this note without having first to fill up any forms. She showed it to the Czech and read out to him several times, 'To whomever it may concern'.

The Czech had some English ready for me. He said that he hoped if he was wounded he would be sent to the hospital where I worked. The German woman said, 'It will be of no use; she works there at night-time and you will be asleep then,' and the Czech answered, 'I arrange then to sleep in daytime.' He was pleased with his answer, thanked me gravely, and together they departed. At first I could hear them talking in the street. The German woman sad, 'I'm sorry for Miss Mallins because she will have to hear all Hansi's stories of internment. That is the trouble with people who go through these experiences; it was the same when my Cousin Karl came out of the concentration camp–talk, talk, talk, and always the same subject. It will be like this with Hansi. Miss Mallins will have to hear these stories again and again.'

'Do you think so?' answered the gentle Czech. 'Poor fellow, poor fellow.'

It was pleasant to be alone now in a quiet room, solitude, and silence, these were the two things which would become each war-day more difficult to get until with cheese and chocolate they would be almost unobtainable.

But Miss Mallins walked again; her footsteps thudded across the floor above me, and then I heard groans and afterwards a quick frightened voice, 'Hush, Hansi! What is the matter, Hansi?–hush!' but it went on–the uneven walking, the groans and the voice filled with fear. Then came the sound of someone running down the stairs and, as soon as this stopped, the knock on my door. It was Miss Mallins calling, 'Lisa, are you there? Lisa come quickly; Hansi is ill.' Lisa, I knew, was the name of the German woman who had left an hour ago. I opened the door. Miss Mallins stood outside; she wore her scarlet coat wrapped round the shoulders of her pyjamas. She wore no shoes at all now, and her feet were flat to the floor like the feet of an Arab. She said, 'Can you help me, please? Hansi has fallen down; he is almost unconscious and I can't move him.' Together we ran back up the stairs. On the floor by the fireplace the refugee lay like a great helpless mammal washed up on a deserted beach. He wore some sort of cretonne pyjamas which also gave him, at times, the look of a vast upturned sofa. The colour of his face seemed to have darkened, and his hair stuck to his forehead with sweat, so that in its painful dampness it no longer looked blond. White saliva came from his lips; we washed it away with Miss Mallins' handkerchief, but each time it came back again. Sometimes he groaned and moved his head from side to side, and because we were afraid that he would get hurt, we put the scarlet coat between his face and the stone fire-fender.

When Miss Mallins tried to telephone to a doctor her hand shook so that she could not dial round the numbers. I had to do this for her and when I got back the answering voice of the medical man it was quite matter of fact. He had the case in hand; the ambulance was on its way. He had already received one message from Miss Mallins; he understood that it was a question of insulin unwisely taken and diet carelessly followed, but soon Dr Heinz would be in hospital and well again.

We had to wait. The flowers on the wooden dining-table were drooping; the coffee-cups had the dregs in them still and on the saucer of each was a dirty spoon. The bread has been put away, but the plate and the large knife remained; the fruit in a glass bowl had a dead look. It seemed as if some beasts had trampled across a tenderly prepared picnic, putting all the guests to flight.

The empty feeling of this room made it difficult for me to recognise the signs of human life around me—the reflection of my own face in the looking-glass on the wall, Miss Mallins' dressing, her hair falling down over her forehead as she fastened her suspenders to her stockings, and the groaning of the collapsed German on the floor. After a while this sound ceased and I went downstairs again to see if the ambulance was arriving. It was quite light outside and very cold, but there was no sign of anyone. We telephoned again to the hospital and they told us that the ambulance had already left. When at last it did arrive, the two stretcher-bearers got down so slowly from their car, they seemed to be living far from our own mood. Without hurrying, they opened the back of the car and took out the folding chair. They went upstairs, but returned again soon without the German. He was too heavy to lift and they telephoned from Miss Mallins' flat for some policemen to help them. They, too, arrived slowly, walking together in a ceremonious way like two cricketers going out to bat.

It seemed a long time before the ill man was brought downstairs. He sat in the chair wrapped round in two blankets looking like a passenger rescued from a shipwreck; his two feet had become uncovered and showed below the blankets very white, one crossed over the other. I thought again of the stories which had raced round the circular mind track of Dr Heinz and all that he had been determined to tell us during the earlier part of the evening. Speech had left him now; all knowledge of his surroundings had gone too; the white saliva was falling from his mouth again.

The policemen and stretcher-bearers had become silent and gentle now. They were very intent on their task of carrying the heavy man along. Miss Mallins walked beside the cortège until Dr Heinz was shovelled from the steel chair into the back of the ambulance. The ambulance driver said 'As e' got 'is gas-mask?' Miss Mallins shook her head. 'Well, 'e's got to 'ave 'is gas-mask to tike to the 'orspital, Miss.' I ran back up the stairs. In Miss Mallins' bedroom I found a square cardboard box. It lay on the arm-chair beside her black hat. On the lid was printed carefully 'Doctor Hans Heinz, 28 Austel Street, SW.' and underneath Dr Heinz had written proudly, 'Supplied to me by the British Government'. When I gave it to Miss Mallins, tiredness and anxiety had brought tears to her eyes. She was not able to say anything but she got silently into the ambulance and with her unconscious lover was driven away.

When I was back in my own flat I thought of the scarlet coat, the dying flowers, the talk of Dr Heinz, the silent Czech solder in British battledress, the clergyman's widow with her interminable biscuits, the ill German with sweat-darkened hair and Miss Mallins with her prejudiced looks but loving expression, and all these images ran through my mind quick as machine-gun fire.

On nights I worked in a hospital; in the daytime I slept. I meant to find Miss Mallins and ask about Dr Heinz, but I did not do this. Surely the German would have got well very quickly and start telling his stories again. As the war went on, the early days seemed remote as memories of adolescence. One day I did see Miss Mallins. I thought, 'Of course I should have heard long ago if Dr Heinz had not recovered, so there's no need to ask now.'

Miss Mallins was wearing the anonymous speckled grey raincoat again. She walked very slowly and I passed her without a word.

Notes on the Texts

BY KATE MACDONALD

There's No Story There

Chapter One. Inspection

Potteries: district of Staffordshire in north-west England, famed for its industrial production of fine porcelain and crockery.

Les Misérables: he is referring to Victor Hugo's novel of 1862, and also the poor of Paris.

Trick Cyclist: slang term for a psychiatrist.

Time and Motion: the gathering of data for business efficiency studies.

noons: the work shift that began at two in the morning and ended at ten in the morning, leaving the afternoon free for shopping or going to the cinema (127).

magazine: the storage building for the finished explosives.

pigeon-toed: walking with her toes pointing inwards, suggesting a fault with her leg muscles or bone positioning.

Group Captain: a senior military rank in the Royal Air Force.

Chapter Two. Cleanway

liberty boat: Edward is at a Naval Training College, and uses the cadets' slang for the transport that will take them ashore on leave. In this case, he's already ashore and he's referring to the bus.

ribbon development: a straggling line of shops, buildings, light industry and houses that had been built out along a main road from a town centre.

scrim-shanking: military slang for avoiding one's appointed duties.

spiritual stays: the automatic protection of the self from emotional damage or inquisitiveness.

treacled-up: slowed down, time impeded, possibly echoing the Mad Hatter in *Alice in Wonderland*.

***Battleship Potemkin*:** the 1925 silent film made in Soviet Russia by Sergei Eisenstein, dramatizing a naval mutiny of 1905.

Hyde Park on a Sunday: the traditional place and day for the right to free speech to be exercised in London, at 'Speaker's Corner'.

knocked 'em in the Old Kent Road: refers to 'Wot Cher! Knocked 'Em In The Old Kent Road', a popular music hall song from 1891. The Old Kent Road, a major thoroughfare in south-east London, had not suffered much bomb damage during the war, though it could have been assumed by those who didn't live there that it had, as it was such a prominent landmark from above.

Blue-band: a civilian rank used in these factories to denote a minor official.

Chapter Three. Joint Production

Burberry: the Burberry raincoat had been adopted in the First World War for service use, and had been a standard men's raincoat thereafter.

little pitchers have long ears: this very old saying, originally noting the acute hearing of children, has the variant of 'big ears', since the 'ears' were the handles on a jug or pitcher, but a spaniel has long ears.

flapjack: a flip-case for face powder or other cosmetics.

pretty hare: her front teeth were probably made more prominent by this arrangement.

PAD: Passive Air Defence, which encompassed camouflage and other kinds of concealment of structures likely to be bombed in air raids.

ROF: Royal Ordnance Factory.

scamping: to do something in an inadequate or unfinished way.

paper-backed detective books: the Penguin Crime series, in a distinctive green and white paper cover.

remarks to the chair: the formal way of managing a meeting's business so that participants' minds are kept on one subject by the chair(man) and don't spiral off into private conversations.

63s: sixty-three shillings. There were twenty shillings in the pound.

stand in a queue: fish was rationed during the war, and in very short supply even when it did arrive in shops.

clear: earn.

Chapter Four. War Hostel

Penguin Special: a series of long essays published in Penguin's orange and white paperback series addressing issues pertinent to the times. Over eighty titles in the series had been published by 1942.

Wrens, Waafs, or Ats: Women's Royal Naval Service (WRNS), Women's Auxiliary Air Force (WAAF) and Auxiliary Territorial Service (ATS), the three women's branches of the British armed services, all with smart uniforms and closer proximity to servicemen.

Sing Sing: a notorious prison in New York State.

Six Little Maids from Sing Sing: a probable confusion of the Asian-sounding name of the prison (actually a derivation from the name of the Native American tribe who had formerly owned the land) with the famous song 'Three Little Maids from School' from Gilbert and Sullivan's comedy operetta *The Mikado*.

turbaned: a soft fabric hat stitched into the shape of an upswept turban was fashionable in the war years, for its comfort, elegance, and for keeping hair in order.

postal order: a convenient way of sending money as a present, which could be cashed at a post office.

a piece of heather or shamrock: flowers that traditionally denoted remembrance and good luck, as well as representing Scotland and Ireland, nationalities working at Statevale.

allotment: the hostels had pieces of ground for residents to grow their own flowers and vegetables, to supplement rations as well as for occupation and exercise.

crêpe-de-chine and triple ninon: both were luxury fabrics, strong but also fine, used for elegant draped garments that needed body as well as lightness.

coupons: dress fabric was rationed in the war, along with most other commodity items, and could only be bought using one's allocation of clothing coupons. May and Linnet made a private transaction in cash.

International Brigade: volunteer forces in Communist-led units supporting the Popular Front government against the Fascist army of General Franco in the Spanish Civil War.

tramp steamer: a ship with no sailing schedule or set ports of call, available for spontaneous hire to anyone in the market.

co-eds: children of both sexes at the same school.

cotton-on: usually meaning to begin to understand, or to take a liking to, Holden uses it here to mean to attach himself to.

escaped from France in 1940: Nazi forces invaded France in 1940.

agent provocateur: secret agent, planted amidst the enemy to sow dissent.

Miss Zero: if a ball rolled into the zero space on a roulette wheel the bank won.

Dr Gallup: American pioneer in sampling public opinion through surveys.

Chapter Five. Time Off

Deb: a debutante, a girl from an upper-class and/or rich family formally presented at court to the King, which marked her entry into formal society.

barracking: robust heckling or challenges to the speaker and his arguments.

How's your father?: popular phrase used as a euphemism for casual sex.

Will Thorne: William Thorne was an influential trades unionist and Labour politician who began his career in Canning Town, east London.

Engels in 'Ighgate: Friedrich Engels wasn't buried in Highgate cemetery, but his collaborator in political philosophy, Karl Marx, was.

like bloody foreign language: one of the signifiers of the local dialect is that 'the' and 'a' were often omitted.

Chapter Seven. Factory Tour

told off: ordered to.

CEMA: Council for the Encouragement of Music and the Arts, a predecessor organisation to the present Arts Council.

ENSA: The Entertainments National Service Association supplied concerts, sketches and shows to British armed forces personnel during the war.

Ascot: Attending the Royal Enclosure at Ascot races (which never ran donkeys) was one of the most exclusive events in the social calendar.

Coronation: George VI's coronation had taken place on 12 May 1937, around six years earlier.

silly symphony: the Silly Symphonies were short comic animated films shown before the main feature at the cinema, and came to be the name for any short comic film.

Chapter Eight. Visit

battledored: shuttlecock and battledore is the old name for the game of badminton.

sky pilot: service slang for a military chaplain, or indeed any kind of clergyman, since they are supposed to be in charge of flying up to heaven.

Rural Dean: a clerical post subordinate to a Bishop, in which the Dean oversees a number of rural parishes.

Chapter Nine. Check Up

Mosley's men: the British Union of Fascists marched in London's East End on 4 October 1936, and were resisted by local Londoners, Jewish and non-Jewish alike.

Chapter Ten. Snowed In

sugar-loaf: tall and conical, with a rounded top.

WVS: Women's Voluntary Services, the main women's voluntary organisation during the war.

careless talk: one of the most well-known government slogans during the war was Careless Talk Costs Lives.

loaf: Cockney rhyming slang for head, as in loaf of bread.

taters: potatoes.

Sheik: reference to *The Sheik*, a massively successful film from 1921, based on the novel by E M Hull, starring Rudolph Valentino. The film made Valentino a huge star, and he was synonymous with playing romantic leading men until his death in 1926.

lilos: rubber inflatable mattresses.

Pioneers: the Royal Pioneer Corps was a British Army corps who worked on light engineering and logistical labour for the Army, in whose ranks refugees and Allied servicemen often served.

Chapter Eleven. Snowed Out

brun: masculine form of 'brunette' for dark-haired.

Lyons Corner House: a chain of cheap and reliable unlicensed restaurants serving snacks and light meals.

MTC: the Mechanised Transport Corps was a civilian organisation that provided women drivers for government and other officials, and for ambulances.

shantung: silk fabic.

coolie hats: distinctive straw hats made in the shape of a wide, shallow cone and tied under the chin, called 'coolie' after their Eastern origin when they first became fashionable in the 1920s among the rich sunbathing set.

sewing bee: a sewing session, designed to encourage greater productivity by working in a group.

Chapter Twelve. Internal Railway

Loofter Wafter: Luftwaffe, the German air force.

Musical Chairman

gallery-girl: a habitual theatre-goer who buys tickets for the cheaper seats.

Home Counties: the counties surrounding London.

old-worlded: imitating an assumed historical past, very often with impossible combinations of architectural styles.

ingle-nooked: a corner seat inside or beside a large fireplace.

quarter day: the traditional time for quarterly payments of rent, or in this case, allowances.

Ido: Ido is a constructed language, deriving from Esperanto.

cleft palate and hair lip: both are types of physical malformation caused during the child's facial development in the womb.

pince-nez: glasses that are supported by sitting on the bridge of the nose without earpieces.

salaried man: a salaried worker was paid their salary monthly, and would speak of their income as so much a year; a wage-earner would receive their pay weekly, and would speak of their income as so much per hour or per week. There is a distinct class difference between the two, with a white-collar worker normally being salaried, denoting greater stability in the post and higher skills in the job market.

Mr Bevin: Ernest Bevin had been General Secretary of one of the largest British trade unions, was a Labour MP and served as Minister for Labour in the wartime coalition government.

smit: smitten, keen on.

scheduled: the Chairman explains what this means further on in the story: 'being scheduled under the Essential Work Orders also means that an employee cannot leave his place of employ without the consent of the National Service Officer. The worker is deprived of his right to sell his labour at a higher rate, but also he is no longer liable to dismissal without a thorough investigation into the causes, and he is guaranteed the right rate of pay for the job.'

wide boy: a man with the air and dress of knowing his way around the black market and other mildly illegal activities.

'Do, do do': a song by George Gershwin in the 1926 musical comedy *Oh Kay!*, written by Guy Bolton and P G Wodehouse.

idiot: the contemporary term used for someone with mental health problems or learning difficulties. This man is clearly suffering from shell-shock or post-traumatic stress disorder.

Exiles in Conversation

cathedral-town tones: from the upper layers of ecclesiastical Establishment society.

Blitz Writing: Night Shift & It Was Different At The Time

by Inez Holden

Inez Holden

Blitz Writing
Night Shift
& It Was Different At The Time

Edited by Kristin Bluemel

Emerging out of the 1940–1941 London Blitz, the drama of these two short works, a novel and a memoir, comes from the courage and endurance of ordinary people met in the factories, streets and lodging houses of a city under bombardment.

Inez Holden's novella *Night Shift* follows a largely working-class cast of characters for five night shifts in a factory that produces camera parts for war planes.

It Was Different At The Time is Holden's account of wartime life from April 1938 to August 1941, drawn from her own diary. This was intended to be a joint project written with her friend George Orwell (he was in the end too busy to contribute), and includes disguised appearances by notable literary figures of the period.

The experiences recorded in *It Was Different At The Time* overlap in period and subject with *Night Shift*, setting up a vibrant dialogue between the two texts.

Inez Holden (1903-1974) was a British writer and literary figure whose social and professional connections embraced most of London's literary and artistic life. She modelled for Augustus John, worked alongside Evelyn Waugh, and had close relationships with George Orwell, Stevie Smith, H G Wells, Cyril Connolly, and Anthony Powell.

The introduction and notes are by Kristin Bluemel, Professor of English at Monmouth University, New Jersey.

Where Stands A Wingèd Sentry

by Margaret Kennedy

Margaret Kennedy

Where Stands
A Wingèd Sentry

A lost Second World War memoir by the author of *The Constant Nymph*

'This is a journal of the tense months between Dunkirk and the start of the Blitz – months when a German invasion of Britain seemed both imminent and inevitable. It's written with a steady intensity; raw worry pokes through the elegant prose, and though there are many vivid details, and moments of wit and levity, this is also an extraordinary meditation of what it means to be free in a world of encroaching tyranny.'

— Lissa Evans, author of *Old Baggage, V for Victory*

Margaret Kennedy's riveting 1941 wartime memoir is *Mrs Miniver* with the gloves off. Her account, taken from her war diaries, conveys the tension, frustration and bewilderment of the progression of the war, and the terror of knowing that the worst is to come, but not yet knowing what the worst will be.

English bravery, confusion, stubbornness and dark humour colour her experiences, in which she and her children move from Surrey to Cornwall, to sit out the war amidst a quietly efficient Home Guard and the most scandalous rumours. *Where Stands A Wingèd Sentry* (the title comes from a hymn) was only published in the USA, and has never been published in the UK before.

Margaret Kennedy (1896–1967) made her name as a novelist with *The Ladies of Lyndon* (1923) and *The Constant Nymph* (1924), and continued publishing until the year before her death.